Robinson Crusoe

-Translated into modern English

ISBN: 978-0-9948396-1-9
First Edition

1.

Start in Life

I was born to a wealthy family in 1632 in York, England. My father was a foreigner from Bremen who moved to England after making his money as a merchandise trader. He left his trade and moved to York, where he married my mother, whose relations were named Robinson. The Robinsons were a very good family in that area, so I was named Robinson Kreutznaer, but by the usual corruption of words in England, we are now called Crusoe.

I had two elder brothers, one who was lieutenant-colonel to an English foot regiment in Flanders, formerly commanded by the famous Colonel Lockhart. He was killed at the battle near Dunkirk against the Spaniards.[1] What became of my second brother I never knew, any more than my father or mother knew what became of me.

Being the third son of the family and not bred to any trade, my head began to be filled early with rambling thoughts. My father, who was very ancient, had given me a competent share of learning – as far as public school goes – and hoped I would study law, but I would only be satisfied by going to sea. My inclination was against the will – well actually, the commands – of my father and against all the persuasions of my mother and other friends. It was almost like they knew the life of misery which was to occur to me.

My father was a wise man and tried to advise me against my choice. He called me one morning into his bedroom, where he was laid up by his gout and kindly disagreed with me on this subject. He asked me why

---

[1] Also known as the Battle of the Dunes, Spain fought the French and English on June 14, 1658 and the center of the English army was commanded by William Lockhart.

I would want to leave his house and my native country, where I would go, and what prospects I had. How would I make my fortune? He told me it was desperate men or aspiring, superior men who went abroad on adventures. Only they would make themselves famous and these people were either too far above me or too far below me. We were middle class, or as my father put it "the upper part of the lower class," which he had found by long experience was the best state in the world. It was best suited to happiness. No misery or hardship, no hard labor and conversely, none of the embarrassment of pride, luxury, ambition and envy of the upper part of mankind. He said this was the state of life which all other people envied. Kings would frequently lament the miserable consequence of being born to greatness. The wisest man prays to have neither poverty nor riches.

We were not exposed to as many changes as the higher or lower part of mankind. I would always find the misfortunes of life were shared among the upper and lower part of mankind, my father said, but the middle...the middle class had the fewest disasters. We were not subjected to as many political disorders as those who, by hard living, luxury and extravagances or by hard labor, want or hunger bring conflict on themselves. It is a natural consequence of their way of living. The middle class was intended for all kind of virtue and enjoyments – peace and abundance were the handmaids of the middle class. Abstinence, moderation, quietness, health, society – all pleasant diversions and desirable pleasures – were the blessings of the middle class. This way men went silently and smoothly through the world and comfortably out of it, not embarrassed by the labor of the hand or of the head, not sold to a life of slavery for daily bread. They are not harassed by circumstances which rob the soul of peace and the body of rest. They are not enraged by the passion of envy or the secret burning lust for great things. They slide gently through the world, sensibly tasting the sweets of living, feeling they are happy and learning by every day's experience to know it more wisely.

After this he pushed me seriously and warmly not to play the young man or to hastily push myself into miseries which nature – and my station in life – have provided against. I was not forced to provide for myself – that my father would do for me. The world is a harsh place and being middle class is what my father was recommending to me. If I wasn't going to be happy in that world, it was my own fault and he would have nothing to answer for, having discharged his duty in warning me. He knew what would hurt me and he would treat me very well if I would stay and settle at home as he directed, but he would not have a hand in my misfortunes if I chose to go away. He closed the conversation by reminding me of my elder brother, who my father also tried to persuade to stay home and not go to the Low Country wars. My father could not prevail, my brother's young desires prompting him to run into the army, where he was killed. Though he said he would not stop praying for me, he did say if I did take this foolish step, God would not bless me and I would have spare time to reflect on having neglected his advice, when there might be no advice to assist in my recovery.

The last part of his discussion was truly prophetic, though I don't suppose my father knew it at the time. I watched tears run down his face, especially when he spoke of my late brother and when he spoke of my having leisure to repent and no help to assist me, he was so moved he broke off and told me his heart was so full he couldn't say any more to me.

I was sincerely affected by this and really, who wouldn't be? I decided not to think about going abroad anymore, but to settle at home according to my father's desire. Regrettably, a few days changed my mind again. To prevent any further insistence from my father, a few weeks later I decided to run away from him. However, I did not act as hastily as you may think. I spoke to my mother at a time when I thought her a little more pleasant than usual, and told her I was so bent on seeing the world that I would never settle for anything less and my father had better give me his permission rather than force me to go without it. I was now eighteen, which was too late to apprentice to a trade or clerk to an attorney. I told her if I did apprentice I would never serve out my time and I would run away from my master before my apprenticeship was over and go to sea. I asked her if she would speak to my father to let me go on one voyage. If I came home again and did not like it, I would never go again and I would promise to diligently recover the time I had lost.

This put my mother into a frenzy. She told me she knew it would serve no purpose to speak to my father. He knew better and would never give his consent to anything which would hurt me so much. She wondered how I could think of any such thing after the discussion I had with my father – with such kind and loving expressions she knew my father had used on me. If I was going to ruin myself, there was no help for me and I would never have their permission. For her part, she would not have a hand in my destruction and I would never be able to say my mother was willing when my father was not.

Though my mother refused to speak to my father, I heard afterwards she reported the conversation to him and my father, after showing great concern, sighed "That boy might be happy if he stays at home but if he goes abroad, he will be the most miserable wretch ever born. I can give no consent to it."

It was almost a year after this that I broke loose and in the interim I was deaf to all proposals of settling into business, and frequently disagreed with my parents, who were against what they knew my inclinations were. I casually went to Hull one day, without the thought of leaving, but one of my friends was about to sail to London in his father's ship and he coaxed me to go with them. It would cost me nothing for my passage and I told neither my father nor my mother, leaving them to hear of it as they might. I did not ask God's blessing or my father's, and without considering the consequences on September 1, 1651 I went on board a ship bound for London. No young adventurer's misfortunes, I believe, began sooner or continued longer than mine. The ship was no sooner out of the Humber River than the wind began to blow and the sea to rise in a terrible way. As I had never been to sea before, I was overwhelmingly nauseous and terrified. I began to now seriously look back on what I had done and how Heaven had judged me for the wickedness of leaving my father's house and abandoning my duty. All the good advice of my parents – my father's tears and my mother's appeals – were now fresh in my mind and my conscience, which was not as hard as it is now, chastised me for being contemptuous of the advice and the breach of my duty to God and my father.

All this happened while the storm increased and the sea rose and fell, though nothing like what I have seen many times since – or even what I saw a few days later – but it was enough to affect me, who was only a young sailor and had never seen anything like it. I expected every wave to swallow us and every time the ship fell in the trough of the sea, I thought we would never rise again. I vowed if it would please God to spare my life this one voyage, once I was on dry land I would go directly home to my father and never set foot on a ship again as long as I lived. I would take his advice and never subject myself to such miseries anymore. Now I plainly saw he was right about the middle station of life, how easy and comfortably he had lived and never been exposed to tempests at sea or troubles on shore and I decided I would, like a true repenting prodigal son, go home to my father.

These wise and sober thoughts continued while the storm lasted and sometime after, but the next day the wind had subsided, the sea was calmer and I began to be a little accustomed to it. I was very solemn that day and still a little seasick. Towards night the weather cleared up, the wind died down and a fine evening followed. The sun went down in a perfectly clear sky and rose the same way the next morning. With little wind and a smooth sea with the sun shining on it, the sight was the most delightful I had ever seen.

I had slept well that night and was no longer seasick and actually very cheerful. I looked with wonder on the sea that was so rough and terrible the day before, and could be so calm and pleasant in such a short period. My friend who had enticed me away, now came over to me. "Well, Bob," he said, clapping me on the shoulder, "how are you after it? I imagine you were frightened last night when it blew a capful of wind,[2] weren't you?"

"A capful you call it?' I replied. "'It was a terrible storm."

"A storm, you fool?" he shot back. "You call that a storm? It was nothing at all. Give us a good ship and space to maneuver and we think nothing of such a squall. You're just a fresh-water sailor, Bob. Come on, let's make a bowl of punch and we'll forget all that. Do you see what charming weather it is now?"

To make short this sad part of my story, we went the way of all sailors. The punch was made and I ended up half-drunk. In that one night's wickedness, I drowned all my sorrow, all my thoughts on my past conduct, all my resolutions for the future. As the sea was returned to smooth and calm after the storm, my fears and anxieties of being swallowed up by the sea were forgotten and all of my old desires returned. I entirely forgot the vows and promises I made in my distress. I found some breaks to think and the serious thoughts did try to return sometimes. But I shook them off and roused from them, like I was in a stupor and applying myself to drinking and company, soon mastered those arts. I had in five or six days a victory over conscience as complete as any young fellow who decided not to be troubled with it. But I was to

---

[2] A sudden breeze.

have another trial still and Providence, as it generally does in such cases, decided to leave me with no excuse. If I would not take this as a rescue, the next time would be so bad, the worst and most hardened wretch among us would confess the danger of it.

Our sixth day at sea we came into Yarmouth Roads. The wind was against us and the weather calm, so we had made little way since the storm. Here we were obliged to drop anchor, with the wind continuing from the southwest. For seven days, many ships from Newcastle came into the same Roads, since it was the common harbor for ships to wait for a wind.

We had not stayed here long and would have drifted up the river, but after we had waited four or five days, the wind blew very hard. The Roads were considered as good as a harbor – the anchorage was good, as was our anchor – so our men were unconcerned and not the least bit worried. They spent the time in rest and fun, but on the morning of the eighth day, the wind picked up and we had all hands at work to lower our topmasts and make everything snug and close, so the ship might ride as easy as possible. By noon the sea was very high and our ship bobbed like a cork. We thought once or twice our anchor had come loose, so our master ordered out the sheet-anchor and we rode with two anchors and the cables veered out to the bitter end.

A terrible storm blew and now I began to see terror and amazement in the faces of the seamen themselves. The master was vigilant in the business of preserving the ship, but I could hear him softly say to himself as he went in and out of his cabin "Lord be merciful to us! We shall all be lost! We shall all be killed!" and so forth. During these first panics I was stupefied, lying still in my cabin on the bottom deck, and cannot describe my mood. I couldn't resume my prayers to God, which I had trampled on and hardened myself against. I thought the bitterness of death had passed and this would be nothing like the first time, but when the master himself came by me and said we would be all lost, I was terrified. I got up out of my cabin and looked out. The sea ran high as mountains and broke on us about every three minutes. When I could look around, I saw nothing except distress all around us. Two ships near us had cut their masts off. A ship about a mile ahead of us had started sinking. Two more ships, were pulled from their anchors and taken by the storm out to sea, their masts snapped clean off. The light ships fared the best, but two or three of them came close by us, running away with only their spritsail out.

Towards evening, the mate and boatswain[3] begged the master of our ship to let them cut away the fore-mast, which he was unwilling to do. The boatswain protested if he did not the ship would founder. The master consented and when they had cut away the fore-mast, the main-mast was so loose and shook the ship so much, they were forced to cut that away as well and make a clear deck.

Anyone may judge what condition I must be in during all this. Me, who was only a young sailor and who had been so afraid before of a little gale. I was ten times more scared of my earlier beliefs and returning from them to the resolutions I had wickedly taken at first, than I was of death itself. These, added to the terror of the storm, put me in a condition words can't describe. But the worst was still to come. The storm continued with such fury the seamen themselves acknowledged they had never seen worse. We had a good ship, but she was full of goods and wallowed in the sea, and every now and then the seamen cried out she would founder.

It was to my benefit that I did not know what they meant by FOUNDER until I asked. The storm was so violent that I saw the master, the boatswain and some others more sensible than the rest praying and expecting the ship would go to the bottom. In the middle of the night and with all the other fears, one of the men shouted we had

---

[3] A ship's officer in charge of equipment and the crew.

sprung a leak. Another said there was four feet of water in the hold.[4] Then all hands were called to pump. At that word, I thought my heart died within me and I fell backwards on the side of my bed where I sat in the cabin. The men revived me and told me I was as able to pump as any other. I stood up and went to the pump, working it very heartily. While we did this, the master saw some light colliers.[5] He knew they would not be able to ride out the storm and would have to run out to sea, and as they would come close to us, he ordered a gun fired as a signal of distress. I didn't know what that meant and thought the ship was breaking up or some other terrible thing happened. I was so surprised I fainted. As everybody had his own life to think of, nobody cared what had happened to me. Another man stepped up to the pump, and shoving me aside with his foot, let me lie, thinking I was dead. It was a long time before I came to.

We worked on, but the water increased in the hold and it was apparent the ship would sink. Though the storm began to subside a little, it was not possible we would make it to port, so the master continued firing guns for help. A light ship, which had ridden it out just ahead of us, sent a boat out to help us. It was extremely dangerous for the boat to come near us and it was impossible for us to get on board, or for the boat to get near the ship's side. The men rowed vigorously and offered their lives to save ours. Our men cast them a rope over the stern with a buoy on it, which after considerable effort and risk they took hold of. We hauled them close to us under our stern and everyone got into their boat. It was no use for them or us to think of reaching their own ship, so everyone agreed to let the boat go, and only pull her in towards shore as much as we could. Our master promised them if the boat was wrecked on shore, he would make it good to their master.

---

[4] The bottom cargo compartment of a ship.
[5] Ships carrying coal.

Partly rowing and partly driving, our boat went away to the north, sloping towards the shore almost as far as Winterton Ness.

We were not much more fifteen minutes out of our ship when we saw her sink, then I understood what was meant by a ship foundering in the sea. I must acknowledge I could barely look up when the seamen told me she was sinking. From the moment they put me into the boat, my heart was dead in me, partly with fright, partly with horror and the thoughts of what was still to come.

While we were in this condition – the men struggling at the oars to bring the boat near shore – we could see several people running along the shore to assist us when we came closer. We made slow progress towards the shore and we couldn't reach the shore until we were passed the lighthouse at Winterton, where the shore falls off to the west towards Cromer and the land broke off some of the violence of the wind. Here we got everyone safe on shore with difficulty. We went on foot to Yarmouth where, as unfortunate men, we were treated with great civility by the town magistrates, who assigned us good quarters, and by certain merchants and ship owners who gave us enough money to take us either to London or back to Hull as we thought fit.

If I had the sense to have gone back to Hull and home, I would have been happy and my father – as in our blessed Savior's parable – had even killed the fatted calf for me. When he heard the ship I went away in sank in Yarmouth Roads, it was a long time before he had any assurances I had not drowned.

But my misfortune pushed me on now with a stubbornness nothing could resist. Though several times I had loud calls from reason to go home, I had no power to do so. I don't know what to call this and I don't believe it is fate that makes us the instruments of our own destruction, even though it is in front of us and we rush in with our eyes wide open. Certainly, nothing but a predisposed and unavoidable misery – which it was impossible for me to escape – could have pushed me forward against the calm reasoning and persuasions of my thoughts, and against the two instructions I had in my first attempt at sea travel.

My friend, who had helped to harden me before, was now less forward than I. The first time he spoke after we returned to Yarmouth was about three days later, since we were separated. It appeared his tone had altered. He looked very miserable, and shaking his head he asked how I was. He told his father who I was, and how I had taken this voyage as a trial. His father, turning to me with a very grave and concerned tone said, "Young man, never to go to sea anymore. You can take this as a plain and visible token that you are not to be a seafaring man."

"Why, sir,' I asked. "Will you not go to sea anymore?

"That is another case,' he replied. "It is my calling and therefore my duty, but since for you this was a trial voyage, Heaven has given you a taste of what you are to expect if you persist. Perhaps this has all happened to us because of you, like Jonah in the ship of Tarshish."[6] He continued. "What are you and why did you go to sea?" I told him some of my story, at the end of which he burst out into a strange kind of passion. "What have I done, that such an unhappy wretch would come into my ship? I would not set foot in the same ship as you again for a thousand pounds." This showed how agitated he was by his loss. After, he talked very gravely to me, urging me to go back to my father and not tempt Providence to my ruin, telling me I might see a visible hand of Heaven against me. "And, young man," he said, "if you do not go back home, wherever you go you will meet with nothing but disasters and disappointments, until your father's words are fulfilled. Depend on it." We parted soon after and I never saw him again. As for me, having some money in my pocket, I travelled to London by land and there, as well as

---

[6] Biblical verse, Jonah 1:3.

on the road, struggled with myself over what course my life would take and whether I would go home or to sea.

Shame stopped me from going home, and it occurred to me how I would be laughed at by the neighbors. I would be ashamed to see not only my father and mother but everybody else. I have since observed many times how strange and irrational the common state of mind is, especially of youth and how the reason which would guide them in such cases, doesn't. They are not ashamed to sin, but are ashamed to repent. They are not ashamed of foolish actions, but are ashamed of returning, which only can make them esteemed wise men.

In this state, I remained for some time, uncertain what actions to take and what course of life to lead. An irresistible reluctance to go home continued and as I stayed away a while, the memory of the distress wore off, and as it subsided, the notion I had to return wore off with it, until at last I laid aside the thought of it and looked out for a voyage.

2.

Slavery & Escape

The evil influence which took me away from my father's house presented the most unfortunate of all enterprises to me. It hurried me into the wild notion of making my fortune and impressed those conceits forcibly on me. It made me deaf to all good advice and to the pleas and even the commands of my father. I boarded a vessel bound for the coast of Africa, or as our sailors vulgarly called it, a voyage to Guinea.

It was my great misfortune that in all these adventures I did not work as a sailor. I might have worked a little harder than ordinary and I would have learned the duty and office of a common sailor. In time, I might have qualified myself as a mate or lieutenant, if not a master. But as it was always my fate to make the worst choice, and having money in my pocket and good clothes on my back, I would always go on board looking like a gentleman. I neither had any business in the ship, nor learned to do any.

It was my luck to fall into pretty good company in London, which does not always happen to such loose and misguided young men as I was. The devil generally does not forget to lay some trap for them very early, but I was lucky. I acquainted myself with the master of a ship who had been on the coast of Guinea and who, having great success there, decided to go again. This captain liked my conversation, which was not unpleasant at the time. He heard me say I wanted to see the world and told me if I would travel with him it would be at no expense. I would be his messmate[7] and his companion and if I brought anything with me, I

---

[7] Someone who shares accommodation.

would have help with trading and perhaps I might meet with some encouragement.

I agreed and entered a strict friendship with this captain, who was an honest, plain-dealing man. I went with him and carried a small amount of merchandise with me which, by the disinterested honesty of my friend the captain, I increased considerably. I carried about £40 worth of toys and trinkets as the captain directed me to buy. I gathered the £40 with the help of some of my relations who I corresponded with and who, I believe got my father – or at least my mother – to contribute that to my first adventure.

This was the only voyage which was successful in all my adventures, which I owe to the integrity and honesty of my friend. Under him I also received a competent knowledge of the mathematics and rules of navigation, learned how to keep an account of the ship's course, take an observation and to basically understand some of the things needed to be understood by a sailor. As he took delight in instructing me, I took delight in learning. This voyage made me both a sailor and a merchant, as I brought home five pounds nine ounces of gold dust for my venture, which at my return yielded me almost £300[8] in London, and this filled me with aspirations which have since completely ruined me. Even in this voyage I had my bad luck too. I was continually sick, being thrown into a violent calenture[9] caused by the excessive heat of the climate, since we were mainly trading on the African coast near the equator.

I was now set up as a Guinea trader. My friend, to my great misfortune, died soon after his return. I decided to go on the same voyage again and I embarked in the same vessel with his former first

---

[8] Though £300 may not sound like much today, in the mid-17th century, it was a tremendous amount of money. To put it into perspective, based on the average earnings in 2016, you would have to make over £650,000 (about $830,000) to put you in the same bracket as Crusoe earned on his first trip.

[9] Feverish delirium

mate and who was now in command of the ship. This was the unhappiest voyage a man had ever made. I had left with my friend's kind and honest widow £200 of my new-gained wealth and although I did not even take £100 with me, I fell into terrible misfortunes. The first thing happened when our ship was headed towards the Canary Islands, or rather between those islands and the African shore. We were surprised in the grey of the morning by a Turkish pirate ship from Salé in Morocco, which chased with all the speed he could make. We crowded as much canvas as our yards would take or our masts would carry to get clear,[10] but the pirate gained on us and came up to us in a few hours. We prepared to fight, our ship having twelve guns and the rogue eighteen. About three in the afternoon we met. Bringing to by mistake across our quarter, instead of across our stern as he intended, we brought eight of our guns to bear on that side and poured in a broadside on him. He veered off again after returning our fire and fired in his small shot from the nearly 200 men he had on board. No one was touched on our ship, since all our men kept under cover. He prepared to attack us again and we prepared to defend ourselves. Sixty men boarded our ship, who immediately cut and hacked the sails and rigging. We pursued them with small shot, half-pikes, [11] powder-chests[12] and the like and cleared our deck of them twice. To cut short this depressing part of our story, our ship was disabled, three of our men were killed and eight wounded. We were forced to surrender and were all taken as prisoners into Salé, a port belonging to the Moors.

My time there was not as dreadful as I thought at first. I wasn't taken through the country to the emperor's court, as the rest of our men were. I was kept by the pirate captain as his prize and made his slave, being

---

[10] Put as many sails up as possible to flee from the pirates.

[11] A short spear-like weapon formerly used by sailors boarding enemy vessels.

[12] A small wooden box containing a charge of gunpowder, old nails or scrap iron, secured over the side of a ship and exploded when an enemy attempted to board.

young and nimble and fit for his business. At this surprising change of circumstance, from a merchant to a miserable slave, I was overwhelmed and now I looked back on my father's prophetic sermon to me – I would be miserable and have nobody to save me. Now the hand of Heaven had taken me and I was devastated without redemption. Sadly, this was only a taste of the misery I was to go through.

As my new patron – or master – had taken me to his house, I hoped he would also take me with him when he went to sea again, believing it would his fate to be taken by a Spanish or Portuguese man-of-war[13] then I would be set free. But this hope was soon taken away. When he went to sea he left me on shore to look after his little garden and do the common drudgery of slaves around his house, and when he came home again from his cruise, he ordered me to lie in the cabin to look after the ship.

I contemplated nothing except my escape and what method I might take to bring it about. I found no way that had the least probability of success and nothing presented itself to make the belief in escape rational, though. I had nobody to tell my plan to who would leave with me – no fellow-slave, no Englishman, Irishman, or Scotchman there but myself. For two years, though I often pleased myself with the thought, I never had the least encouraging prospect of putting it in practice.

After about two years, an odd circumstance presented itself which again put the old thought of making an escape attempt into my head. My patron was at home longer than usual without outfitting his ship. I heard he needed money and once or twice a week, he would take the ship's pinnace[14] and go out to sea fishing. He always took me and young

---

[13] Warship

[14] A small boat, typically with sails, forming part of the equipment of a warship or other large vessel.

Maresco with him to row the boat. We made him very happy and I proved very handy at catching fish, to the extent that sometimes he would send me with one of his Moorish kinsmen, and the youth – the Maresco, as they called him – to catch a dish of fish for him.

Going fishing on a calm morning, a fog rose so thick that, though we were not even half a league[15] from shore, we lost sight of it. We didn't know where or which way we were rowing. We toiled all day and night and when morning came we found we had headed off to sea instead of pulling in to shore and we were at least six miles from shore. However, we got in again with a great deal of work and some danger, since the wind began to blow hard in the morning and we were very hungry.

Our patron, cautioned by this disaster, decided to take more care of himself in the future. We brought our English ship's longboat he had taken and he decided not to go fishing anymore without a compass and some provisions. He ordered the carpenter of his ship – who was also an English slave – to build a little cabin in the middle of the longboat, with a place to stand behind to steer and haul home the mainsheet[16] and with room for a hand or two to stand and work the sails. She sailed with what we call a shoulder-of-mutton sail.[17] The boom moved over the top of the cabin, which lay very snug and low and had room for him to stay with a slave or two, a table to eat on and small lockers to put in some bottles of liquor he thought fit to drink as well as his bread, rice, and coffee.

We went out fishing in this boat frequently and as I was the handiest at catching fish for him, he never went without me. He decided to go out in this boat, either for pleasure or for fish, with a few distinguished Moors from Salé. Overnight he sent on board the boat a larger supply of provisions than ordinary and had ordered me to get ready three

---

[15] A former measure of distance by land, usually about three miles.
[16] A sheet used for controlling and trimming the mainsail of a sailing boat.
[17] A triangular sail carried on a boat's mast, named from its shape.

fusees[18] with gunpowder and shot, since they were going to try some bird hunting for sport as well as fishing.

I got all things ready as he had directed and waited the next morning with the boat washed clean, her ancient [19] and pendants out and everything to accommodate his guests. Before long, my patron came on board alone and told me his guests had put off going, due to some business that fell through and ordered me, with the man and boy – as usual – to go out and catch them some fish. His friends were to dine at his house and he commanded that as soon as I got some fish I would bring them to his house, all of which I prepared to do.

Right then, notions of liberation darted into my thoughts. Now I had a little ship at my command and since my master was gone, I prepared to furnish myself, not for fishing but for a voyage. The only problem was I didn't know, and I didn't consider where I would steer – just anywhere to get out of that place.

My first idea was to make a pretense to speak to the Moor, to get something for our survival on board. I told him we must not presume to eat our patron's bread. He said that was true, so he brought a large basket of biscuits and three jars of fresh water into the boat. I knew where my patron's case of bottles was – which by the brand was pirated from an English ship – and I took them to the boat while the Moor was on shore so he thought they were already there. I also carried a about a fifty-pound lump of beeswax into the boat with a section of twine, a hatchet, saw and a hammer, all of which were great use to us afterwards. Another trick I tried on him was: his name was Ismael, but they called him Moely. So I called to him "Moely, our patron's guns are on board the boat. Can you not get a little gunpowder and shot? We

---

[18] A type of light musket.
[19] Flag

may kill some alcamies (a type of bird) for ourselves and I know he keeps the gunner's stores in the ship."

"Yes," he said, "I'll bring some." He brought a large leather pouch, which held a pound and a half of gunpowder and another which had about five pounds of shot and some bullets, and put them all into the boat. At the same time, I had found some of my master's gunpowder in the cabin, which I filled one of the large bottles with, pouring what was in it into another. Equipped with everything needed, we sailed out of the port to fish. The castle at the entrance of the port knew who we were and took no notice of us, and we were less than a mile out of the port before we hauled in our sail and started to fish. The wind blew from the north-northeast, which was against my wishes, because if it had blown from the south, I could have easily made the coast of Spain, and at least reached the bay of Cadiz. But I decided that, blow which way it would, I would be gone from that horrid place and leave the rest to fate.

After we had fished some time and caught nothing – when I had fish on my hook I would not pull them up, so he would not see them – I said to the Moor, "This will not do. This does not serve our master. We must go farther off." He, thinking no harm, agreed and being in the head of the boat, set the sails. As I had the helm, I ran the boat out nearly three miles farther and then came to a stop, as if I would fish. Giving the boy the helm, I stepped forward to where the Moor was, and making as if I was going down to get something behind him, I took him by surprise with my arm under his waist and tossed him overboard. He came up immediately like a cork and begged to be taken in, told me he would go all over the world with me. He swam so strong after the boat that he would have reached me very quickly as there was only a little wind. I stepped into the cabin, and grabbing one of the shotguns, I pointed it at him and told him I had done him no harm and if he would be quiet I would do him none. "But," I said, "you swim well enough to reach the shore and the sea is calm. Make your way to shore and I will do you no harm, but if you come near the boat I'll shoot you through the head, because I am determined to have my freedom." He turned himself around and swam for shore, and I have no doubt he reached it with ease since he was an excellent swimmer.

I could have been content to have taken this Moor with me and drowned the boy, but there was no way I could trust him. When he was gone, I turned to the boy and said to him, "Xury, if you will be faithful to me, I'll make you a great man. But if you will not stroke your face to be true to me" – which meant, swear by Muhammad and his father's beard – "I must throw you into the sea too." The boy smiled and spoke so innocently that I could not distrust him, and swore to be faithful to me and go all over the world with me.

While I was in view of the Moor who was swimming, I headed out to sea with the boat, so they might think I had gone towards the Straits' mouth – as anyone who had their wits would do. Who would have supposed we sailed on to the south, to the truly Barbarian coast, where whole nations of negroes were sure to surround us with their canoes and destroy us, where if we went on shore we would be eaten by savage beasts, or more merciless savages of the human kind?

At dusk, I changed my course and steered directly south, bending my course a little towards the east to keep close to shore. Having a fair wind and a smooth, quiet sea, I believe by the next afternoon when I first made land, I was at least 150 miles south of Salé – well beyond the Emperor of Morocco's dominions, or any other king, since we saw no people. My fear of the Moors was so great, I would not stop or go on shore. The wind continued for five days, then with the wind shifting to the south, I concluded if any vessels were chasing me, they also would now give up. I decided to head for the coast and weighed anchor in the mouth of a little river. I didn't know what, where, what latitude, what country, what nation, or what river. I neither saw, nor desired to see any people – the principal thing I wanted was fresh water. We came into this creek in the evening, deciding to swim on shore as soon as it was dark and discover the country. But as soon as it was dark, we heard horrible noises – the barking, roaring and howling of unknown wild creatures. The poor boy was ready to die from fear and begged me not to go on shore until daylight. "Well, Xury," I said, "then I won't. But we may see men in daylight who will be as bad to us as those lions."

"Then we give them the shoot gun," said Xury, laughing, "make them run wey." Xury spoke English by talking among us slaves. I was glad to see the boy so cheerful, and I gave him a dram[20] out of our patron's case of bottles to cheer him up. After all, Xury's advice was good and I took it. We dropped our little anchor and lay still all night. I say still, since we did not sleep. In a couple hours we saw huge creatures – we did not know what to call them – of all sorts come down to the seashore and run into the water, wallowing and washing to cool themselves and they made hideous howling and yelling I had never in my life.

Xury was terribly frightened and so was I, but we were both more frightened when we heard one of these mighty creatures swimming towards our boat. We could not see him, but we heard by his blowing that he was a monstrously huge and furious beast. Xury said it was a lion and it might be true for all I know. Poor Xury pleaded with me to weigh anchor and row away. "No," I said, "Xury, we can slip our cable[21] and go off to sea. They cannot follow us far." I had no sooner said that when I saw the creature (whatever it was) within two oars' length, which surprised me. I immediately stepped to the cabin door and picking up my gun fired at him. He instantly turned around and swam towards the shore again.

It is impossible to describe the horrid noises, hideous cries and howling on the edge of the shore as well as higher within the country at

---

[20] A small drink
[21] Disengage (a ship's anchor) when leaving a port in haste.

the noise from the gun, something I have reason to believe those creatures had never heard before. This convinced me there was no going on shore at night on that coast, and how to venture on shore in the day was another question too. To fall into the hands of any savages would have been as bad as to fall into the hands of the lions and tigers. At least we were equally nervous of the danger.

Even with this terror, we were forced to go on shore somewhere for water since we didn't have a pint left in the boat. Xury said if I would let him go on shore with one of the jars, he would find out if there was any water and bring some to me. I asked him why would he go? Why not me and he stay in the boat? The boy answered with so much warmth, I loved him for it. "If wild mans come, they eat me, you go wey."

"Well, Xury, we will both go and if the wild mans come, we will kill them. They won't eat either of us." I gave Xury a piece of bread to eat and a shot of liquor out of our patron's case of bottles and we hauled the boat in as close the shore as we thought was suitable and waded on shore, carrying nothing but our guns and two jars for water.

I did want to go out of sight of the boat, fearing canoes with savages coming down the river. The boy, seeing a low place about a mile up country, rambled to it and eventually I saw him come running towards me. I thought he was pursued by some savage or frightened by some wild beast and I ran towards him to help him. When I came closer to him I saw something hanging over his shoulders, which was a creature he had shot, something like a hare but a different color with longer legs. We were very glad and it was very good meat, but the great joy poor Xury came with was to tell me he had found good water and seen no wild mans.

We found out after we did not need to take such pains for water, since a little higher up the creek where we were, we found the water fresh when the tide was out. We filled our jars and feasted on the hare he had killed and prepared to go on our way, having seen no footsteps of any human creature in that part of the country.

As I had been on a voyage to this coast before, I knew the islands of the Canaries and the Cape de Verde Islands as well, lay not far off the coast. However, I had no instruments to know what latitude we were in and not exactly remembering what latitude they were in, I did not know where to look for them, otherwise I might easily have found some of these islands. My hope was, if I stayed along this coast until I came to that part where the English traded, I would find some vessels which would help us and take us in.

By my best calculation, I now must be at that country which, lying between the Emperor of Morocco's dominions and the negroes, lies wasted and uninhabited, except by wild beasts. The negroes, having abandoned it and gone farther south in fear of the Moors, and the Moors not thinking it worth inhabiting since it was barren. Both have abandoned it because of the exceptional number of tigers, lions, leopards and other furious creatures which live there. The Moors use it only for their hunting, where they go like an army with a few thousand men at a time. Undeniably, for nearly a hundred miles on this coast we saw nothing but a wasted, uninhabited country by day and heard nothing but the howling and roaring of wild beasts by night.

Once or twice in the daytime I thought I saw the Pico of Tenerife – the top of the Tenerife Mountain in the Canaries – and had a great mind to venture out in hopes of reaching it. But having tried twice, I was forced in again by opposing winds and the sea getting too rough for my little vessel. I decided instead to pursue my first strategy and keep along the shore.

Several times I had to land for fresh water after we had left this place. Once, early in morning we anchored by a little point of land, which was high and we went farther in. Xury, whose eyes were more around him than it seems mine were, called softly to me and told me it would be best if we go farther off the shore. "Look, over there is a terrible monster on the side of that hill, fast asleep." I looked where he pointed and saw a terrible monster indeed. It was a terrifyingly large lion which was laying on the side of the shore, under the shade of a precipice that hung a little over him.

"Xury," I said, "you go on shore and kill him."

Xury looked frightened. "Me kill! He eat me at one mouth!" – one mouthful he meant. I said no more to the boy, but told him to stay still. I took our biggest gun, which was almost musket-bore, and loaded it with a good charge of gunpowder with two slugs, and put it down. Then I loaded another gun with two bullets[22] and the third (as we had three pieces) I loaded with five smaller bullets. I took the best aim I could with the first gun and tried to shoot him in the head, but he laid with his leg raised a little above his nose. The slugs hit his leg around the knee and broke the bone. He got up, growling at first, but finding his leg broken fell again. He then got up on three legs and gave the most hideous roar I ever heard. I was a little surprised I had not hit him in the head. I picked up the second piece immediately and though he began to move off, fired again and shot him in the head, and had the pleasure to see him drop and make a slight noise, struggling for life. Then Xury took heart, and had me let him go on shore. The boy jumped into the water and, taking a little gun in one hand, swam to shore with the other hand. Coming close to the creature, he put the muzzle of the piece to his ear and shot him in the head again, which killed him.

This was game to us, but this was no food and I was very sorry to lose three charges of powder and shot on a creature that was good for nothing to us. However, Xury said he would have some of him. He came

---

[22] When this was written in 1719, the term bullet was more likely a musket ball. The word bullet comes from the 16th-century French term *boulet* meaning 'small ball'

on board and asked me to give him the hatchet. "For what, Xury?" I asked.

"Me cut off his head," he said. However, Xury could not cut off his head, but he cut off a foot and brought it with him, and it was a monstrously large one.

I thought to myself the skin of him might, one way or other, be of some value to us. I decided to take off his skin if I could. Xury and I went to work on him, but Xury was a much better workman at it, since I did not know how to do it. It took us both the whole day, but at last we got off the hide of him, and spreading it on the top of our cabin, the sun dried it in two days' time and afterwards it served me as a blanket to lie on.

3.

Wrecked on a Desert Island

After this stop, we went south continually for about twelve days, living very sparingly on our provisions and going no more often to the shore than we needed for fresh water. My plan was to make it to the river Gambia or Senegal – anywhere near the Cape de Verde – where I hoped to meet with some European ship. And if I did not, I did not know what course to take, except to head for the islands or die there among the negroes. I knew all the ships from Europe, which sailed either to the coast of Guinea or to Brazil or the East Indies, headed for this cape and I put my whole fortune on this single point – either I must meet with some ship or must die.

After the twelve days, I began to see the land was inhabited and in a few places as we sailed by, we saw people stand on the shore to look at us. We could also see they were quite black and naked. I was thinking of going on shore to them once, but Xury advised against it, saying "No go, no go." However, I hauled in closer to shore so I might talk to them, and they ran along the shore following me a fair way. I observed they had no weapons in their hand, except one who had a long slender stick, which Xury said was a lance and they could throw them a long way with good aim. So, I kept at a distance but talked with them by signs as well as I could, particularly making signs for something to eat. They signaled to me to stop my boat and they would fetch me some meat. I lowered the top of my sail and stayed there waiting. Two of them ran up into the country and in less than half-an-hour came back, bringing with them two pieces of dried meat and some corn. We didn't know what either was but we were willing to accept it. How to get the food was our next issue, since I would not venture on shore to them and they were just as afraid of us. But they took a safe way for all of us. They brought it to the shore and put it down, then went and stood a long way off until we got it on board, and then came close to us again.

We made signs of thanks to them since we had no way of paying them. But then an opportunity offered itself to please them wonderfully. While we were by the shore two mighty creatures came, one pursuing the other with great fury, from the mountains towards the sea. Whether it was the male pursuing the female, or whether they were in sport or in rage, we could not tell, any more than we could tell whether it was usual or strange, but I believe it was the latter. Those ravenous creatures seldom appear except at night and the people were terribly frightened, especially the women. The man who had the lance did not flee from them, but the rest did. As the two creatures ran into the water, they did not try to attack any of the negroes, but plunged into the sea and swam around, as if they had come for their pleasure. One of them began to get closer to our boat than I expected, but I was ready for him. I had loaded my gun as fast as possible and asked Xury to load both the others. As soon as he came within each, I fired and shot him in the head. Immediately he sank down into the water, but rose instantly and plunged up and down, struggling for life. He immediately headed for the shore, but between the wound and the water, he died just before he reached the shore.

It is impossible to express the astonishment of these poor creatures at the noise and fire of my gun. Some of them were even ready to die from fear and fell down in terror, but when they saw the creature dead in the water and that I made signs to them to come to the shore, they felt encouraged and began to search for the creature. I found him by his blood staining the water. With the help of a rope slung around him which I gave the negroes to haul, they dragged him on shore and found it was a very interesting leopard, spotted, fine and splendid. The negroes held up their hands in admiration of what I had killed him with.

The other creature, frightened with the flash of fire and the noise of the gun, swam on shore and ran to the mountains from where they came. From that distance, I could not tell what it was. The negroes wished to eat the flesh of this creature, so I was willing to have them take it as a favor from me which, when I made signs to them to take it, they were very thankful. Immediately they started to work on him. Though they had no knife, with a sharpened piece of wood they took off his skin as well, if not better, than we could have done with a knife. They offered me some of the meat, which I declined, pointing out I would give it to them. I made signs for the skin, which they gave me very freely and then brought me a lot more of their food which, though I did not understand, I accepted. I then made signs to them for some water and held out one of my jars to them, turning it upside down to show that it was empty and I wanted to have it filled. They called immediately to some of their friends and two women brought a large earthenware jug. I sent Xury on shore with my jars and he filled all three of them. The women were as naked as the men.

I was now equipped with roots and corn and water. Leaving my friendly negroes, I headed forward for about eleven more days, without trying to go near the shore until I saw the land run out a long way into the sea, about 15 miles ahead of me. The sea was very calm and I kept a large offing[23] to make the point. At about six miles, I plainly saw land on the other side, towards the sea. I concluded with certainty this was the Cape de Verde and the Cape de Verde Islands. However, they were still far off and I didn't know what was best for me to do – if I were taken by a fresh gust of wind, I might reach neither one.

____

[23] The more distant part of the sea in view

Xury had the helm while I was pondering this dilemma and I stepped into the cabin and sat down. Suddenly, the boy cried out, "Master, master, a ship with a sail!" The foolish boy was frightened out of his wits, thinking it must be some of his master's ships sent to pursue us, but I knew we were far enough out of their reach. I jumped out of the cabin and immediately saw not only the ship, but that it was a Portuguese ship and, as I thought, was bound for the coast of Guinea for negroes. But when I observed the course she steered, I was convinced they were headed some other way and did not plan to come any closer to shore. I headed out to sea as much as I could, determined to speak with them if possible.

Even with all the speed my sails could gather, I would not be able to catch up to them and they would be gone before I could make any signal to them. After I had tried my best and thought the situation hopeless, they saw through their telescopes it was a European boat, which they supposed must belong to some ship that was lost. They shortened sail[24] to let me come up. I was encouraged by this and as I had my patron's ancient on board, I waved it to them as a signal of distress and fired a gun, both which they saw. They told me they saw the smoke, though they did not hear the gun. In about three hours' time I came up next to them.

They asked me what I was, in Portuguese, Spanish and French, but I understood none of them. At last a Scotch sailor on board called to me. I answered him and told him I was an Englishman and I had escaped out of slavery from the Moors at Salé. They then asked me to come on board and very kindly took me and all my goods aboard.

It was an overwhelming joy to me that I was rescued from the miserable and almost hopeless condition I was in. I immediately offered all I had to the captain of the ship, in return for my rescue. He

---

[24] To reduce the amount of sail, thereby slowing a ship down

generously told me he would take nothing from me and all I had would be delivered safe to me when we arrived in the Brazils. He said, "I have saved your life on no other terms than I would hope to be saved myself and it may, one time or other, be my fate to be in the same condition. Besides, you will be so far away from your own country when I take you to the Brazils. If I take from you what you have, you will starve and then I only take away the life I have given. No, no, Seignior Inglese (Mr. Englishman), I will carry you there in charity and those things will help to buy your existence there and your passage home again."

As much as he was charitable in this offer, he was just as much in the execution to a tittle [25] since he ordered the seamen to not touch anything I had. Then he took everything into his own possession and gave me back an exact inventory, even my three earthen jars.

He saw my boat was very good and told me he would buy it from me for his ship's use, asking what I wanted for it. I told him he had been so generous to me that I could not put a price on the boat and left it entirely to him. He told me he would give me a note to pay 80 pieces of eight[26] for it in Brazil and if anyone offered me more, he would make up the difference. He also offered me 60 pieces of eight more for my boy Xury, which I despised the thought of. Not that I was unwilling to let the captain have him, but I didn't want to sell the freedom of a poor boy who had assisted me so faithfully in obtaining my own. When I let him know my reason, he agreed and offered me this instead: he would give the boy his freedom in ten years if he turned Christian. Xury said he was willing to go to him, so I let the captain have him.

We had a very good voyage to the Brazils and I arrived in the Bay de Todos los Santos – All Saints' Bay – 22 days later. I was once more

---

[25] A tiny amount or part of something.
[26] Modern equivalent of about £8,000.

brought from the most miserable of all conditions of life and I now had to consider what to do next with myself.

The generous treatment the captain gave me I can never remember enough. He would take nothing from me for my passage, gave me twenty ducats[27] for the leopard's skin and forty for the lion's skin which I had in my boat and made sure everything I had in the ship was punctually delivered to me. What I was willing to sell he bought from me, such as the case of bottles, two of my guns and a piece of the lump of beeswax – I had made candles from the rest. I made about 220 pieces of eight from all my cargo and with this I went on shore in the Brazils.

I had not been there long before I was recommended to the house of a good honest man like himself, who had an INGENIO (a plantation and a sugarhouse), as they call it. I lived with him for some time and acquainted myself with the planting and making of sugar. Seeing how well the planters lived and how they got rich quick I decided if I could get a license to settle there, I would become a planter too. In the meantime, I decided to find some way to get the money I had left in London sent to me. To do this, I got a letter of naturalization and I did this when I purchased as much uncured[28] land as my money would buy and formed a plan for my plantation and settlement – one which was suitable to the stock I proposed to receive from England.

I had a neighbor from Lisbon, but with English parents. His name was Wells and he was in the same circumstances as I was. I call him my neighbor, because his plantation lay next to mine and we got on very sociably together. My inventory was low – as was his – and we planted food rather than anything else for about two years. However, we began to grow and our land began to come to order, so the third year we planted some tobacco and each made a large piece of ground ready for

---

[27] The ducat was a coin which traditionally carried about 1/10 ounce of gold, so 20 ducats would be about 2oz. of gold.

[28] Not taken care of, or in this case, not cultivated

planting sugarcane the next year. But we both wanted help and now I found, more than ever, I had done wrong in parting with my boy Xury.

Sadly, for me to do wrong when I never did right was no great wonder. I could do nothing else but go on. I was working opposite to my natural ability and contrary to the life I delighted in, and I abandoned my father's house and ignored all his good advice. I was finally coming into the very middle class which my father advised me to stay in. If I decided to go on with it, I might as well have stayed at home and never have fatigued myself in the world as I had done. I often used to say to myself, I could have done this as well in England, among my friends. Instead, I went off 5,000 miles to do it among strangers and savages in a wilderness and at such a long distance as to never hear from any part of the world that had the least knowledge of me.

I used to look on my condition with the greatest regret. I had nobody to talk with except this neighbor now and then. No work could be done except by the labor of my hands and I used to say I lived just like a man cast away on some desolate island, who had nobody there but himself. But how fair has it been – and how would all men think – that when they compare their present conditions with others that are worse, Heaven may have them make the exchange and they would be convinced of their previous happiness. How fair has it been, that the truly solitary life I thought about, on a desolate island, would be my luck. I had so often unfairly compared it with the life I led, which if I had continued I would probably have been exceeding prosperous and rich.

I was settled in my business on the plantation when my kind friend, the captain who rescued me at sea, went back. The ship remained there, lading[29] and preparing for his voyage nearly three months. When I told him what little money I had left behind in London, he gave me this

---

[29] Loading a ship with cargo

friendly and sincere advice: "Seignior Inglese," (as he always called me) "if you will give me letters and a procuration[30] with orders to the person who has your money to send your effects to Lisbon, I will direct that person to give me items which are appropriate for this country and I will bring you them, God willing, when I return. But, since human affairs are all subject to changes and disasters, request only £100 sterling, which you say is half your stock, and take your chances. If it comes safe, you may order the rest the same way and if things go wrong, you will still have the other half." This was such excellent and friendly advice, I was convinced it was the best course of action. I prepared letters for the gentlewoman who I had left my money with and a procuration to the Portuguese captain, as he desired.

I wrote the widow a full account of all my adventures – my slavery, escape and how I met the Portuguese captain at sea, his humanity and what condition I was in now, with all necessary directions for my money. When this honest captain came to Lisbon he found a way – with the help of the English merchants there – to send over not only the order, but also my story to a merchant in London, who told her every detail. She not only delivered the money, but out of her own pocket sent the Portugal captain a very substantial present for his humanity and charity to me.

The merchant in London sent this £100 in English goods directly to the captain in Lisbon, and he brought them all safe to me to the Brazils. Without my direction – since I was too young in my business to think of them – he had taken care to have all sorts of tools, ironwork and utensils necessary for my plantation and which were of great use to me.

When this cargo arrived I thought my fortune made and I was surprised by the joy of it. My good agent – the captain – put out the £5, which my friend had sent him as a present, to purchase and bring me

---

[30] Power of attorney

over a servant, under bond for six years' service. He would not accept any consideration, except a little tobacco which I insisted upon, being my own produce. And this wasn't all. Since my goods were all made in England – such as cloth, baize[31] and things particularly valuable and desirable in the country – I found they sold at a very high profit. I had more than four times the value of my first cargo and was now infinitely beyond my poor neighbor – in the advancement of my plantation, I mean. The first thing I did was buy myself a negro slave and another European servant, in addition to the one who the captain brought me from Lisbon.

But as abused prosperity is often the means of our greatest adversity, so it was with me. The next year I had great success in my plantation. I raised fifty large rolls of tobacco, which was more than I needed to trade for necessities among my neighbors. These fifty rolls, each being more than 100 pounds, were well cured and put aside for the return of the fleet from Lisbon. Now increasing in business and wealth, my head began to be full of projects and undertakings beyond my reach, which are often the destruction of the best heads in business. Had I continued in the situation I was now in, I would have had all the happy things happen to me which my father so sincerely recommended – a quiet life which he had so sensibly described the middle class to be full of. But I was still to be the willful agent of all my own miseries. To increase my fault and double the thoughts I had – which in my future sorrows I would have leisure to make – these mistakes were made by my obstinate, foolish inclination to wandering abroad. I pursued that inclination, in contradiction to doing myself good in a plain pursuit of those prospects, which nature and Providence both presented me with and to make my duty.

---

[31] A coarse felt-like material that is typically green, used for covering billiard and card tables.

I could not be satisfied now. As I had done once already by breaking away from my parents, I must go and leave the happiness I had being a rich and thriving man in my new plantation, only to pursue a rash and extreme desire of rising faster than nature allowed. I threw myself down again into the deepest hole of human misery a man ever fell into.

Having now lived almost four years in the Brazils and beginning to prosper splendidly on my plantation, I had not only learned the language, but had made friends with my fellow planters, as well as among the merchants at the port of St. Salvador. While talking to them, I had frequently given them an account of my two voyages to the coast of Guinea, how I traded with the negroes there and how easy it was on the coast to trade with trivial items – beads, toys, knives, hatchets, bits of glass, and the like – and to receive back not only gold dust, Guinea grains, elephants' teeth, etc., but also negroes for the service of the Brazils, in large numbers.

They always listened very attentively to my conversations, especially to the buying of negroes, which was a trade at that time. It was a trade which was only carried on by *assientos*, or by permission of the kings of Spain and Portugal, so that few negroes were bought, and these were excessively expensive.

After having a serious conversation with my acquaintances, three of them came to me next morning and told me they had been thinking a lot about what I had said. They came to make a secret proposal and after commanding me to secrecy, they told me they wanted to outfit a ship to go to Guinea. They all had plantations like mine and were straitened[32] for nothing so much as servants. Since it was a trade that could not be carried on, because they could not publicly sell the negroes when they came home, they wanted to make one voyage only, bring the negroes on shore privately and divide them among their own

---

[32] Had very low supply

plantations. The question was whether I would be their supercargo[33] in the ship, to manage the trading part on the coast of Guinea. In payment, they offered me an equal share of the negroes for my work.

This was a fair proposal, had it been made to anyone who had not had a plantation of his own to look after, which was becoming very extensive and with good stock. But for me, who just had to go on as I had for the last few years and who, in that time, was worth probably £4,000 sterling – and that was increasing too – for me to think of such a voyage was the most preposterous thing a man in such circumstances could be guilty of.

But I was born to be my own destroyer and couldn't resist the offer, any more than I could restrain my first rambling desires when my father's good advice was lost on me. I told them I would go with all my heart, if they would look after my plantation in my absence and dispose of it as I saw fit if I failed. This they all promised to do, putting it in writing. I made a formal will, disposing of my plantation and belongings in case of my death, making the captain of the ship who had saved my life my beneficiary, but asking him to dispose of my belongings as I had directed in my will – half of the proceeds being to himself and the other to be shipped to England.

I took all possible care to preserve my possessions and to keep up my plantation. Had I used half as much forethought in this, I certainly never would have gone away from such a prosperous and thriving enterprise and gone on a sea voyage with all its hazards, to say nothing of the reasons I had to expect misfortune.

But I blindly obeyed the dictates of my imagination rather than my reason. The ship was outfitted, the cargo loaded and all things prepared by my partners, I went on board September 1, 1659, the same day eight

---

[33] A representative of the ship's owner on board a merchant ship, responsible for overseeing the cargo and its sale.

years earlier I left my father and mother at Hull to rebel against their authority and the fool to my own interests.

Our ship was about 120 tons, carried six guns and 17 men, including the master, his boy and myself. We had on board no large cargo, just toys which were fit for our trade with the negroes, such as beads, bits of glass, shells, and other trifles, especially little telescopes, knives, scissors, hatchets and so on.

We set sail to the north on our own coast, planning to head over to the African coast when we came to about ten degrees northern latitude, which was the standard course in those days. We had very good weather – only excessively hot – all the way along our coast, until we came to Cape St. Augustine. From there, keeping further out to sea, we lost sight of land and steered as if we were bound for the isle Fernando de Noronha,[34] holding our course and leaving those islands to the east. In this course, we passed the equator in about twelve days' time and were by our last observation at 7°22' North latitude, when a violent hurricane took us by surprise. It began from the southeast, came around to the northwest, then settled in the northeast. From there it blew in such a terrible way, that for twelve days we could do nothing but sail away in front of it and let it carry us where fate and the fury of the winds directed. During those twelve days I expected every day to be swallowed up and nobody on the ship expected to save their lives.

Besides the terror of the storm, we had one of our men die of fever and one man and the boy washed overboard. Around the twelfth day, the weather cleared a little and the master made an observation as well as he could and found he was around 11° north latitude, but he was 22° west of Cape St. Augustine. He found he was on the coast of Guiana near the north part of Brazil, between the Amazon and Orinoco River

---

[34] Fernando de Noronha is a volcanic archipelago about 350 kilometers off Brazil's northeast coast.

and began to consult with me what course he should take, since the ship was leaky and disabled and he was going directly back to the coast of Brazil.

I was positively against that and looking over the charts of the coast of America with him, we concluded there was no inhabited country until we came within the circle of the Caribbean Islands. We decided to head for Barbados, which by keeping out to sea to avoid the indraft of the Gulf of Mexico we might easily reach, we hoped, in about fifteen days. We realized we could not possibly make our voyage to the coast of Africa without some assistance both to our ship and to ourselves.

With this plan, we changed course and steered to the northwest to reach some of our English islands, where I hoped for relief. But our voyage was otherwise preordained. At latitude 12°18', a second storm came on us which carried us away with the same hastiness westward and drove us so out of the way of all human commerce, that had all our lives been saved, we were more likely to be devoured by savages than ever returning to our own country.

In this distress and with the wind still blowing very hard, one of our men shouted, "Land!" and we had barely run out of the cabin, hoping to see where in the world we were, when the ship struck on a sandbar. With her motion being stopped so suddenly, the sea broke over her so violently that we expected to have died immediately. We immediately huddled together to shelter us from the foam and spray of the sea.

It is not easy for anyone who has not been in the same situation to understand the alarm of men in such circumstances. We didn't know where we were – whether an island or the mainland, whether inhabited or not. As the rage of the wind was still great, though less than at first, we knew the ship wouldn't hold for very long without breaking into pieces unless the winds miraculously turned around. We sat looking at one another and expected death every moment, and every man accordingly prepared for another world. There was little or nothing more for us to do. Our present comfort – and all the comfort we had – was against our expectation, the ship did not break and the master said the wind began to decrease.

Though we thought the wind did subside a little, the ship was stuck on the sand, and stuck too firmly for us to expect to get it off. We were in an awful state and had nothing to do but think about saving our lives as best as we could. We had a boat at our stern just before the storm, but she was staved[35] when hurled against the ship's rudder, then she broke away and either sunk or was driven off to sea, so there was no hope from her. We had another boat on board, but how to get her off into the sea was doubtful. However, there was no time to debate, since we thought the ship would break into pieces at any minute – and some told us she was broken already.

In this distress the mate of our vessel took hold of the boat, and with the help of the rest of the men got her slung over the ship's side. Getting everyone into her we let go and committed all eleven of us to God's mercy and the wild sea. Though the storm had subsided considerably, the sea ran extremely high on the shore, and might well be called DEN WILD ZEE, as the Dutch call the sea in a storm.

And now our case was very dismal. We all saw clearly the sea went so high that the boat could not survive and we would inevitably have drowned. As to making sail, we had none, though if we had we couldn't have done anything with it. With heavy hearts we worked at the oar towards the land, like men going to execution. We all knew when the boat came near the shore she would be broken in a thousand pieces by the breaking of the waves. We committed our souls to God in the most solemn way. With the wind driving us towards the shore, we hurried our destruction with our own hands, pulling as well as we could towards land.

---

[35] Broken by piercing it roughly

What the shore was – rock or sand, steep or shallow – we did not know. The only hope we had was, if we could find some bay or the mouth of some river, we might run our boat in or get under the protection of the land. But nothing like this appeared. As we approached the shore, the land looked more frightful than the sea. After we had rowed – or actually were driven – about five miles, a raging mountain-like wave came rolling astern[36] of us and plainly told us to expect the COUP DE GRACE.[37] It took us with such a fury that it overturned the boat instantly and separating us from the boat as well as from one another, gave us no time to say, "O God!" as we were all swallowed up in a moment.

Nothing can describe the confusion I felt when I sank into the water. Although I swam very well, I could not rescue myself from the waves to draw a breath, until a wave carried me a vast way on to the shore, and having spent itself, went back and left me on land, but half dead with the water I took in. Seeing myself closer to the mainland than I expected, I had enough presence of mind, as well as breath left, to get on my feet and attempt to make it to land as fast as I could before another wave returned. I soon found it was impossible to avoid. I saw the sea come after me as high as a large hill and as furious as an enemy, which I had no strength to contend with. My business was to hold my breath and raise myself on the water if I could. Swimming to preserve my breathing and pilot myself towards the shore, my greatest concern was now the sea, since it would carry me towards shore when it came in but could also carry me back again when it went back towards the sea.

The wave that came on me again buried me almost thirty feet deep in its body and I could feel myself carried with a massive force and

---

[36] Behind.

[37] A final shot given to kill a wounded person.

swiftness in towards the shore. I held my breath and swam forward with all my might. I was ready to burst from holding my breath when I felt myself rising up, and to my immediate relief I found my head and hands shoot out above the surface of the water. Though it was barely two seconds I could keep myself above water, it relieved me greatly, gave me breath and new courage. I was covered again with water a long time but I held out. Finding the wave had spent itself and began to return to the sea, I plowed forward against the return of the waves and felt the ground again with my feet. I stood still a few moments to recover my breath until the waters left, then ran with what strength I had further towards the shore. But this did not deliver me from the fury of the sea, which came pouring in after me again. Twice more I was lifted by the waves and carried forward as before.

The last of these had nearly been fatal to me, since the sea had hurried me along as before and thrust me against a piece of rock with such force that it left me almost unconscious and helpless. The blow hit my side and chest and beat the breath out of me. Had it immediately returned, I would have been strangled in the water. But I recovered a little before the return of the waves and seeing I would be covered again with water, I decided to hold on tight to a piece of the rock and hold my breath until the wave went back. Since the waves were not as high as at first and being closer to land, I held on until the wave subsided and then ran again, which brought me so close to shore that the next wave, though it went over me, did not swallow me up and carry me away. The next run I took, I got to the mainland where, to my great comfort, I clambered up the cliffs of the shore and sat down on the grass, free from danger and out of the reach of the water.

I was now safe on shore and began to look up and thank God that my life was saved. I believe it is impossible to express what the ecstasies and joys of the soul are, when it is saved out of the grave. When a criminal has a noose around his neck, and just about to be hanged, has a reprieve brought to him – I do not wonder that they bring a surgeon to let him bleed[38] the moment they tell him of it, so the surprise does not drive the animal spirits from the heart and overwhelm him.

"Sudden joys, like griefs, confuse at first."

I walked along the shore lifting my hands and my whole being, wrapped up in contemplation of my rescue, making a thousand gestures and motions which I cannot describe, thinking about all my comrades who had drowned and there was not one soul saved except myself. As for them, I never saw them afterwards or any sign of them, except three of their hats, one cap and two shoes.

I looked at the stranded vessel. The break and froth of the sea was so big, I could hardly see it and I thought: Lord! How was it possible I could get on shore? After I had comforted myself with my present condition, I began to look around me to see what kind of place I was in and what was next to be done. Soon I found my comforts subside and I had a terrible thought. I was wet, had no clothes to change into and nothing to eat or drink to comfort me. I did not see any prospect ahead of me except dying of hunger or being consumed by wild beasts. What was particularly troubling to me was I had no weapon, either to hunt and kill any creature for food, or to defend myself against any other creature that might want to kill me. I had nothing with me except a knife, a tobacco pipe and a little tobacco in a box. This was all my provisions and threw me into such terrible anguish that for a while I ran about like a madman. With night approaching, I dejectedly considered what would happen if there were any predatory beasts in that country, as at night they always come abroad for their prey.

---

[38] Bloodletting, as described here, is the withdrawal of blood from a patient to cure or prevent illness and disease. In Defoe's time, it was common to apply leeches to a person to remove some blood to make sure the bodily fluids (or humours) were in proper balance. Obviously, not an advisable medical practice.

The only remedy offering itself was to get up into a thick bushy tree like a fir which grew near me, where I decided to sit all night and consider the next day what death I would die since I saw no prospect of life. I walked about a furlong[39] from the shore to see if I could find any fresh water to drink, which I did to my great joy. Having drank and put a little tobacco in my mouth to prevent hunger I went to the tree, and getting up into it, tried to place myself so if I would sleep I wouldn't fall. I cut a short stick like a truncheon[40] for my defense, took up my accommodation and being extremely tired, I fell fast asleep and slept as comfortably as I believe few could have done in my condition and found myself more refreshed than, I think, I ever was on such an occasion.

---

[39] 220 yards.
[40] A policeman's baton.

4.

First Weeks on the Island

When I woke up it was broad daylight, the weather clear and the storm weakened so the sea did not rage and swell as before. But what surprised me most was the ship was lifted off in the night from the sand and was driven up almost as far as the rock I first mentioned, where I had been bruised by the wave smashing me against it. Being a mile from where I was on shore and the ship seeming to stand upright, I wished myself on board, so I could at least save some necessities for my use.

When I came down from my apartment in the tree, I looked around me again and the first thing I saw was the boat, on land about two miles to my right, as the wind and the sea had tossed her up. I walked as far as I could on the shore to get to her but found an inlet of water between me and the boat which was about half a mile wide. I came back for now, intent on getting at the ship where I hoped to find something for my survival.

A little after noon the sea was very calm and the tide ebbed so far out that I could come within a quarter of a mile of the ship. My grief was renewed now. If we had kept on board we would have all been safe and I would not be so miserable as I now was, left entirely destitute of all comfort and company. This forced tears to my eyes again but as there was little relief in that, I decided if possible to get to the ship. I pulled off my clothes – since the weather was hot to the extreme – and went in the water, but when I came to the ship I did not know how to get on board. Though she lay aground and high out of the water, there was nothing within my reach to grab on to. I swam around her twice, and the second time I spied a small piece of rope – which I wondered why I did not see it at first – hung down by the fore-chains. It was low enough that with great difficulty I got hold of it and by the help of that rope I got up into the forecastle[41] of the ship. Here I found the ship had bulged and had a great deal of water in her hold, but she laid on the side of a bank of hard sand, so her stern was lifted up on the bank and her head low, almost to the water. Because of this all her quarter was free and all that was in that part was dry. My first work was to search and to see what was spoiled and what was not. First, I found all the ship's provisions were dry and untouched by the water. Being very hungry, I went to the bread room and filled my pockets with biscuits and ate it as I went around looking for other things since I had no time to lose. I also found some rum in the great cabin, which I took a large shot from and which I needed to cheer me up for what was ahead. Now I wanted nothing except a boat to equip me with all the things I expected would be essential to me.

It was pointless to sit and wish for what I didn't have and this adversity stirred me into motion. We had several spare yards of sail, two or three large wooden spars and a spare topmast in the ship. I decided to work with these and I flung as many of them overboard as I could manage, tying each one with a rope so they would not float away. When this was done I went down the ship's side, and pulling them to me, I tied four of them together at both ends as well as I could to make a raft. Laying a couple of short pieces of plank on them crossways, I found I could walk on it very well but the pieces were too light and it was not able to bear much weight. I went to work, and with a carpenter's saw I cut the spare topmast into three lengths and added them to my raft with a great deal of difficulty. The hope of supplying

---

[41] The forward part of a ship below the deck, traditionally used as the crew's living quarters.

myself with necessities encouraged me to go beyond what I would have been able to do on any other occasion.

My raft was now strong enough to bear any reasonable weight. My next care was what to load it with and how to preserve what I placed on it from the surf, though I did not consider this for too long. Considering what I most wanted, I got three of the seamen's chests, which I had broken open and emptied and lowered them down on my raft. The first of these I filled with provisions – bread, rice, three Dutch cheeses, five pieces of dried goat's meat and the small remainder of European corn, which had been put aside for some chickens we brought with us, but were now dead. There had been some barley and wheat but to my great disappointment, the rats had eaten or spoiled it all. As for liquor, I found several cases of bottles belonging to our skipper, in which were some cordial waters[42] and about five or six gallons of rack.[43] These I stowed by themselves, since there was no need to put them in the chest, or any room for them. While I was doing this, the tide began to come in and I was mortified to see my coat, shirt and waistcoat, which I had left on the shore, swim away. As for my breeches,[44] which were only linen and open-kneed, I swam on board in them and my stockings. Now I was rummaging for clothes, which I found enough of, but took no more than I wanted for my current needs, since I had set my eye on other things – such as tools to work with on shore. It was after a long search I found the carpenter's chest, which was definitely a very useful prize to me, and much more valuable than a shipload of gold would have been at that time. I got it down to my raft without losing time to look in it, as I basically knew what it contained.

My next care was for some ammunition and arms. There were two very good shotguns in the great cabin and two pistols. These I secured

---

[42] Liqueurs
[43] Wine
[44] Pants

first, with some powder-horns, a small bag of shot and two rusty old swords. I knew there were three barrels of gunpowder in the ship, but did not know where our gunner had stowed them. With considerable searching, I found them – two of them dry and good, though the third was waterlogged. Those two I got to my raft with the weapons. Now I was well loaded and began to think how I would get to shore with them, having neither sail, oar, nor rudder, and the least bit of wind would have overturned all my navigation.

Three things encouraged me: smooth, calm sea; the tide was rising; and what little wind there was blew me towards the land. Besides the tools in the chest, I found two saws, an axe and a hammer and having found a few broken oars belonging to the boat, I put to sea. For a mile, my raft went very well, except I found it go a little distant from where I had landed before. I realized there was some inward flow of water and consequently I hoped to find some river, which I might use as a port to get to land with my cargo.

As I imagined, so it was. In front of me there appeared a little opening of land and I found the strong tidal current pushed into it, so I guided my raft as well as I could to keep in the middle of the stream.

But here I could have suffered a second shipwreck which, if I had, I know it would have broken my heart. Knowing nothing of the coast, my raft ran aground at one end of it on a submerged sandbank, and not being aground at the other end, it would have taken very little for all my cargo to slip off the end that was afloat and to fall into the water. I put my back against the chests to keep them in their places, but could not thrust the raft off with all my strength and I dared not move. Holding up the chests with all my strength, I stood that way nearly half-an-hour, in which time the rising water brought me a little more level. A little after, the water still rising, my raft floated again and I thrust her off with the oar into the channel and then heading up higher, I found myself in the mouth of a little river with land on both sides and a strong tidal current running up. I looked on both sides for a proper place to get to shore, as I was not willing to be driven too high up the river. I was hoping to see some ships at sea and decided to place myself as near the coast as I could.

I spied a little cove on the right shore of the creek, where I guided my raft with great difficulty. At last I got so near that, reaching ground with my oar, I could shove her directly in. But here I almost dipped my cargo into the sea again, since the shore here was steep. There was no place to land, except where one end of my raft was so high that it would endanger my cargo again. All I could do was wait until the tide was at the highest, anchoring the raft with my oar. I held the side of it close to the shore near a flat piece of ground which I expected the water would flow over – and so it did. As soon as there was enough water, I pushed her on that flat piece of ground and fastened her there by sticking my two broken oars into the ground, one on each side and I stayed there until the water ebbed away and left my raft and all my cargo safe on shore.

My next work was to view the country, seek a proper place for my habitat and where to stow my goods to secure them. I did not know where I was – the continent or an island, inhabited or not, in danger from wild beasts or not. There was a hill less than a mile from me which rose very steep and which seemed higher than some other hills in a ridge to the north. I took out one of the shotguns, one of the pistols and a horn of gunpowder. Armed, I travelled for discovery up to the top of that hill where, after great difficulty, I got to the top. To my great pain, I found I was on an island surrounded by the sea. No land could be seen except some rocks, which were a long way off, and two small islands which lay about nine miles to the west.

I also found the island I was on was barren, and uninhabited except by wild beasts, though I didn't see any. I saw plenty of birds, but did not know what kind and when I killed them, I could not tell what was fit for eating and what wasn't. Coming back, I shot at a large bird I saw sitting in a tree on the side of a large forest. I believe it was the first gun that had been fired there since the creation of the world. I had no sooner fired, then from all parts of the wood ascended countless number of birds of many sorts, making a confused screaming and crying, but I did not know what kind any of them were. As for the creature I killed, its color and beak resembled a kind of hawk, but it had no talons or claws more than common. Its flesh was carrion,[45] and fit for nothing.

Satisfied with this discovery, I came back to my raft and began to bring my cargo on shore, which took me the rest of that day. I did not know what to do with myself at night, nor where to rest, as I was afraid to lie down on the ground, not knowing if some wild beast might devour me – though as I found afterward, there was really no need for those fears.

As well as I could, I barricaded myself with the chest and boards I had brought on shore and made a kind of hut for that night's lodging. As for food, I did not know how to supply myself, except that I had seen a few creatures like hares run out of the wood where I shot the bird.

I now began to consider that I might get a lot of things out of the ship which would be useful to me, particularly some of the rigging and sails and other things which might come to land. I decided to make another voyage on board, if possible. And as I knew the first storm that blew could break her in pieces, I decided to set all other things aside until I had everything out of the ship I could get. Then I called a council – in my thoughts – to see whether I would take back the raft, but this appeared impossible. I decided instead to go as before when the tide was down, only I stripped before I went from my hut, having nothing

---

[45] Unfit for food

on but my chequered[46] shirt, a pair of linen drawers, and a pair of pumps[47] on my feet.

I got on board the ship as before and prepared a second raft. Having had the experience of the first, I made this one not so bulky, nor loaded it so hard. I brought away several things very useful to me: in the carpenter's supplies, I found a few bags full of nails and spikes, a large screw-jack,[48] a dozen hatchets and above all, that most useful thing, a grindstone. All these I secured, together with several things belonging to the gunner, particularly three iron crowbars, two barrels of musket bullets, seven muskets, another shotgun with a small quantity of gunpowder, a large bagful of small shot and a large roll of lead sheathing – but this was so heavy, I could not hoist it up to get it over the ship's side.

Besides these things, I took all the men's clothes I could find, a spare topsail, a hammock and some bedding and with this I loaded my second raft and brought them all safe on shore, to my very great comfort.

I was worried during my absence from the land that my provisions might be devoured on shore. When I came back though, I found no sign of any visitor, except a creature like a wild cat which sat on one of the chests and which, when I came towards it, ran away a little distance, then stood still. She sat very composed and unconcerned and looked me in the face, as if she wanted to be acquainted with me. I pointed my gun at her, but since she did not understand it, she was perfectly unconcerned and didn't run away. I tossed her a bit of biscuit, though I was stingy with it, as my stock was not great. I spared her a bit and she went to it, smelled it and ate it, and looked for more – but I could spare no more. I thanked her and she marched off.

---

[46] Plaid.
[47] A man's leather shoe.
[48] A screw-operated jack for lifting. Interestingly, this is the first use of the word ever, so it could be said Defoe invented the word.

Having got my second cargo on shore – though I was obliged to open the barrels of powder and bring them in smaller parcels since they were too heavy – I went to work to make a little tent with the sail and some poles which I cut for that purpose. Into this tent I brought everything I knew would spoil with either rain or sun and I piled all the empty chests and casks up in a circle around the tent, to fortify it from any sudden attempt from either man or beast.

When I had done this, I blocked up the door of the tent with some boards and an empty chest set on end outside. Spreading one of the beds on the ground, laying my two pistols at my head and my gun at length by me, I went to bed for the first time and slept very quietly all night. I was extremely tired – the night before I had barely slept and had worked very hard all day to get all those things from the ship and get them on shore.

I believe I had the biggest warehouse ever for one man, but I was still not satisfied and while the ship sat upright, I thought I should get everything out of her I could. Every day at low tide I went on board and took away something or other. The third time I went I carried away as much of the rigging as I could, as well as all the small ropes and twine I could get, a piece of spare canvas – which we used to mend the sails – and the barrel of wet gunpowder. I brought away all the sails, only I had to cut them in pieces and bring as much at a time as I could, as they were no longer useful as sails, just as pieces of canvas.

What comforted me more was last of all. After I had made five or six voyages and thought I had nothing more to expect that was worth my meddling, I found a large hogshead[49] of bread, three large runlets[50] of rum, a box of sugar and a barrel of fine flour. This was surprising to me, because I had given up expecting any other supplies, except what was

---

[49] Barrel.
[50] Cask.

spoiled by the water. I soon emptied the hogshead of the bread and wrapped it up, parcel by parcel, in pieces of the sails and I also got all this safe on shore.

The next day I went again and now, having plundered the ship of what was portable, I began with the cables. Cutting the great cable into pieces I could move, I got two cables and a hawser[51] on shore, with all the ironwork I could get. Having cut down the spritsail-yard, and the mizzen-yard[52] and everything I could to make a large raft, I loaded it with all these heavy goods and came away. But my good luck now began to leave me. This raft was so awkward and so overloaded, after I had entered the little cove where I had landed the rest of my goods, it overturned and threw me and all my cargo into the water. As for myself, it was no great harm – I was near the shore – but my cargo was mostly lost, especially the iron, which I thought would have been of great use to me. However, when the tide was out, I got most of the pieces of the cable ashore, and some of the iron, though with infinite effort. I had to dip into the water for it, a job which exhausted me. After this, I went every day on board and brought away what I could get.

I had now been on shore thirteen days and had been on board the ship eleven times, in which time I had brought away all that one pair of hands was capable, though I truly believe if the calm weather held, I would have brought away the whole ship, piece by piece. Preparing the twelfth time to go on board, the wind began to increase. However, at low water I went on board, and though I thought nothing more could be found, I discovered a locker with drawers in it. In one I found two or three razors and one pair of large scissors, with about a dozen good knives and forks. In another I found about £36 worth of money – some

---

[51] A large rope used for securing a ship.
[52] The spritsail-yard and mizzen-yard were both spars, which were attached to the masts and the sails would hang from them.

European coins, some Brazil, some pieces of eight, some gold and some silver.

I smiled to myself at the sight of this money. "Oh drug!' I said aloud, "what are you good for? You have no worth to me, not even worth taking off the ground. One of those knives is worth all this heap. I have no use for you – remain where you are and go to the bottom as a creature whose life is not worth saving." But on second thought I took it, and wrapping all this in a piece of canvas, I began to think about making another raft. While I was preparing, the sky clouded over and the wind began to grow and in a quarter of an hour it gusted from the shore. It was in vain to pretend to make a raft with this wind and it was my business to be gone before the tide came in, otherwise I might not be able to reach the shore at all. I dropped myself down into the water and swam across the channel between the ship and the sands, and even that with difficulty, partly with the weight of the things I carried and partly the roughness of the water. The wind grew very quickly and before it was high tide a storm blew in.

I got home to my little tent, where I lay with all my wealth around me, very secure. It blew very hard all night and in the morning when I looked out, no more ship was to be seen! I was a little surprised, but was satisfied I had lost neither time nor diligence getting everything out of her which was useful to me and there was little left in her I was able to bring away even if I had had more time. I now stopped thinking about the ship or of anything out of her, except what might come on shore, as pieces of her did afterward, but those things were of small use to me.

I now thought about securing myself against either savages, if any would appear, or wild beasts, if any were on the island. I had many thoughts of how to do this and what kind of dwelling to make, and whether I would make a cave in the earth or a tent on the earth. In short, I decided on both, and it would be proper to give an account of how I did this.

I soon found the place I was in was not fit for my settlement, because it was on a low ground like a moor near the sea and I believed it would not be safe and more particularly, because there was no fresh water near it. I decided to find a healthier and more convenient spot of ground.

I thought of what would be best for me: health and fresh water, as I just mentioned; shelter from the heat of the sun; security from ravenous creatures, whether man or beast; a view of the sea, so if God had sent any ship in sight, I wouldn't lose the opportunity for my rescue, which I was not willing to banish from my expectation.

In search of a proper place, I found a little plain on the side of a hill, whose front was as steep as a house-side and so nothing could come down on me from the top. On the one side there was a hollow place, worn a little way in, like the entrance of a cave but there was not really any cave or way in at all.

On the flat of the plain, just before this hollow place, I decided to pitch my tent. This plain was not more than a hundred yards across and about twice as long, and lay like a lawn in front of my door and the end of it descended irregularly down to the low ground by the seaside. It was on the northwest side of the hill so it was sheltered from the heat every day, until it came to a southwest sun which, in those countries, is nearly sunset.

Before I set up my tent I drew a half-circle in front of the hollow, which took in about twenty yards in its diameter. In this half-circle, I pitched two rows of strong stakes, driving them into the ground until they stood firm like piles, the biggest end being out of the ground more than five and a half feet and sharpened on the top. The two rows did not stand more than six inches from one another.

Then I took the pieces of cable I had cut from the ship and laid them in rows, one on top of another within the circle. Between these two rows of stakes I placed other stakes inside, leaning about two and a half feet high against them, like a spur to a post and this fence was so strong neither man nor beast could get into it or over it. This cost me a great deal of time and labor, especially cutting the piles in the woods, bringing them and driving them into the earth.

The entrance I made into this place was not by a door but by a short ladder to go over the top which, when I was in, I lifted up after me. I was completely fenced in and fortified from all the world and consequently slept secure in the night, which otherwise I could not have done. Though as it appeared afterwards, there was no need for all this caution from the enemies who I thought I was in danger from.

Into this fortress, I carried all my riches, provisions, ammunition and stores, with infinite labor. I made a large tent to preserve me from the rains which in one part of the year are very violent there, I made a double tent – one smaller tent inside and one larger tent above it, and covered the uppermost with a large tarpaulin, which I had saved among the sails. And now I no longer laid in the bed I had brought on shore but in a hammock, which was a very good one and belonged to the mate of the ship.

When I had done this, I began to work my way into the rock. Bringing through my tent all the earth and stones I dug out, I stacked them inside my fence, like a terrace, so it raised the ground inside about a foot and a half. And so, I made a cave just behind my tent, which served me like a cellar to my house.

It took a lot of work and several days before all these things were brought to perfection. Therefore, I must go back to some other things which took up some of my thoughts. At the same time, after I had planned to set up my tent and make the cave, a rainstorm fell from a thick, dark cloud. A sudden flash of lightning occurred and after that a great clap of thunder, as is naturally the effect. I was not so much surprised with the lightning as I was with the thought which darted into my mind as swift as the lightning itself – Oh, my gunpowder! My heart sank when I thought at one blast all my powder might be destroyed, which not only my defense but my food entirely depended on. I was not anxious about my own danger though, had the gunpowder caught fire, I would never have known who had hurt me.

Such an impression this made on me that after the storm was over I put aside all my work building and fortifying, and applied myself to make bags and boxes to separate the powder and keep it in little packages, in the hope that it wouldn't all catch fire at once. I finished this work in about a fortnight[53] and I think my powder, which in all was about 240 pounds, was divided in not less than a hundred packages. As to the barrel that had been wet, I did not think any danger from that so I placed it in my new cave, which I called my kitchen, and the rest I hid up and down in holes among the rocks so it would not get wet, marking very carefully where I laid it.

While I did this, I went out at least once a day with my gun to divert myself as well as to see if I could kill anything fit for food and acquaint myself with what the island produced. The first time I went out, I discovered there were goats on the island, but they were so shy, so subtle and so fast, it was the most difficult thing in the world to come up behind them. I was not discouraged at this though, not doubting I might now and then shoot one, and it soon happened. After I had found their haunts, I laid waiting for them. If they saw me in the valleys, though they were on the rocks, they would run away frightened. But if they were feeding in the valleys and I was on the rocks, they took no notice of me. From this I concluded their sight was so directed downward they did not easily see objects above them. Afterwards I always climbed the rocks first to get above them and then frequently had a fair mark.

---

[53] Two weeks

The first shot I made at these creatures, I killed a she-goat which had a little kid by her she still suckled and this saddened me greatly. When the old one fell, the kid stood still by her until I came and picked her up, and when I carried the old one on my shoulders, the kid followed me to my enclosure. I laid down the mother and took the kid in my arms and carried it over my pale,[54] in hopes of taming it, but it would not eat so I was forced to kill it and eat it myself. These two supplied me with meat for a long time, since I ate sparingly and saved my supplies – my bread especially – as much as possibly I could.

Having now fixed my habitat, I found it necessary to have a place to make a fire and fuel to burn. What I did, how I enlarged my cave and what conveniences I made, I will give a full account of in time. But now I must give a little account of myself and of my thoughts about living.

I had a dismal prospect for my future. As I was cast away on that island by a violent storm, hundreds of miles out of the ordinary course of mankind, I had good reason to consider it a judgement of Heaven that in this desolate place and in this desolate manner, I would end my life. The tears would plentifully run down my face when I had these thoughts. Sometimes I would argue with myself why Providence would so completely ruin His creatures and leave them so miserable, so without help, so abandoned and so entirely depressed that it would hardly be rational to be thankful for such a life.

But something always happened to me to control these thoughts and to scold me. One day, while walking with my gun by the seaside, I was very thoughtful on my present condition, when reason disagreed with me the other way: "It is true you are in a desolate condition but remember, where are the rest? Was there not eleven of you in the boat? Where are the ten? Why were they not saved and you lost? Why were you singled out? Is it better to be here or there?" And then I pointed to

---

[54] Fenced-in area

the sea. All evils are considered with the good that is in them and with what worse could happen.

Then it occurred to me how well equipped I was for my survival and what would have happened (which was 100,000:1) if the ship had not floated from the place where she first struck and was pushed so close to the shore that I had time to get all these things out of her. What would have been my situation if I had been forced to live in the condition in which I first came on shore, without the necessities of life or the supplies to acquire them? I said to myself "What would I have done without a gun, without ammunition, without any tools to make anything, without clothes, bedding, a tent or any covering?" Now I had all these in sufficient quantity and could provide myself and could live without my gun when my ammunition was spent, and I had a tolerable view of surviving, without any want, as long as I lived. I considered from the beginning how I would deal with the accidents that might happen and for the future, not only after my ammunition was spent, but after my health and strength would decay.

And now started my sad, silent life, such as was never heard of in the world before. I will start at the beginning and continue in order. It was by my account the 30th of September when I first set foot on this horrid island, when the sun, being in its autumnal equinox,[55] was almost over my head. I estimated I was at 9°22' north of the equator.

After I had been there about ten or twelve days, I thought I would lose my estimate of time without books, pen and ink and would even forget the Sabbath days. To prevent this, with my knife I cut on a large post in capital letters – and making it into a large cross, I set it up on the shore where I first landed "I came on shore here on the 30th September 1659." On the sides of this square post I cut a notch every day and every seventh notch I crossed the rest, and every first day of

---

[55] Around the first days of fall

the month as long as the rest and so I kept my calendar, or weekly monthly and yearly estimate of time.

Among the many things I brought out of the ship, I got several things of less value but not at all less useful to me, which I omitted before: pens, ink and paper, several packages in the captain's, mate's, gunner's and carpenter's possession; three or four compasses, some mathematical instruments, dials, telescopes, charts and books of navigation, all which I huddled together, whether I might want them or not. Also, I found three very good Bibles which came in my cargo from England and which I had packed up among my things as well as some Portuguese books, among them a couple of Popish[56] prayer books and several other books, all of which I carefully secured. I must not forget we had in the ship a dog and two cats, of whose eminent history I may say something. I carried both the cats with me and as for the dog, he jumped out of the ship himself and swam on shore to me the day after I went with my first cargo and was a trusty servant to me many years. I wanted nothing he could fetch me, nor any company he gave me. I only wanted him to talk to me, but that would not do. As I observed before, I found pens, ink and paper, and I used these very carefully. While my ink lasted, I kept things very exact but after that was gone I could not, since I could not make any ink by any means I could devise.

Now I thought I wanted many things besides what I had gathered. Of these, ink was one; a spade, pickaxe and shovel to dig or remove the earth; needles, pins and thread. This want of tools made everything I did difficult and it was nearly a whole year before I had finished my little encampment. The piles, or posts, which were as heavy as I could lift, took a long time cutting and preparing in the woods, and far more time bringing home. I sometimes spent two days cutting and bringing home one of those posts and a third day in driving it into the ground.

---

[56] Disparaging term for Roman Catholic

For this I got a heavy piece of wood at first, but then remembered one of the iron crowbars which, though I found it, made driving those posts very laborious and tedious work. But why was I concerned with the tediousness of anything I had to do, since I had enough time? And I did not have any other employment when that was completed, at least that I could anticipate, except exploring the island to look for food which I did, almost every day.

I now began to seriously consider the circumstances I was reduced to. I drew up the state of my affairs in writing – not so much to leave them to anyone who might come after me – but to get my thoughts out and not rehash them daily and drive myself crazy. As reason was becoming the master over my hopelessness, I began to see everything as good against evil, so I would have something to distinguish my situation from one far worse. I stated very impartially, like debtor and creditor, the comforts I enjoyed against the miseries I suffered:

Evil: I am a castaway on a horrible, desolate island, devoid of all hope of recovery.

Good: But I am alive and did not drown, as all my shipmates did.

Evil: I am singled out and separated from all the world to be miserable.

Good: But I am singled out, too, from all the ship's crew, to be spared from death and He who miraculously saved me from death can deliver me from this condition.

Evil: I am divided from mankind – a solitaire; one banished from human society.

Good: But I am not starving and dying on a barren place with no food.

Evil: I have no clothes to cover me.

Good: But I am in a hot climate, where if I had clothes, I could hardly wear them.

Evil: I am without any defense or means to resist any violence of man or beast.

Good: But I am castaway on an island where I see no wild beasts to hurt me as I saw on the coast of Africa and what if I had been shipwrecked there?

Evil: I have nobody to speak to or relieve me.

Good: But God wonderfully sent the ship close enough to shore so I have as many things to either supply my wants or enable me to supply myself as long as I live.

Overall, here was an absolute testimony that there was barely any condition in the world so miserable but there was something positive to be thankful for in it. Let this direct you from the most miserable of all experiences in this world. We may always find something in it to comfort ourselves from evil, on the credit side of the account. Being a little more comfortable with my condition, and abandoning looking out to sea to spy a ship, I begun to arrange my way of living and to make things as easy as I could.

I have already described my habitat, which was a tent under the side of a rock, surrounded with a strong fence of posts and cables. I might now call it a wall, since I raised a wall of sod up against it, about two feet thick on the outside. After some time (I think it was a year and a half) I raised rafters from it, leaning against the rock, and covered it with trees boughs and such things as I could get to keep out the rain, which I found sometimes were very violent.

I have already written how I brought all my goods into this yard and into the cave which I had made behind me, but I must also write that at first, this was a confused heap of goods, which were in no order and took up all my space. I had no room to turn around, so I decided to enlarge my cave and work farther into the ground – it was a loose, sandy soil which gave way easily to me. When I found I was safe from beasts of prey, I worked sideways to the right and into the rock. Then turning to the right again, worked my way out and made a door to come outside of my fortification. This gave me not only a back way to my tent and to my storehouse but also gave me room to store my goods.

And now I began to make things I found necessary, particularly a chair and a table. Without these I was not able to enjoy the few comforts I had in the world – I could not write or eat or do several other things with pleasure without a table, so I went to work. And here I must observe every man may be, in time, master of every mechanic art. I had never handled a tool in my life and yet in time, by labor, application and skill I found I could make anything, especially if I had the tools. I even made an abundance of things without tools and some with no more tools than an adze[57] and a hatchet – things which perhaps were never made that way before and with infinite labor. For example, if I wanted a board, I had no other way but to cut down a tree, set it on an edge before me, and cut it flat on either side with my axe, until it was as thin as a plank and then make it smooth with my adze. It is true, by this method I could only make one board out of a whole tree, but I had no remedy for this except patience, any more than I had for the exceptional amount of time and labor it took me to make a plank or board. But my time or labor was worth very little and so it was employed this way as well as any other.

I made a table and a chair out of the short pieces of boards I brought on my raft from the ship. But when I had made some boards like the ones above, I instead made large shelves – a foot and a half wide –all along one side of my cave to lay all my tools, nails and ironwork to separate everything so I could easily find them. I knocked pieces into the wall of the rock to hang my guns and all things that would hang up. Had my cave been seen by anyone, it looked like a general storage area of all necessities and had everything ready, and it was a great pleasure

---

[57] An axe-like tool

to see all my goods in such order and specially to find my stock of all necessities so great.

It was here I began to keep a journal of every day's work. At first, I was in too much of a hurry and too agitated, and my journal would have been full of many dull things. For example:

September 30th

After I had got to shore and escaped drowning, instead of being thankful to God for my deliverance, I vomited with the large quantity of salt water which had got into my stomach and recovering myself a little, I ran around the shore wringing my hands and beating my head and face, exclaiming at my misery, and crying out, 'I was ruined, ruined!' until, tired and faint, I was forced to lie down on the ground to rest, but dared not sleep for fear of being devoured.

Some days after this and after I had been on board the ship, and got all that I could out of her, I could not hold back from getting up to the top of a little mountain and looking out to sea in hopes of seeing a ship. At a vast distance, I spied a sail and pleased myself with the hopes of leaving and then after looking steadily until I was almost blind, I lost it and sat down and cried like a baby and increased my misery by my foolishness.

Having somewhat gotten over these things and settling my household staff and habitat, made a table and a chair and all as handsome around me as I could, I began to keep my journal – which I will give you the copy of as long as it lasted, since having no more ink, I was forced to leave it off.

5.

Builds a House
& The Journal

September 30th, 1659 – I, poor miserable Robinson Crusoe, being shipwrecked during a terrible storm, all the rest of the ship's company drowned and myself almost dead, came on shore on this dismal, unfortunate island, which I called 'The Island of Despair."

October 1st – In the morning I saw, to my great surprise, the ship had floated with the high tide and was pushed on shore much nearer the island. I hoped if the wind subsided I might get on board and get some food and necessities out of her. It also renewed my grief at the loss of my comrades who, if we had all stayed aboard, might have saved the ship or at least they would not have all drowned. Had the men been saved, we might have built a boat out of the ruins of the ship to take us to some other part of the world. I spent most of this day thinking about this, but seeing the ship almost dry, I went on the sand as close as I could and then swam on board. It also continued raining, though with no wind at all.

From the 1st of October to the 24th – I spent all these days getting everything I could out of the ship, which I brought on shore on rafts. Lots of rain also in the days, though with some intervals of fair weather. It seems this was the rainy season.

October 20th – I overturned my raft and all the goods I had on it, but being in shallow water and everything being heavy, I recovered many of them when the tide was out.

October 25th – It rained all night and day, with some gusts of wind blowing a little harder than before, during which time the ship broke in pieces and was not seen anymore, except the wreck of her, and that only at low water. I spent this day covering and securing the goods which I had saved, so the rain would not spoil them.

October 26th – I walked along the shore almost the whole day to find a place to make my habitat, very concerned about securing myself from any attack in the night from wild beasts or men. Towards night, I found a proper place under a rock face and marked my encampment which I decided to strengthen with a wall made of double posts, lined inside with cables and turf.

From the 26th to the 30th I worked very hard in carrying all my goods to my new home, though some part of the time it rained exceedingly hard.

The 31st in the morning, I went out on the island with my gun, to hunt for some food and discover the country. I killed a she-goat and her kid followed me home, which I also killed because it would not feed.

November 1 – I set up my tent and lay there for the first night, making it as large as I could, with stakes driven in to swing my hammock on.

November 2 – I set up all my chests, boards and the pieces of timber which made my rafts, and with them formed a fence around me, slightly inside the place I had marked out for my fortification.

November 3 – I went out with my gun and killed two birds like ducks, which were very good food. In the afternoon, I started making a table.

November 4 – This morning I began to organize my work times – going out with my gun, time to sleep and time of diversion - viz.[58] every

---

[58] Viz. appears quite often in Robinson Crusoe, though for the most part it is redundant. It is an archaic term for "for example."

morning I walked around with my gun for a few hours if it did not rain, then worked until about eleven o'clock; eat what I had to live on; from twelve to two I napped, as it was quite hot; then in the evening, to work again. The working part of this day and of the next I worked at making my table since I was a terrible workman, though time and necessity made me a completely natural mechanic soon after, as I believe anyone else would.

November 5 – I went with my gun and my dog and killed a wild cat. Her skin was soft but her meat was good for nothing. Every creature I killed I took off the skins and preserved them. Coming back by the seashore, I saw many types of seabirds which I did not understand, but was surprised and almost frightened by two or three seals which, not knowing what they were, got into the sea and escaped me.

November 6 – After my morning walk I went to work on my table again and finished it, though not to my liking, but it was not long before I learned to mend it.

November 7 – Now it began to be fair weather. The 7th to the 10th and part of the 12th (the 11th was Sunday) I worked on a chair and with a lot of trouble got it to a tolerable shape, though never enough to please me and even while I made it I pulled it apart several times. I soon neglected keeping track of Sundays, since I omitted my mark for them on my post and forgot which was which.

November 13 – This day it rained, which was very refreshing and cooled the earth, but it was accompanied with terrible thunder and lightning, which frightened me as I thought it would light my gunpowder. As soon as it was over, I decided to separate my stock of powder into as many little packages as possible so it posed no danger.

November 14-16 – These three days I spent making little square boxes to hold about a pound or two of gunpowder. Putting the powder in, I put it in places as secure and remote from one another as possible.

On one of these three days, I killed a large bird that was good to eat, but I did not know what to call it.

November 17 – I began to dig behind my tent into the rock, to make room for my further convenience. There were three things I really wanted for this work – a pickaxe, a shovel and a wheelbarrow or basket. I stopped my work and began to contemplate how to make some tools. As for the pickaxe, I used the iron crowbars, which were good but heavy. The next thing was a shovel or spade. This was so necessary I could do nothing effectively without it, but I didn't know what kind to make.

November 18 – The next day while searching the woods, I found a tree like what they call the iron-tree in the Brazils for its exceeding hardness. With a lot of work and almost wrecking my axe, I cut a piece from it and brought it home, which was also difficult since it was remarkably heavy. Little by little I made it into a shovel, its handle shaped exactly like ours in England though with no iron end on it. The excessive hardness of the wood – and since I had no other way – meant it took me a long while to make. It did not last long, though it served well enough for my use, just never as a shovel.

I was still lacking, as I wanted a basket or a wheelbarrow. A basket I could not make, having no twigs that would bend to make wicker-ware. As to a wheelbarrow, I thought I could make everything but the wheel, and that I had no idea how to make. Besides, I had no possible way to make the iron sockets for the axle, so I gave up. To carry the dirt I dug out of the cave, I made a thing like a trough which the laborers carry mortar up to the bricklayers. This was not as difficult as making the shovel. This, the shovel and my attempt at a wheelbarrow, took me four days – except for my morning walk with my gun, which I seldom missed and very seldom did not bring home something fit to eat.

November 23 – I put aside all other work while making these tools, but when they were finished I went on, and working every day, as my strength and time allowed, I spent eighteen days widening and deepening my cave, so it would hold my goods conveniently. During this time, I worked to make this cave spacious enough to accommodate a warehouse, a kitchen, a dining room and a cellar. As for my lodging, I kept to the tent, except sometimes in the wet season it rained so hard I could not keep myself dry. This made me cover all inside my fort with long rafters leaning against the rock and load them with flags and large tree leaves, like a thatch.

December 10 – I began to think my cave was finished, when suddenly – it seems I had made it too large – a large amount of earth fell from the top on one side. So much fell that it frightened me – and not without reason – if I had been under it, I wouldn't have needed a gravedigger. I had now a great deal of work to do over again. I had the loose earth to carry out and, more importantly, I had the ceiling to prop up, so I would be sure no more would come down.

December 11 – I went to work on it and got two posts pitched upright to the top, with two pieces of boards crossing over each post. I finished the next day and setting more posts up with boards, I had the roof secured in about a week and the posts, standing in rows, served me as partitions in the house.

December 17 – From this day to the 20th I placed shelves and knocked nails in the posts to hang everything up that could be. Now I began to be in some order.

December 20 – I carried everything into the cave and began to furnish my house. I set up some pieces of boards like a dresser to put my food on, but boards began to be very scarce. Also, I made me another table.

Dec. 24 – Much rain all night and all day. Nothing moving outside.

Dec. 25 – Rain all day.

Dec. 26 – No rain and the earth much cooler than before and more pleasant.

Dec. 27 – Killed a young goat and hurt another, which I caught and led home on a string. When I had it at home, I bound and splinted its leg, which was broken. I took such care of it that it lived and the leg grew as strong as ever but, because I nursed it so long, it grew tame and fed on the little lawn at my door and would not go away. This was the first time I entertained a thought of breeding some tame creatures so I might have food when my powder and shot was gone.

Dec. 28-31 – Very hot and no breeze, so that there was no movement, except in the evening for food. This time I spent putting all my things in order inside.

January 1 – Very hot still but I went out early and late with my gun and relaxed in the middle of the day. This evening, going farther into the valleys at the center of the island, I found there were plenty of goats, though exceedingly shy and hard to come near. I decided to bring my dog and see if I could hunt them down.

Jan 2 – I went out with my dog and sicced him on the goats but I was mistaken when they all turned on the dog and he knew his danger too well, since he would not come near them.

Jan. 3 – I began my fence which, being still suspicious of being attacked by somebody, I decided to make very thick and strong. Since I described this wall already, I purposely omit what was said in the journal. I will say from the 2nd of January to the 14th of April I was building, finishing and perfecting this wall, though it was no more than about twenty-four yards long with the door of the cave being in the center behind it.

All this time I worked very hard, the rains hindering me several days, or sometimes weeks on end, but I thought I would never be perfectly secure until this wall was finished. It is hard to believe what overwhelming labor everything was done with, especially bringing posts out of the woods and driving them into the ground since I made them much bigger than I needed to.

When this wall was finished and the outside double fenced with the turf raised up close to it, I believed if any people were to come on shore they would not see anything like a habitation and it was a good thing too, as you will see.

During this time, I made my rounds in the woods every day when the rain permitted me and made frequent discoveries in these walks of something or other to my advantage. Particularly, I found a type of wild pigeons which builds nests in the holes of the rocks and taking some young ones, I succeeded in taming some. But when they grew older they flew away, perhaps because they were hungry, since I had nothing to give them. After, I frequently found their nests and got their young ones, which were very good meat. And now, I found myself craving many things, which I thought at first it was impossible to make and with some of them it was. For instance, I could never make a cask to be hooped.[59] I had a small cask or two, but I could never make one, though I spent many weeks at it. I could not put in the heads, or join the staves[60] close enough to one another so they would hold water, so I gave up on that as well. I had no candles so as soon as it was dark, which was generally by seven o'clock, I was forced to go to bed. I remembered the lump of beeswax I had during my African adventure but I had none of that now. The only solution I had was when I had killed a goat, I saved the tallow[61] and with a little clay dish I had made and baked in the sun, I added an oakum[62] wick and made a lamp. This gave me light, though not a clear, steady light like a candle. In the middle of my work while rummaging through my things, I found the little bag which had been filled with corn for the poultry – not for this voyage, but I suppose when

---

[59] The iron rings around a barrel or cask.
[60] Lengths of wood fixed side by side to make a barrel, as opposed to the verb "to stave" which meant forcibly put a hole in something.
[61] Hardened fat used to make candles.
[62] Loose fiber obtained by untwisting old rope.

the ship came from Lisbon. The little bit of corn that had been in the bag was devoured by the rats and I saw nothing in the bag but husks and dust. Wanting the bag for some other use – I think it was to put gunpowder in – I shook the husks of corn out of it on one side of my fortification, under the rock face.

It was a little before the heavy rains I just mentioned that I threw this stuff away, not remembering I had thrown anything there. About a month later I saw some stalks of something green shooting out of the ground, which I thought might be some plant I had not seen. I was surprised and astonished when, after a little longer time, I saw about a dozen ears of perfect green barley come out, the same kind as our European – or actually our English – barley.

It is impossible to express the astonishment and confusion I had now. I had previously acted on no religious foundation at all. I had very few notions of religion in my head and had not entertained any sense of anything other than chance or, as we lightly say, what pleases God. But after I saw barley grow there, in a climate which I knew was not proper for it and since I did not know how it got there, it startled me and I began to suggest that God had miraculously caused His grain to grow without any seed and it was purely for my nutrition on that wild, miserable place.

This touched my heart and brought tears to my eye and I began to bless myself that such a wonder of nature would happen on my account. What was stranger, because I saw it near the barley along the side of the rock, was some other straggling stalks, which proved to be stalks of rice – which I knew because I had seen it grow in Africa when I was ashore there.

I not only thought these were the pure productions of Providence for my care, but thinking there was more I went all over that part of the island, peering in every corner and under every rock, but I could not find any. At last I realized I shook a bag of chickens' meal out and then the wonder began to cease. I must confess my thanks to God's providence began to decline too, on the discovering all this was nothing but what I had done. I should have been thankful for so strange and unforeseen a delivery as if it had been miraculous – it was really the work of Providence to me, that would decide a dozen grains of corn would remain unspoiled, when the rats had destroyed all the rest, as if it had been dropped from heaven. It was also the work of Providence that I would throw it out in that place where, being in the shade of a high rock, it sprang up immediately. If I had thrown it anywhere else at that time, it would have been burnt up and destroyed.

I carefully saved the ears of barley, which was about the end of June. Saving every ear, I decided to plant them all again, hoping in time to have enough to supply me with bread. It was not until the fourth year that I could allow myself a little of this barley to eat and even then, sparingly. I lost all I planted the first season by not observing the proper time – I planted it just before the dry season, so it never came up at all. Besides this barley, there were about thirty stalks of rice, which I preserved with the same care and for the same use – to make bread or food. I found ways to cook it without baking, though I also did that after some time.

But now I return to my Journal.

I worked very hard the last few months to get my wall done and the 14th of April I closed it up, planning to go into it by a ladder over the wall, so there was no sign on the outside of my home.

April 16 – I finished the ladder, so I went up it to the top, then pulled it up after me and let it down inside. This was a complete enclosure to me – inside I had enough room and nothing could come at me from outside unless it could first mount my wall.

The next day after the wall was finished I almost had all my work ruined and myself killed. As I was busy inside behind my tent, just at the entrance into my cave, I was terribly frightened when the earth came crumbling down from the roof of my cave and from the edge of the hill over my head. Two of the posts I had set up in the cave cracked horribly. I was completely scared but thought nothing of the cause, only thinking the top of my cave had fallen in, as some of it had done before. Out of fear I would be buried inside, I ran to my ladder and not thinking myself safe there either, I got over my wall, fearing pieces of the hill would roll down on me. I had no sooner stepped on solid ground, then I plainly saw it was a terrible earthquake. The ground I stood on shook three times in about eight minutes, with three shocks that would have overturned the strongest building on the earth. A huge piece of rock which stood about half a mile from me next to the sea fell down with a terrible noise like I never heard in all my life. I noticed the sea itself was put into violent motion by it and I believe the shocks were stronger under the water than on the island.

I was so much amazed, having never felt anything like it or spoke with anyone who had, that I was stunned. The motion of the earth made my stomach sick, like someone tossed at sea, but the noise of the falling rock woke me from my confusion and filled me with horror. I thought of nothing except the hill falling on my tent and all my household goods and burying everything and this sunk my soul for a second time.

After the third shock was over and I felt no more for some time, I began to regain my courage, though not enough to go over my wall again, fearing being buried alive. I sat still on the ground, depressed and sad and not knowing what to do. All this time I did not have the least serious religious thought – nothing but the common "Lord have mercy on me!" and when it was over that went away too.

While I sat there, the sky grew cloudy and overcast as if it would rain. Soon after the wind rose little by little, and in less than half-an-hour it blew an awful hurricane. The sea was suddenly covered with foam and froth. The shore was covered with the breaking waves, the trees were torn up by the roots and it was a terrible storm. This lasted about three hours then began to subside. Two hours later it was quite calm and began to rain very hard. All this time I sat on the ground, terrified and dejected when it came to me that these winds and rain were the consequences of the earthquake – the earthquake itself was over and I could venture into my cave again. With this thought my spirits began to revive – and the rain also helped to persuade me – I went in and sat down in my tent. The rain was so violent that my tent was ready to be beaten down with it and I was forced to go into my cave, very afraid and uneasy, fearing it would fall on my head. This violent rain forced me to a new work – to cut a hole through my new fortification, like a drain, to let the water go out, which would otherwise have flooded my cave. After I had been in my cave for some time with no more aftershocks, I began to be more composed. And now to support my spirits, which needed it, I went to my little store and took a small sip of rum which I did now and again very sparingly, knowing I could have no more when that was gone. It continued raining all that night and the better part of the next day so I could not go out, but my mind being more collected, I began to think of what I should do, concluding if the island was subject to these earthquakes, there would be no living in a cave. I must consider building a little hut in an open place which I could surround with a wall, as I had done here, and make myself secure from wild beasts or men. I concluded if I stayed where I was, I would certainly be buried alive.

With these thoughts, I decided to move my tent from where it stood, which was just under the hanging precipice of the hill and which, if it was shaken again, would certainly fall on my tent. I spent the two next days – the 19th and 20th of April – deciding where and how to move my home. The fear of being swallowed up alive meant I never slept peacefully but the anxiety of lying outside without any fence was almost equal to it. When I looked around and saw how everything was put in order, how pleasantly concealed I was and how safe from danger, it made me unwilling to move. It occurred to me it would require a lot of time for me to do this and I must be satisfied where I was, until I had formed a camp for myself and had secured it to move to it. I composed myself and decided I would quickly go to work to build a wall with posts and cables in a circle as before, and set up my tent in it when it was finished, but I would risk staying where I was until it was finished. This was the 21st.

April 22 – I thought how to put this in motion, but I was at a loss for tools. I had three large axes, an abundance of hatchets – we carried the hatchets for trade with the Indians – but with a lot of chopping and cutting knotty hardwood, they were all full of notches and dull. Though I had a grindstone, I could not turn it and grind my tools too. I spent as much thought on this as a statesman would have given a grand point of politics or a judge on the life and death of a man. I ended up making a wheel with a string to turn it with my foot so I would have both my hands free. I had never seen anything like it in England, though I have since noticed it is very common there. Besides, my grindstone was very large and heavy. This machine cost me a full week's work to bring it to perfection.

April 28, 29 – These two whole days I took grinding my tools, with my machine for turning my grindstone performing very well.

April 30 – Noticing my bread had been low a long time, I inspected it and reduced myself to one biscuit a day, which made me very sad.

May 1 – In the morning, looking towards the sea and with the tide being low, I saw something lying on the shore bigger than ordinary. It looked like a cask and when I came to it, I found a small barrel and a few pieces of the shipwreck, which were driven on shore by the last hurricane. Looking towards the wreck itself, I thought it seemed to lie higher out of the water than it used to do. I examined the barrel which was driven on shore, and soon found it was a barrel of gunpowder but it was soaked and the powder was caked as hard as stone. However, I rolled it farther on shore for the present, and went on the sand as near as I could to the wreck of the ship, to look for more.

6.

Ill and Conscience-Stricken

When I came down to the ship I found it strangely moved. The forecastle, which before was buried in sand, was heaved up at least six feet and the stern, which was broken in pieces and apart from the rest by the force of the sea, was tossed up and thrown on one side. The sand was thrown so high on the side next to her stern, where before I could not come within a quarter of a mile of the wreck without swimming I could now walk up to her when the tide was out. I was surprised by this at first, but soon concluded it must have been done by the earthquake. This violence caused the ship to be more broken open than before, so many things came on shore daily, which the winds and water rolled to the land.

This completely diverted my thoughts from the plan of moving my home and I kept busy searching to see if I could get into the ship but I found the inside was choked up with sand. As I had learned not to let this depress me, I decided to pull everything I could to pieces, concluding everything I could get from her would be of some use or other to me.

May 3 – I began with my saw and cut a piece of a beam, which I thought held some of the quarter-deck together. When I had cut it through, I cleared away the sand as best as I could from the side but with the tide coming in, I had to give up for now.

May 4 – I went fishing, but did not catch one fish I would dare eat until I was tired of my sport. When I was just going to leave, I caught a young dolphin. I had made a long line of some rope, but I had no hooks.

I frequently caught as much fish as I cared to eat, which I dried in the sun and ate them dry.

May 5 – Worked on the wreck. Cut another beam apart and brought three large fir planks off from the decks, which I tied together and made to float on shore when the tide came on.

May 6 – Worked on the wreck. Got several iron bolts out of her and other pieces of ironwork. Worked very hard and came home very tired and had thoughts of giving up.

May 7 – Went to the wreck again not intending to work, but found the weight of the wreck had broken itself apart, the beams being cut. Several pieces of the ship seemed to lie loose and the inside of the hold lay so open that I could see into it, but it was almost full of water and sand.

May 8 – Went to the wreck and carried an iron crowbar to wrench up the deck, which now lay clear of the water. I wrenched off two planks and brought them on shore with the tide. I left the iron crowbar in the wreck for the next day.

May 9 – Went to the wreck and with the crowbar made my way into the body of the wreck. I felt several casks and loosened them with the crowbar but could not break them up. I also felt a roll of English lead and could move it, but it was too heavy to lift.

May 10-14 – Went every day to the wreck and got several pieces of timber, boards and two or three hundred pounds of iron.

May 15 – I took two hatchets to try to cut off a piece of the lead roll by placing it on the edge of one hatchet and driving it with the other, but since it was in about a foot and a half of water, I could not make any blow to drive the hatchet.

May 16 – It had blown hard in the night and the wreck appeared more broken by the force of the water. I stayed so long in the woods to get pigeons for food that the tide prevented me from going to the wreck that day.

May 17 – I saw some pieces of the wreck blown on shore about two miles away and decided to see what they were. It was a piece of the bow, but too heavy for me to carry.

May 24 – Everyday until now I worked on the wreck, and with hard labor I loosened some things so much with the crowbar that with the first flowing tide several casks floated out as well as two of the seamen's chests. But with the wind blowing from the shore, nothing came to land that day except pieces of timber and a barrel which had some Brazil pork in it, but the salt water and the sand had spoiled it. I continued this work every day to the 15th of June, except when it was necessary to get food, which I always decided was when the tide was high so I would be ready when it ebbed out. By now I had enough timber, planks and ironwork to build a good boat, if I had known how. I also got, at several times and in several pieces, nearly one hundred pounds of the sheet lead.

June 16 – Going down to the seaside, I found a large turtle. This was the first I had seen, which was my misfortune, not any defect of the place or because they were scarce. Had I happened to be on the other side of the island, I might have had hundreds of them every day as I found afterwards, but perhaps had paid dearly for them.

June 17 – I spent cooking the turtle. I found in her three-score[63] eggs and her meat was to me, at that time, the most savory and pleasant I ever tasted in my life, having had no meat except for goat and bird since I landed in this horrid place.

June 18 – Rained all day and I stayed inside. I thought the rain felt cold and I was somewhat chilly, which I knew was unusual in that latitude.

June 19 – Very ill and shivering, as if the weather had been cold.

June 20 – No rest all night, violent pains in my head and feverish.

---

[63] Sixty

June 21 – Very ill. Frightened almost to death about my sad condition – to be sick and with no help. Prayed to God for the first time since the storm off Hull, but barely knew what I said, or why, my thoughts being all confused.

June 22 – A little better but very anxious about my sickness.

June 23 – Very bad again, cold and shivering and then a violent headache.

June 24 – Much better.

June 25 – A very violent ague,[64] the fit held me seven hours. Cold and hot with sweats after it.

June 26 – Better and having no food to eat, took my gun, but found myself very weak. However, I killed a she-goat and got it home with a lot of difficulty and broiled some of it and ate. I would have been pleased to stew it and made some broth, but had no pot.

June 27 – The shivering was so violent again that I lay in bed all day and did not eat or drink. I was ready to die of thirst but I was so weak, I did not have the strength to stand up or to get myself any water to drink. Prayed to God again, but was light-headed. When I was not, I was so oblivious I did not know what to say. All I could do was lay there and cry, "Lord, look on me! Lord, pity me! Lord, have mercy on me!" I suppose I did nothing else for two or three hours until, the fit wearing off, I fell asleep and did not wake up until far in the night. When I awoke, I found myself refreshed, but weak and very thirsty. However, as I had no water in my home, I was forced to lie there until morning and went to sleep again. In this second sleep, I had this terrible dream: I thought I was sitting on the ground outside of my wall, where I sat when the storm blew after the earthquake. I saw a man descend from a great black cloud, in a bright flame of fire and stand on the ground. He was as bright as a flame, so I could barely look towards him. His

---

[64] A fever or shivering fit

expression was indescribably awful. When he stepped on the ground I thought the earth trembled, just as it had done during the earthquake, and the air looked as if it was filled with flashes of fire. As soon as he was on the earth, he moved forward towards me with a long spear in his hand to kill me. When he came to higher ground some distance away, he spoke to me – or I heard a voice so dreadful it is impossible to express the terror of it. All I can say I understood was this: "These things have not brought you to repentance, now you will die." At those words, I thought he lifted the spear to kill me.

No one who will ever read this will expect that I would be able to describe the horrors of my soul at this terrible vision. I mean, even though it was a dream, I dreamt of those horrors. It is also not possible to describe the impression that remained in my mind when I woke up and found it was only a dream.

I had, sadly, no divine knowledge. What good instruction I had received from my father was worn out by eight years of uninterrupted, seafaring wickedness, and constant conversations with only those who were, like myself, wicked and profane to the last degree. I do not remember that I had, in all that time, one thought which either looked up towards God, or inwards on my own ways. Only a certain stupidity of soul, without desire of good or conscience of evil, had entirely overwhelmed me. I was a hardened, unthinking, wicked creature among our common sailors, not having the least sense of either of the fear of God while I was in danger, or of thankfulness to God when I was rescued from it.

Through all the variety of miseries that had happened to me up until now, I never had one thought of it being the hand of God or that it was a just punishment for my sin of rebellion against my father, my present sins – which were great – or a punishment for the general course of my wicked life. When I was on the desperate expedition on the desert shores of Africa, I never thought what would happen to me, or one wish for God to direct me where to go, or keep me from the dangers of voracious creatures or cruel savages. I did not think of a God or a Providence, and acted like a mere brute from the principles of nature and common sense only, and hardly even that. When I was rescued by the Portugal captain, well treated and dealt with justly, charitably and honorably, I had not the least bit of gratitude in my thoughts. When I was shipwrecked again, abandoned and in danger of drowning on this island, I was remorseless and did not think it was a judgment. I only said to myself often that I was an unfortunate dog and born to always be miserable.

It is true, when I first got on shore here and found all my ship's crew drowned and myself spared, I was ecstatic and had the grace of God assisted, might have become true appreciation. But it ended where it began, being glad I was alive, without looking back on the goodness of the hand which had singled me out to be preserved when all the rest were destroyed, or questioned why Providence had been so merciful to me. It's the same joy seamen generally have after they are safely ashore from a shipwreck, which they drown in the next bowl of punch and forget almost as soon as it is over. All the rest of my life was like it. Even afterwards, when I had made sense of how I was castaway on this dreadful place, out of the reach of humankind, with no hope of relief or prospect of recovery, as soon as I saw a prospect of living and I would not starve, all the sense of my condition wore off. I began to be very relaxed, applied myself to the work of my preservation, and was far enough from being worried about this being a judgment from heaven, or that the hand of God was against me. These were thoughts which very seldom entered my head.

The growing of the barley had some influence on me at first and began to touch me with seriousness, if I thought it had something miraculous in it. But as soon as that thought was removed, the impression that was raised from it wore off also. Even the earthquake, though nothing could be more terrible or more directed by the invisible Power which directs such things, no sooner was the first fright over, then the impression it had made went away as well. I had no more sense of God or His judgments – much less of my circumstances being from His hand – than if I had been in the most prosperous condition of life.

But now, when I began to be sick and an unhurried view of the miseries of death placed itself before me, when my spirits began to sink, exhausted with the violence of the fever, now my conscience that had slept so long began to wake up and I began to criticize myself about my past life. I had evidently provoked the justice of God to deal with me in so vindictive a manner by the uncommon wickedness of my past. These thoughts burdened me for two of three days while I was in this poor state of mind, and in the violence of the fever as well as the dreadful criticisms of my conscience, forced some words from me like praying to God, though I can't say for sure if they were a prayer.

It was the voice of mere fright and distress. My thoughts were confused and the horror of dying in such a miserable condition started to make me hysterical. In these panics I did not know what my tongue might express. It would exclaim, "Lord, what a miserable creature I am! If I were sick, I would certainly die without help and what will happen to me!" Then the tears burst out of my eyes and I could say nothing for a long while. In this interval, my father's good advice and prediction came to mind– if I took this foolish step, God would not bless me, and I would have leisure to look back on ignoring his advice when there would be no advice to assist me. "Now," I said aloud, "my dear father's words have come true. God's justice has overtaken me and I have nobody to help or hear me. I rejected the voice of Providence, which mercifully put me where I might have been happy and calm. But I would neither see it myself nor learn to know the blessing of it from my parents. I left them to mourn over my folly and now I am left to mourn under the consequences of it. I ignored their help and assistance, they would have made everything easy for me and now my struggles are too great for even nature itself to support, and no assistance, no help, no comfort, no advice." Then I cried out, "Lord, help me because I am in great distress." This was the first prayer, if I may call it so, that I had made for many years.

But to return to my Journal.

June 28 – Having been somewhat refreshed with the sleep I had and the fever gone, I got up and though the fright and terror of my dream was extreme, I considered the fever would return the next day and now was my time to get something to refresh and support myself when I would be ill. The first thing I did was fill a large square bottle with water and set it on my table, in reach of my bed. To take the chill off the water, or if the fever returned, I put about a quarter of a pint of rum in it and mixed them together. Then I got a piece of the goat's meat and broiled it on the coals, but could only eat a very little. I walked around, but was very weak, very sad and heavy-hearted because of my miserable condition, dreading the return of my mental state the next day. At night, I made a supper of three of the turtle's eggs, which I roasted in the ashes and ate in the shell, and this was the first bit of meat I had ever asked God's blessing for – that I could remember – in my whole life. After I had eaten, I tried to walk but found myself so weak that I could hardly carry a gun and since I never went out without it, I went only a little way and sat down on the ground, looking out on the sea, which was very calm and smooth. As I sat here, I thought: What is this earth and sea, of which I have seen so much? Where is it produced? And what am I, and all the other creatures wild and tame, human and brutal? Where are we? Sure, we are all made by some secret Power, who formed the earth and sea, the air and sky. And who is that? Then it followed most naturally, it is God who has made all. Well, then it came on strangely. If God has made all these things, He guides and governs them all since the Power that could make all things must certainly have power to guide and direct them. If so, nothing can happen in the great circuit of His works, either without His knowledge or without His decisions.

And if nothing happens without His knowledge, He knows I am here, and am in this dreadful condition. And if nothing happens without His decisions, He has decided all this would happen to me. Nothing occurred to me to contradict any of these conclusions and therefore it rested on me with force – it must be God who decided all this would happen to me. I was brought into this miserable circumstance by His direction, He who has the sole power, not just over me, but over everything that happened in the world. And it followed: Why has God done this to me? What have I done to be punished in this way? My conscience stopped me in that inquiry, as if I had blasphemed, and I thought it spoke to me like a voice.

"Lowlife! Do you ask what you have done? Look back on a terrible, wasted life and ask yourself what have you NOT done? Ask, why is it you weren't destroyed long ago? Why were you not drowned in Yarmouth Roads, killed in the fight when the ship was taken by the Salé warship, devoured by the wild beasts on the coast of Africa, or drowned HERE, when all the crew died except you? You ask what have *I* done?" I was struck dumb with these thoughts, astonished and did not have a word to say. I didn't answer myself but stood up, thoughtful and sad, walked back to my retreat and went up over my wall, as if I was going to bed. But my thoughts were sadly disturbed and I was not inclined to sleep. I sat down in my chair and lit my lamp as it began to get dark. Now, as the anxiety of the return of my mental state terrified me, it occurred to me the Brazilians take no drugs except their tobacco for almost all psychological states and I had a piece of a roll of tobacco in one of the chests, which was well cured, and some that was green and not quite cured.

I went, directed by Heaven no doubt. In this chest I found a cure both for soul and body. I opened the chest and found the tobacco and the few books I had saved. I took out one of the Bibles which I mentioned before, and until now didn't have the time or inclination to consider. I took it out and brought it and the tobacco with me to the table. I did not know what to use the tobacco for in my current state of mind, or whether it was good for it or not, but I tried several experiments with it to see if it would hit one way or other. I took a piece of leaf and chewed it in my mouth, which at first almost stupefied my brain, the tobacco being green and strong and I was not used to this anymore. Then I took some and steeped it an hour or two in some rum and decided to take a dose of it when I lay down. Lastly, I burnt some on a pan of coals, and held my nose over the smoke as long as I could bear it. In the intervals I took up the Bible and began to read but my head was too disturbed by the tobacco to read, at least at that time.

Having opened the book casually, the first words I saw were "Call on Me in the day of trouble and I will deliver you, and you will worship Me." These words were very suitable and made an impression on me when I read them, though not so much as they did after. As for being DELIVERED, the word had no meaning to me. The thing was so remote, so impossible in my anxiety that I began to say, as the children of Israel did when they were promised meat, "Can God spread a table in the wilderness? Can God Himself deliver me from this place?" Since it was many years later that any hopes appeared, this often prevailed on my thoughts, but the words made a great impression on me and I often considered them. It was now late and the tobacco had, as I said, dozed my head so much I became drowsy. I left my lamp burning in the cave, in case I wanted anything in the night, and went to bed. Before I laid down, I did something I had never done in all my life – I kneeled and prayed to God to fulfil the promise to me, that if I called on Him in the day of trouble, He would deliver me. After my broken and imperfect prayer was over, I drank the rum where I had steeped the tobacco, which was so strong and rank from the tobacco that I could barely get it down and immediately went to bed.

It flew up into my head violently but I fell into a sound sleep, and woke up around three o'clock in the afternoon the next day – but I still think to this day I slept all the next day and night and until three the day after. This is the only explanation I have for losing a day out of my calculation in the days of the week, as it appeared I had done some years later. If I had lost it by crossing and re-crossing my lines, I would have lost more than one day, but certainly I lost a day in my account and never knew which way. When I awoke I found myself remarkably refreshed and my spirits lively and cheerful. I was stronger than I was the day before and my stomach better and I was hungry. In short, I had no fever the next day, but continued for the better. This was the 29th.

The 30th I was well again and I went out with my gun, but did not want to travel too far. I killed a seabird or two, something like a brandgoose[65] and brought them home, but did not look forward to eating them, so I ate some more of the turtle's eggs, which were very good. This evening I took more of my medicine – the tobacco steeped in rum – which I thought did me good the day before, only I did not take so much this time and I did not chew any of the leaf or hold my head over the smoke. However, I was not so well the next day as I hoped I would have been. I had a little bit of the cold again, but it was not much.

July 2 – I took the medicine all three ways, taking the same doses except I doubled the quantity which I drank.

July 3 – I was rid of the fever for good, though I did not recover my full strength for some weeks after. While I was gathering my strength, my thoughts went to the Scripture "I will deliver thee" and the

---

[65] Wild goose

impossibility of my rescue stayed on my mind. As I was discouraging myself with such thoughts, I realized I had pondered my rescue so much that I disregarded the liberation I had received and I asked myself these questions: Have I not been rescued – and wonderfully too – from the most distressed state? And what notice had I taken of it? Had I done my part? God had delivered me, but I had not worshipped Him – I had not been thankful for the rescue and how could I expect greater liberation? This touched my heart greatly and immediately I knelt and gave God thanks for my recovery from my sickness.

July 4 – In the morning I took the Bible and beginning at the New Testament, I seriously began to read it and decided to read a while every morning and every night – not tying myself to the number of chapters, but as long as my thoughts would engage me. It was not long after I went seriously to this work that I found my heart more deeply and sincerely affected by the wickedness of my past life. The impression of my dream revived and the words, "All these things have not brought you to repentance" ran seriously through my thoughts. I was sincerely begging God to give me repentance when it unexpectedly happened, the same day I was reading the Scripture, I came to these words: "He is exalted a Prince and a Savior, to give repentance and to give remission." I threw down the book and with my heart and my hands lifted up to heaven, in joy I cried out 'Jesus, you son of David! Jesus, you glorious Prince and Savior! Give me repentance!" This was the first time I could say, in the true sense of the words, I prayed in all my life. Now I prayed with a sense of my condition and a true Scriptural view of hope, founded on the encouragement of the Word of God. From this time, I began to hope that God would hear me.

Now I began to interpret the words mentioned above, "Call on Me, and I will deliver you,' differently than I had ever done before. I had no notion of anything being called DELIVERANCE except for being delivered from the captivity I was in. Though I was free, the island was certainly a prison to me in the worst sense of the word. But now I learned to take it in another sense. Now I looked back on my past life with such horror, and my sins seemed so terrible that my soul looked for nothing from God except release from the load of guilt that bore down on me. As for my solitary life, it was nothing. I did not pray to be rescued from it or think of it – it did not compare to this. And I add this part here, to hint to whoever will read this: whenever they come to a true sense of things, they will find relief from sin a much greater blessing than relief from illness.

But, leaving this part, I return to my Journal.

My state now began to be, though not less miserable, much easier to my mind being directed by a constant reading of the Scripture and praying to God. I had a great deal of comfort inside, which until now I knew nothing of. Also, my health and strength returned, so I tried to provide myself with everything I wanted and make my life as normal as I could.

From the 4th of July to the 14th I walked around with my gun in my hand, like a man who was slowly gathering up his strength after an illness. It is hard to imagine how low I was and how I weak I was. The medication I used was completely new and perhaps had never cured a fever before and I can't recommend anyone to practice by this experiment. Though it did cure my fever, it weakened me, as I had frequent convulsions in my nerves and limbs for some time. I also learned that being outside in the rainy season was the nastiest thing to my health ever, especially in those rains which came with storms and hurricanes. The rain which came in the dry season was almost always accompanied with such storms and I found that rain was much more dangerous than the rain which fell in September and October.

7.

Agricultural Experience

I had now been on this unhappy island for more than ten months. All possibility of rescue was taken away from me and I firmly believed no human had ever set foot on that place. Having now secured my home, I had a great desire to make a more complete discovery of the island, to see what other creations I might find.

On the 15th of July I began to take a more exact survey of the island itself. I went up the creek first where I brought my rafts on shore. After I walked about two miles up, the tide did not flow any higher and it was only a little brook of very fresh running water. Being the dry season, there was hardly any water in some parts of it – at least not enough to run. On the banks of this brook I found many pleasant meadows, plain, smooth and covered with grass. On the rising parts of them where I supposed the water never overflowed, I found a large amount of green tobacco growing strong. There was a diversity of other plants, which I had no understanding about, but may have virtues of their own. I searched for the cassava root, which the Indians in all that climate make their bread from, but I could not find any. I saw large aloe plants, but did not understand them. I saw several wild sugarcanes, but since they were uncultivated, they were imperfect. I satisfied myself with these discoveries this time, and came back thinking what I might do to know the benefit and goodness of any of the fruits or plants I had discovered, but to no avail. I had made so little observation while I was in the Brazils that I knew little of the plants in the field, or at least very little that might serve any purpose now.

The next day, the sixteenth, I went the same way again and going further than I had the day before, I found the brook and the savannahs cease and the country become more forested than before. Here I found different fruits – particularly melons on the ground and grapes on the trees. The vines had spread over the trees and the clusters of grapes were very ripe and rich. This was a surprising discovery and I was beyond happy, but I was cautious and would only eat them sparingly, remembering when I was ashore in Barbary, several Englishmen who were slaves were killed eating grapes when they were thrown into fluxes[66] and fevers. But I found an excellent use for these grapes which was to dry them in the sun and keep them as raisins which I thought would be – as indeed they were – wholesome and pleasant to eat when no grapes could be had.

I spent all that evening there and did not go back to my home which, by the way, was the first night I had not slept at home. I got up in a tree, where I slept well, and the next morning proceeded on my discovery, travelling nearly four miles, as I judged by the length of the valley. I kept heading north, with a ridge of hills on the south and north side of me. At the end of this march I came to an opening where the country seemed to descend to the west and a little spring of fresh water, which came out of the side of the hill by me, ran the other way, due east. The country appeared so fresh, so green, so flourishing, everything being in a constant verdure[67] of spring that it looked like a planted garden. I descended a little on the side of that delicious valley, surveying it with a secret kind of pleasure, though mixed with my other worrying thoughts. To think, this was all my own and I was king and lord of all this country and had a right of possession. And if I could make it known, I would have it as an inheritance just like any lord of a manor in

---

[66] A much more pleasant term for dysentery or diarrhea.
[67] The fresh green color of lush vegetation

England. There was an abundance of cocoa trees, orange, lemon and citron trees, all wild and very few bearing any fruit – at least not then. The limes I gathered were not only pleasant to eat but very wholesome, and I mixed their juice with water, which made it very cool and refreshing. I now had enough to gather and carry home and I decided besides storing the grapes, I would also store limes and lemons to supply myself during the wet season, which I knew was approaching. To do this, I gathered a large heap of grapes in one place, a smaller heap in another and a large bunch of limes and lemons in another. Taking a few of each with me I travelled home, deciding to come again and bring a bag – or what I could make – to carry the rest home. Having spent three days on this journey I came home, but before I got there the grapes had spoiled – the richness of the fruit and the weight of the juice broke and bruised them and they were good for nothing. As to the limes, they were good, but I could only bring back a few.

The next day was the nineteenth. I went back, having made two small bags to bring home my harvest. I was surprised when I found my heap of grapes spread around, trampled to pieces and dragged around and mostly eaten. I concluded there were some wild creatures which had done this, but I didn't know what they were. As I could not lay them in heaps or carry them in a sack without them being crushed under their own weight, I took another course. I gathered a large quantity of the grapes and hung them in trees so they would dry in the sun. As for the limes and lemons, I carried as many back as I could.

When I came home from this journey, I thought about the fruitfulness of that valley, the pleasantness of the situation and the security from storms on that side of the water and the forest. I concluded I had pitched my tent somewhere which was – by far – the worst part of the country. I began to consider moving my home and looking for a place as safe as where I was now – if possible, that pleasant, fruitful part of the island.

I thought about this for some time, the appeal of the place tempting me but when I though more about it, I considered I was now by the seaside, where it was at least possible that something advantageous might happen to me and the same ill fate that brought me here might bring some other unhappy wretches to the same place. Though it was improbable any such thing would ever happen, to enclose myself among the hills and woods in the center of the island was to keep me captive on the island for the rest of my life, so I should not move. However, I was so enamored with this place, I spent a lot of my time there for the remaining part of July and on second thought, I decided not to move. I built a little kind of a bower[68] and surrounded it at a distance with a strong fence, as high as I could reach and well staked and filled between with brush. Here I stayed very secure, sometimes two or three nights at a time, always going over it with a ladder so I now had my country house and my coastal house and this work took me to the beginning of August.

I had just finished my fence and began to enjoy my labor when the rains came, and made me stick close to my first home. Though I had made me a tent like the other with a piece of a sail and spread it very well, I did not have the shelter of a hill to keep me safe from storms, or a cave behind me to retreat into when the rains were extraordinary.

I had finished my bower and began to enjoy myself and on the 3rd of August, the grapes I had hung up were completely dried and were excellent raisins. I began to take them down from the trees and I was glad I did, since the rains which followed would have spoiled them and I would have lost the best part of my winter food, since I had more than two hundred large bunches of them. No sooner had I taken them all down and carried most of them home to my cave then it began to rain. From the 14th of August it rained almost every day until the middle of

---

[68] A country cottage

October and sometimes so violently that I could not leave my cave for several days.

In this season, I was surprised when my family increased in size. I had been concerned over the loss of one of my cats – who I thought had died, but had run away. She came home about the end of August with three kittens. I thought this strange because, though I had killed a wild cat with my gun, I thought it was very different from our European cats. The kittens were the same kind of house-breed as the old one and since both my cats were females, I thought it very strange. But from these three cats I was so harassed with cats that I was forced to kill them like vermin and to chase them from my house as much as possible.

From the 14th of August to the 26th there was incessant rain, so much so I could not leave and I was now very careful not to get wet. In this confinement, I began to run out of food but venturing out twice, I killed a goat one day. The last day I found a very large tortoise, which was a treat to me and my menu was something like this: I ate a bunch of raisins for my breakfast, a piece of the broiled goat or turtle meat for my lunch – as I was unlucky enough to have no pot to boil or stew anything – and two or three of the turtle's eggs for my supper.

During this confinement, I worked a few hours each day enlarging my cave and worked towards one side until I came to the outside of the hill, I made a door out, which came beyond my fence, so I came in and out this way. But I was not at ease being so open. Before, I was in a complete enclosure. Now I thought I lay exposed and open for anything to come in at me, though I never saw any living thing to fear – the biggest creature I had seen on the island was a goat.

September 30th – I was now at the unhappy anniversary of my landing. I counted up the notches on my post and found I had been on shore 365 days. I spent this day as a solemn fast, setting it aside for religious exercise, throwing myself on the ground with the most serious humility, confessing my sins to God, acknowledging His righteous judgments on me and praying to Him to have mercy on me through Jesus Christ. Not having tasted anything for twelve hours, I ate a biscuit and a bunch of grapes and went to bed, finishing the day as I began it. All this time I had not observed the Sabbath day. At first, I had no sense of religion on my mind and after some time had stopped distinguishing the weeks by making a longer notch than ordinary for the Sabbath day, and so did not really know what any of the days were. But now, having totaled up the days, I found I had been there a year, so I divided it into weeks, and set aside every seventh day for a Sabbath, though I found at the end of my account I had lost a day or two in my calculation. A little after this, my ink began to fail and so I used it more sparingly, writing down only the most remarkable events of my life without continuing a daily memorandum of other things.

The rainy season and the dry season now began to appear regularly to me and I learned to divide them to provide for them accordingly but I am going to relate one of the most discouraging experiments that I made.

I have mentioned I had saved the few ears of barley and rice and I believe there were about thirty stalks of rice and about twenty of barley. After the rains, I thought it was the proper time to plant it. I dug up a piece of ground as best as I could with my wooden spade and dividing it into two parts, I planted my grain. But as I was planting, I decided I would not plant it all at first – because I did not know when the best time for it was – so I planted about two thirds of the seeds, leaving about a handful of each. I was thankful afterward, since not one grain of what I planted this time grew. The dry months followed and the soil had no rain after the seed was planted and they never came up until the wet season – then it grew as if it had been freshly planted. Finding my first seed did not grow, which I imagined was by the drought, I looked for a wetter piece of ground to make another trial in. I dug up a piece of ground near my new cottage and planted the rest of my seeds in

February, a little before the vernal equinox.[69] This planting, having the rainy months of March and April to water it, sprung up very nicely and yielded a very good crop. Having only part of the seeds left and not daring to plant all I had, my whole crop amounted to less than half a peck[70] of each kind. This experiment made me master of my domain and now I knew exactly when the proper season was to plant and that I might expect two seeding times and two harvests every year.

While this grain was growing I made a little discovery, which was useful to me after. As soon as the rains ended and the weather began to settle, which was around November, I made a visit to where my cottage was. Though I had not been there in months, everything was just as I left them. The double hedge I had made was not only firm and complete, but the stakes I had cut out of some trees had all shot out and grown long branches, much as a willow tree usually shoots the first year after cutting its head. I don't know what kind of tree these stakes were cut from. I was surprised and very pleased to see the young trees grow. I pruned them and had them grow as much alike as I could. It is incredible how beautiful they grew in three years. The hedge made a circle about twenty-five yards in diameter and the trees soon covered it making a complete shade, sufficient to lodge under the whole dry season. This made me decide to cut some more stakes and make a hedge like this in a semi-circle around the wall of my first dwelling. Placing the trees in a double row eight yards away from my first fence, at first they were a fine cover to my habitat and afterward served as a defense.

The seasons here can generally be divided not into summer and winter as in Europe, but into the rainy and the dry seasons. Half of February, all of March and half of April were the rainy season. Half of

---

[69] First day of spring.
[70] About four quarts.

April, all of May, June, and July, and half of August were the dry season. Half of August, all of September and half of October – rainy, then dry until the second half of February.

The rainy seasons sometimes held longer or shorter as the winds happened to blow but this was the general observation I made. After my experience with the ill consequences of being outside in the rain, I took care to supply myself with provisions beforehand so I would not have to go out and I sat indoors as much as possible during the wet months. I had a lot to do, as I tried to make many things which I had no way to provide myself with except by hard and constant labor. Particularly, I tried many ways to make a basket, but all the twigs I could get were so brittle that they would do nothing. It was advantageous that when I was a boy, I used to take great delight in standing at a basket maker shop in the town where my father lived, to see them make their wicker-ware. And being – as boys usually are – very willing to help and a great observer of the way they worked, I had the ability but not the materials. Then I remembered the twigs of that tree where I cut my stakes and they might possibly be as tough as the sallows,[71] willows and osiers in England, and I decided to try. The next day I went to my country house and cutting some of the smaller twigs, I found them usable. The next time I came prepared with a hatchet to cut down a number. These I set up to dry inside my hedge and when they were fit for use I carried them to my cave and here, during the wet season, I busied myself making baskets to carry earth or anything I wished. They were ugly, but I made them sufficiently usable for my purpose. Afterward, I took care to never be without them and as my wicker-ware decayed, I made more – especially strong, deep baskets to place my grain, instead of sacks.

----

[71] A type of shrubby willow.

Having mastered this difficulty – and using a world of time to do it – I tried if possible to see how to supply two wants. I had no containers to hold any liquid, except two casks which were almost full of rum and some glass bottles – some medium-sized and some large for water, spirits, etc. I had no pot to boil anything, except a large one I saved out of the ship and which was too big for what I wanted – to make broth or stew a bit of meat by itself. The second thing I would have loved was a tobacco-pipe, but it was impossible to me to make one. However, I found a gadget for that, too. That dry season I planted my second rows of stakes and worked at making baskets, when another business took up more time than I could spare.

8.

Surveys his Position

I mentioned before that I wanted to see the whole island and I had travelled up the brook to where I built my cottage and where I had an opening to the sea on the other side of the island. I now decided to travel across to the seashore on that side. Taking my gun, a hatchet, my dog and a more gunpowder and shot than usual, with two biscuits and a large bunch of raisins in my pouch, I began my journey. When I had passed the valley where my cottage stood, I came within view of the sea to the west, and being a very clear day, I saw land. I could not tell whether it was an island or a continent, but it was very high, extending from the west to the southwest for a long distance. By my guess it was at least 50 or 60 miles away.

I could not tell what part of the world I was in, except I knew it must be part of America and must be near the Spanish dominions. Perhaps it was inhabited by savages where, if I had landed, I would be in a worse condition than I was now. Therefore, I accepted the inclinations of Providence and believed everything was for the best. I silenced my mind with this and stopped worrying myself with fruitless wishes of being there.

Besides, after some thought I considered if this land was the Spanish coast I would certainly see some vessel pass one way or other but if not, then it was the savage coast between the Spanish country and Brazils, where the worst of savages are found, since they are men-eaters, and will murder and devour all the human bodies that fall into their hands.

With these considerations, I walked very leisurely forward. I found the side of the island where I now was much nicer than mine – the open fields sweet, adorned with flowers and grass and full of very fine forests. I saw an abundance of parrots, and would have liked to catch one, if possible, to keep as a pet and teach it to speak to me. I did, after some hard work, catch a young parrot after I knocked it down with a stick and brought it home. It was years before I could make him speak, but at last I taught him to call me by name.

I was exceedingly unfocused during this journey. I found hares and foxes in the low grounds, but they differed greatly from all the other kinds I had met with and I could not convince myself to eat them, though I killed several. I had no need to be adventurous since I didn't need food, though what I found was very good, especially the goats, pigeons and turtle, which added to my grapes, Leadenhall Market[72] could not have furnished a table any better. My circumstance was awful, but I had great reason to be thankful I was not driven to any extreme for food and had lots to choose from, even dainties.[73]

I never travelled more than two miles a day, but I took so many turns and twists to see what discoveries I could make, by the time I decided to sit down for the night I was weary and tired. Then I either rested in a tree or surrounded myself with a row of stakes set upright in the ground so no wild creature could come at me without waking me.

As soon as I came to the seashore, I was surprised to see I had settled on the worst side of the island. Here, the shore was covered with countless turtles, but on the other side I had found only three in a year and a half. There was also an infinite number of various birds, some I had seen and some not, and many of them very good meat but I did not know the names of any, except the penguins.

I could have shot as many as I pleased, but was very careful with my gunpowder and shot and would have killed a she-goat if I could, which

---

[72] Leadenhall Market still exists today in the center of London as an upscale shopping destination and food market.
[73] Delicacies.

would give me more food. Though there were many goats here, more than on my side the island, but it was much more difficult to get near them, since the country was flat and even and they saw me much sooner than when I was on the hills.

This side of the country was much more pleasant than mine but I had not the least inclination to move, since I was happy in my home and it was like I was here on a journey. I travelled along the seashore towards the east, I suppose about twelve miles and then setting up a large pole on the shore as a marker, I decided I would go home again. The next journey I took would be on the other side of the island east from my dwelling and around until I came to my post again.

I took another way back than I went, thinking I could easily keep all the island in my view so I could not miss finding my first dwelling. But I found myself mistaken. After walking about two or three miles, I found myself in a very large valley surrounded by hills, and those hills were covered with trees so I could not see which was my way by any direction except that of the sun, and not even then, unless I knew the position of the sun at that time of the day. To my further misfortune, the weather proved hazy for three or four days while I was in the valley, and not being able to see the sun, I wandered around very uncomfortably. At last I was forced to find the seaside, look for my post and come back the same way I went. I turned homeward, but the weather was very hot, and my gun, ammunition, hatchet and other things were very heavy.

In this journey, my dog surprised a kid,[74] and held it. Running to take hold of it, I caught it and saved it from the dog. I had a good mind to bring it home if I could, as I had often thought if it might be possible to get a kid or two and raise a breed of tame goats, which might supply me when my powder and shot was gone. I made a collar for this little

---

[74] Young goat.

creature and with a string I always carried, led him along – with some difficulty – until I came to my cottage and there I fenced him in and left him, since I was very impatient to get home, as I had been absent more than a month.

I cannot express how satisfied I was to get to my old hutch,[75] and lie down in my hammock. This little nomadic journey, without a place to stay had been so unpleasant, that my own house, as I called it to myself, was a perfect settlement compared to that. It made everything around me so comfortable, I decided I would never go far away from it again while I stayed on the island.

I relaxed here a week, to rest and entertain myself after my long journey. Most of the time was taken up in the weighty affair of making a cage for my Polly, who now began to be domesticated and well acquainted with me. Then I began to think of the poor kid I had penned up in my little circle and decided to go and bring it home or give it some food. I went and found it where I left it and it had almost starved. I went and cut branches of whatever shrubs I could find and threw it over, and having fed it, I tied it as I did before to lead it away. But it was so tame from being hungry, I didn't need to tie it, since it followed me like a dog and as I continually fed it, the creature became so loving, so gentle and so fond, that from that time on, it also became one of my domestics and would never leave me afterwards.

The rainy fall season had now come, and I spent the 30th of September in the same solemn manner as before, being the second anniversary of my landing on the island. With no more prospect of being rescued than the first day I came there, I spent the whole day in humble and thankful acknowledgment of the many wonderful mercies I had given to me, and without which it might have been infinitely more

---

[75] Strangely, this is a word for rabbit cage. Defoe must be using a colloquialism, much like saying you are returning to your "old hole in the wall."

miserable. I gave humble and hearty thanks that God had been pleased to discover it was possible I might be happier in this solitary condition than I would have been in the liberty of society, and in all the pleasures of the world. Also, that He could completely make up to me the deficiencies of my solitary state and the need for society, by His presence and the communications of His grace to my soul, supporting, comforting and encouraging me to depend on His providence here, and hope for His eternal presence in future.

It was now I began to feel how much happier the life I led was – with all its miserable circumstances – than the wicked, cursed, abominable life I had led. Now I exchanged my joys for my sorrows. My desires altered, my affections changed their gusts and my delights were completely new from what they were when I came ashore, or even for the past two years.

Before, as I walked around either hunting or exploring, the anguish of my soul would break out on me suddenly and my heart would die within me. I used to think of the woods, the mountains and the deserts and how I was a prisoner, locked up with the eternal bars and bolts of the ocean, in an uninhabited wilderness, without rescue. This would break out on me like a storm and make me wring my hands and cry like a child. Sometimes it was during my work and I would immediately sit down and sigh, and look at the ground for an hour or two and this was even worse. If I could burst into tears or vent my anger with words, it would go away and the grief, having exhausted itself, would subside.

But now I began to exercise my mind with new thoughts. Every day I read the word of God and applied all the comforts of it to my present state. One morning, being very sad, I opened the Bible on these words, "I will never, never leave you or abandon you." Immediately it occurred what these words were to me. Why else would they be directed at me, just when I was mourning over my condition, as one abandoned by God and man? "Well then," I said, "if God does not abandon me, how bad can it be, or what does it matter? Though the world had forgotten me, if I had the whole world and would lose the kindness and blessing of God, there would be no comparison in the loss?"

From this moment, I knew it was possible for me to be happier in this deserted, solitary condition than I would have ever been in any other place in the world, and with this thought I gave thanks to God for bringing me to this place. I don't know what it was, but something shocked my mind at that thought, and I dared not speak the words. "How did you become such a hypocrite," I said aloud, "to pretend to be thankful for a state which, however you may try to be happy with, you would rather pray energetically to be delivered from?' So, I stopped there, though I could not say I thanked God for being there, I thanked God for opening my eyes to see my former life, to feel sorrow for my wickedness and repent. I had never opened the Bible, but my soul blessed God for directing my friend in England, to pack it up among my goods and for helping me afterwards to save it out of the wreck of the ship.

In this state of mind, I began my third year, and though I have not given the reader an in-depth account of my work this last year as in the first, in general I was very seldom idle, regularly dividing my time between the several daily jobs I gave myself. My first duty was to God and reading the Scriptures, for which I constantly set aside time thrice[76] every day. Exploring with my gun for food generally took three hours every morning when it did not rain. The organization, cutting, preserving and cooking of what I had killed or caught – this took the better part of the day. In the middle of the day, when the sun was at its zenith, the heat was too much to go out in and four hours in the evening was all the time I could work, the only exception being that sometimes

---

[76] Three times.

I changed my hours of hunting and working, and went to work in the morning and out with my gun in the afternoon.

It should be noted this short time allowed for labor does not indicate how exceedingly hard the work was. The lack of tools, help and skill all added to the difficulty of the work. For example, it took 42 days to make a board for a long shelf which I wanted in my cave. But two sawyers,[77] with their tools and a saw-pit, would have cut six of them out of the same tree in half a day.

I needed to cut down a large tree, because my board was so wide. It took three days to cut down this tree, two more cutting off the branches and reducing it to a piece of timber. With tremendous hacking and hewing[78] I reduced both sides of it until it was light enough to move. Then I turned it and made one side of it smooth and flat as a board from end to end. Then, turning that side downward, cut the other side until I the plank was about three inches thick and smooth on both sides. Anyone may judge the work of my hands in such a piece, but labor and patience carried me through that and many other things. I only observe this to show the reason why so much of my time went away with so little work – what might be easily done with help and tools was a massive effort and required an extraordinary amount of time to do alone and by hand. Nevertheless, with patience and labor I got through everything that my circumstances made necessary for me to do, as will appear by what follows.

I was now in the months of November and December and expecting my crop of barley and rice. The ground I had manured[79] and dug up for them was not great since my seeds for each was less than the quantity of half a peck – remember, I had lost one whole crop by planting in the dry season. But now my crop looked very promising, when I found I

---

[77] A person who saws timber for a living.
[78] Cutting.
[79] Fertilized.

was in danger of losing it all again by enemies of several sorts, which were barely possible to keep from it. At first, the goats and wild creatures I called hares who, tasting the sweetness of the leaf, stayed night and day and ate it as soon as it came up.

I saw no solution for this except to make an enclosure around it with a hedge, which I did with a lot of work, especially since it required speed. As my land suitable for farming was small, I had it well fenced in about three weeks' time. Shooting some of the creatures in the daytime, I had my dog guard it at night, tying him up to a stake at the gate where he would stand and bark all night long. In a short period, my enemies abandoned the place and the grain grew very well, and began to ripen quickly.

But as the beasts ruined me while my grain was growing, now the birds were as likely to ruin me now when the ears sprouted. Going to see how it grew, I saw my little crop surrounded with birds, which stood watching until I was gone. I immediately shot at them, since I always had my gun with me. I shot, then a little cloud of birds, which I had not seen at all, flew from among the grain itself.

I predicted in a few days they would devour all my hopes, that I would starve and never be able to raise a crop at all. I didn't know what to do. I decided not to lose my grain, if possible, and I would watch it night and day. I went to see what damage was already done and found they had spoiled a lot of it, but as it was too green for them, the loss was not so great and the remainder was likely to be a good crop if it could be saved.

I stayed by it to load my gun and then leaving, I could easily see the thieves sitting on all the trees near me, as if they only waited until I was gone. As I walked off, I was no sooner out of their sight than they dropped down one by one into the grain again. I had no patience to stay until more came, knowing every grain they ate now was a peck-loaf[80] to me. Coming up to the hedge, I fired again and killed three of them. This was what I wished for. I picked them up and served them as we serve notorious thieves in England – I hanged them in chains as a terror to the rest of them. It is impossible to imagine this would have the effect it did, as the birds not only would not come near the grain, but they left that part of the island and I never saw a bird near the place as long as my scarecrows hung there. I was very glad and near the end of December – which was our second harvest of the year – I reaped my grain.

I needed a scythe or sickle[81] to cut it down and all I could do was make one as well as I could out of one of the broadswords, which I saved among the arms out of the ship. Since my first crop was small, I had no difficulty cutting it down. I reaped it in my own way, cutting nothing off but the ears and carried it away in a large basket I had made. At the end of all my harvesting, I found out my half-peck of seed had given me nearly two bushels of rice, and about two and a half bushels of barley by my guess, since I had no measure at that time.

This was very encouraging and I expected, in time, it would please God to supply me with bread. And here I was perplexed again, as I neither knew how to grind or make meal, nor how to clean it and part it. And if I made meal, how would I make bread from it? And if I knew how to make bread, I didn't know how to bake it. I added these things to my list of desires for my pantry, for lack of a better word. I decided not to taste any of this crop but to preserve it all as seed for the next season and in the interim to use all my study and hours of working to accomplish the great work of providing myself with bread.

---

[80] A loaf of bread made from a peck of flour, historically speaking, though this would be about 11 pounds of flour today.

[81] Traditional tools used for harvesting corn. Today, the best-known use of a scythe is as the Grim Reaper's implement of doom.

I truly now worked for my daily bread. I believe few people have thought much about the multitude of little things necessary in the providing, producing, curing, dressing, making and finishing this one loaf of bread. I, who was reduced to a mere state of nature, found this was my daily discouragement and was made more cognizant of it every hour, even after I had got the first handful of grain which, as I have said, came up unexpectedly.

First, I had no plough to turn up the earth and no spade or shovel to dig it. I conquered this by making a wooden spade, but this did my work in a wooden manner and it cost me a lot of days to make it without iron. It not only wore out sooner but made my work harder and performed much worse. I lived with this and was happy to work it out with patience and bear the bad performance. When the corn was planted, I had no harrow,[82] and was forced to go over it myself, dragging a heavy tree branch over it, rather than rake or harrow it. When it was growing, I had no tools to fence it, secure it, mow or reap it, cure and carry it home, thrash, part it from the chaff and save it. I wanted a mill to grind it, sieves to sift it, yeast and salt to make it into bread and an oven to bake it in, but all these things I did without, but the grain was still a great comfort and advantage to me. All this made everything laborious and tedious to me, but my time wasn't much of a loss to me because, as I had divided it, a certain part of each day was selected for this work. Because I had decided to use none of the grain for bread until I had more, I had the next six months to apply myself exclusively, by labor and invention, to provide myself with the proper utensils to make the grain fit for my use.

---

[82] An implement for breaking up and smoothing out the surface of the soil.

9.

A Boat

I had to prepare more land, since now I had enough seed to plant more than an acre. Before I did this, I had at least a week's work to make a spade which, when it was done, was a sorry one, very heavy and required double the labor to work with it. I got through that and planted my seeds in two large flat pieces of ground, as close to my house as I could and fenced them in with a good hedge. This took me at least three months, because a lot of that time was the wet season, when I could not go out. When it rained, I stayed indoors and worked. I diverted myself by talking to my parrot and teaching him to speak. I quickly taught him to know his own name and to speak it out loud, "Polly," was the first word I heard spoken on the island by any mouth but my own. This was not my work, but an assistance to my work. Now, I had a large job on my hands. I had long tried to understand how to make some earthenware pots which I really wanted, but did not know how to make. Considering the heat of the climate, I did not doubt if I could find clay, I might bake some pots in the sun that might be hard and strong enough to bear handling and hold anything that was dry and needed to be kept that way. This was necessary for preparing the grain and I decided to make some as large as I could, to stand like jars and hold what would be put into them.

It would make the reader pity me – or laugh at me – to tell how many awkward ways I took trying to make these pots. What odd, misshapen, ugly things I made. Many of them caved in and many more fell over since the clay was not stiff enough to bear its own weight. Still many more cracked from the over-violent heat of the sun and even more fell to pieces by only moving them both before and after they dried, and finally, after working hard to find the clay – to dig it, bring it home and work it – I could not make more than two large earthen ugly things (I cannot call them jars) after two months' labor.

As the sun baked these two very dry and hard, I lifted them very gently and set them down again in two large wicker baskets, which I had made on purpose for them so they wouldn't break. Since there was a little room to spare between the pot and the basket, I stuffed it full of the rice and barley straw and I thought they would hold my dry grain and perhaps the meal.

Though I failed so much in my design of large pots, I made several smaller things with better success, such as little round pots, flat dishes, pitchers, and pipkins[83] and anything my hand turned to, and the heat of the sun baked them quite hard.

But all this was not my goal, which was to get an earthenware pot to hold liquid and bear the fire, which none of these could do. That happened after making a large fire for cooking my meat. When I went to put it out, I found a broken piece of one of my earthenware containers in the fire, burnt as hard as a stone and red as a tile. I was pleasantly surprised to see it and said to myself, certainly they might be made to burn whole, if they would burn broken.

This had me study how to build my fire to make it burn some pots. I had no notion of a potter's kiln, or of glazing them with lead – though I had some lead to do it with – but I placed three large pipkins and a few pots in a pile, one on top of the other, and placed my firewood all around it, with a large heap of embers under them. I plied the fire with fresh fuel on the outside and on the top, until I saw the pots on the inside red-hot all the way through and observed they did not crack at all. When I saw them clear red, I let them stand in that heat about five

---

[83] A small earthenware pot.

or six hours, until I found one of them, though it did not crack, did melt since the sand which was mixed with the clay melted by the violence of the heat and would have become glass if I had gone on. I let the fire die down gradually until the pots began to lose the red color. Watching them all night, so the fire didn't die down too fast, by the morning I had three very good (I will not say handsome) pipkins and two other earthenware pots, as hard burnt as could be desired, and one of them perfectly glazed with the running of the sand.

After this experiment, I had every sort of earthenware for my use, but their shapes were very different, since I had no way of making them except as children make mud pies, or as a woman would make pies who never learned to make pastry.

The joy I felt for such a trivial thing was equal to none when I found I had made an earthenware pot that would bear the fire and I was impatient to wait until they were cold before I set one on the fire again with some water in it to boil me some meat, which it did admirably. With a piece of a kid I made some very good broth, though I wanted oatmeal and several other ingredients necessary to make it as good as I would have wanted.

My next concern was to get a stone mortar to stamp or beat some grain in, since there was no way I would perfect the art of a stone mill with one pair of hands. To supply this need, I was at a great loss. Of all the trades in the world, I was as completely unqualified as a stone-cutter as for any other job, and I didn't have any tools to do it. I spent many days looking for a stone big enough to cut hollow, and make it fit for a mortar. I couldn't find any, except what was in the solid rock and which I had no way to dig or cut out. The rocks on the island were not hard enough and were all of a sandy, crumbling stone, which neither would bear the weight of a heavy pestle, nor would break the grain without filling it with sand. After a great deal of time lost searching for a stone, I gave up and decided to look for a large block of hard wood, which I found much easier. Getting one as big as I had strength to move, I made it round and formed it on the outside with my axe and hatchet. Then with the help of fire and infinite labor, made a hollow place in it as the Indians in Brazil make their canoes. After this, I made a heavy pestle out of ironwood. This I prepared and put aside until I had my next crop of grain, which I decided to grind into meal to make bread.

My next difficulty was to make a sieve to part it from the bran and the husk, without which I did not think it possible to have any bread. This was difficult to think about, since I had nothing to make it with, even a fine thin canvas to filter the meal through. And here I was at a full stop for many months and I really didn't know what to do. I had no linen left except what was mere rags. I had goat's hair, but didn't know how to weave or spin it and even if I had known how, there were no tools to work it with. The only solution I found was I remembered I had, among the seamen's clothes saved out of the ship, some muslin[84] neckcloths and with some pieces of these I made three small sieves appropriate for the work, which I used for years.

The baking part was the next thing to be considered, and how I would make bread once I had the grain even though I had no yeast. There was no way to get this, so I did not concern myself much about it, but I needed an oven. I found an experiment for that also: I made some earthenware pots which were wide but not deep – about two feet in diameter and no more than nine inches deep. These I burned in the fire, as I had done the others and when I wanted to bake, I made a roaring fire on my hearth, which I had paved with some square tiles of my own baking but I would not call them square.

When the firewood had pretty much burned down to embers, I pulled them forward on the hearth to cover it all over, and I let them lie until the hearth was very hot. Then sweeping away all the embers, I set

---

84 A cravat or necktie made from unbleached cotton

down my loaf or loaves, and burying the earthenware pot in them, put the embers around the outside of the pot, to keep in and add to the heat. As good as the best oven in the world, I baked my barley loaves and soon became a good pastry cook as well, as I made myself several cakes and puddings from the rice, but I made no pies having nothing to put in them, except the meat of birds or goats.

You may wonder how this took most of my third year living here, but in the intervals of these things I had my new harvest to manage. I reaped my grain when it was in season and carried it home as well as I could and laid it up in my large baskets until I had time to rub it out, since I had no floor to thrash it on or tool to thrash it with.

And now, with my stock of grain increasing, I really wanted to build my barn bigger. I wanted a place to store it in since the increase in grain now yielded me so much that I had about twenty bushels each of barley and rice, so much so that I decided to begin to use it freely as my bread had been gone quite a while. Also, I decided to see what quantity would be sufficient for a whole year, so I only had to plant once a year. I found the forty bushels of barley and rice were much more than I could eat in a year, so I decided to plant only the same quantity every year that I had the last, in hopes that would fully provide me with bread and so on.

While I did this, my thoughts ran frequently on the prospect of the land I had seen from the other side of the island. I sometimes secretly wished I was on shore there, thinking that seeing the mainland and an inhabited country, I might find some way or other to take myself further and perhaps at last find some means of escape.

But I made no allowance for the dangers of such an undertaking and how I might fall into the hands of savages, perhaps far worse than the lions and tigers of Africa. I would run the danger of being killed and perhaps eaten, as I had heard the people of the Caribbean coast were cannibals and I knew by the latitude that I could not be far from that shore. Supposing they were not cannibals, they might still kill me, as many Europeans who had fallen into their hands had before, even when there were twenty of them. All these things I well considered, but gave me no fears at first and my head ran greatly on the thought of getting over to the shore.

Now I wished for my boy Xury and the longboat with shoulder-of-mutton sail, with which I sailed over a thousand miles on the coast of Africa, but this was in vain. Then I thought I would go and look at our ship's boat which, as I have said, was blown up on shore when we were first cast away. She lay almost where she did at first and was turned by the force of the waves upside down against a high ridge of rough sand, but with no water near her. If I had men to refit and launch her into the water, the boat would have done well enough and I might have gone back into the Brazils with her easily enough. Unfortunately, I could no more turn her and set her upright than I could move the island. I went to the woods and cut levers and rollers and brought them to the boat determined to try, telling myself that if I could turn her over, I could repair the damage she had received and I could go to sea in her very easily. I spared no pains in this piece of fruitless toil and spent, I think, three or four weeks at it, finding at last it was impossible to heave it up with my little strength. I even tried digging away the sand to undermine it and make it fall, setting pieces of wood to thrust and guide it right in the fall.

But when I had done this, I was unable to move it or to get under it, much less move it forward towards the water. I was forced to give up and though I gave up the hopes of the boat, my desire to venture to the mainland increased, rather than decreased.

I wondered if it was possible to make myself a canoe like the natives of those climates make without tools out of a large tree trunk. I not only thought this was possible, but easy, and satisfied myself with the thoughts of making it and with having much more use for it than any of the negroes or Indians. I did not consider the inconveniences I had, such as no help to move it into the water. This was much harder for me to overcome than the need of tools could be to them. After I had chosen a vast tree in the woods and cut it down with considerable trouble, and with my tools chopped the outside into the shape of a boat and burned the inside to make it hollow., what then? After all this, what use was it if I must leave it where I found it because I didn't have the manpower to launch it into the water?

One would have thought while I was making this boat I must have had the smallest inkling of how I would get it into the sea. But, my thoughts were so intent on my sea voyage that I never once considered how I would get it off the land and it was easier for me to guide it over forty-five miles of sea than over forty-five fathoms[85] of land to set it afloat in the water.

I went to work on this boat like the biggest fool. I pleased myself with the plan without determining whether I was ever able to undertake it. The difficulty of launching my boat came often into my head but I put a stop to my inquiries with the foolish answer, "Let me make it first. I'm sure I will find some way to get it to the sea when it is done."

This was a most preposterous method but my eagerness prevailed, and to work I went. I felled a cedar tree and I wonder if Solomon ever had one like it when building the Temple of Jerusalem. It was 5'10" diameter at the lower part near the stump, and 4'11" in diameter at the end of twenty-two feet, after which it lessened for a while, then parted into branches. It was with infinite labor that I felled this tree. I was twenty days hacking and hewing it at the bottom; I was fourteen more getting the branches and limbs and the vast spreading head cut off; it cost me a month to shape it to something like the bottom of a boat, so it might swim upright as it ought to do. It cost me nearly three months more to clear the inside, and work it to make an exact boat of it. This I

---

[85] Old measure of sea depth equal to six feet

did without fire, only with a mallet and chisel and by hard labor, until I had made a very handsome canoe, big enough to carry 26 men and consequently big enough to carry me and all my cargo.

When I was done, I was extremely delighted with it. The boat was much bigger than any canoe made from one tree I ever saw in my life. Many a weary stroke it had cost and had I gotten it into the water, I kid you not, I would have begun the craziest voyage, and the most unlikely ever tried.

But all my devices to get it into the water failed me, though they cost me infinite labor too. It was about a hundred yards from the water, but the first inconvenience was it was up hill towards the creek. To take away this discouragement, I decided to dig into the ground and make a slope. I began, and it cost me an extraordinary amount of pain (but I don't begrudge pains when my deliverance is in view), but when this was worked through and the difficulty managed, I still couldn't move this canoe. Then I measured the distance and decided to cut a canal to bring the water up to the canoe, as I could not bring the canoe down to the water. I began this work and when I calculated how deep and how wide it had to be dug, working by myself it would have taken ten or twelve years, so with great reluctance I gave up on this attempt as well.

This saddened me greatly and now I saw, though too late, the folly of beginning a project before we count the cost and before we judge our own strength to go through with it.

In the middle of this work I finished my fourth year here and kept my anniversary with the same devotion, and with as much comfort as ever before. By a constant study and serious application to the Word of God, and by the assistance of His grace, I gained a different knowledge from what I had before. I entertained different notions of things. I looked on the world now as a remote thing which I had nothing to do with, no expectations from and certainly, no desire for. I had nothing to do with it and was never likely to have, or so I thought.

I was removed from all the wickedness of the world. I had neither the lusts of the flesh, the lusts of the eye, nor the pride of life. I had nothing to desire – I had all I was now capable of enjoying. I was lord of the whole manor or if I pleased, I could call myself king or emperor over my whole country. There were no rivals. I had no competitor, nobody to dispute sovereignty or command with me. I could have raised shiploads of grain, but had no use for it. I had enough tortoise, but one was as much as I could put to any use. I had enough timber to have built a fleet of ships and I had enough grapes to have made wine or raisins to load into that fleet when it was built.

But all I could make use of was all that was valuable to me. I had enough to eat and supply my wants and what was the rest to me? If I killed more meat than I could eat, the dog or vermin would eat it. If I planted more grain than I could eat, it would spoil. The trees I had cut down were lying to rot on the ground, as they were only useful as fuel and for that, I had no need except to cook my food.

Experience taught me that all the good things in this world are no good to us unless we can use them and whatever we collect to give to others, we enjoy just as much as we can use, and no more. The greediest, grumbling cheapskate in the world would have been cured of greed if he had been in my situation, since I possessed infinitely more than I knew what to do with. I had no room for desire, except of things which I did not have and they were insignificant, though of great use to me. I had some money, gold and silver worth about £36 sterling. Sadly, it was useless to me and often thought I would have given a handful of it for a gross[86] of tobacco pipes or for a hand-mill to grind my grain. No, I would have given it all for a sixpenny-worth[87] of turnip and carrot seed out of England, or for a handful of peas and beans and a bottle of

---

[86] 144

[87] 2½ pence

ink. As it was, I had no benefit from it, but there it lay in a drawer and grew moldy with the damp of the cave in the wet seasons. If I had a drawer full of diamonds, it would be the same – they were of no value to me, because of no use.

I had now brought my life to appoint which was much simpler than it was at first, both in mind and body. I frequently sat down to eat meat with thankfulness, and admired the hand of God's providence, which had spread my table in the wilderness. I learned to look more on the bright side of my condition and less on the dark side and to consider what I enjoyed rather than what I wanted. This sometimes gave me comfort which I take notice of here, to tell those discontented people who cannot comfortably enjoy what God has given them, because they see and crave something He has not given them. All our dissatisfaction about what we want springs from the lack of thankfulness for what we have.

Something else I thought about which made me feel better – and would make anyone else in my condition as well – was to compare my present condition with what I at first expected it would be or, more precisely, what it would have been, if the good providence of God had not wonderfully ordered the ship to be thrown closer to shore, so I could get everything out of her for my relief and comfort. Without this, I would have had no tools to work, weapons for defense or gunpowder and shot for getting my food.

I spent whole hours – sometimes whole days - telling myself in the liveliest colors how I would have acted if I had got nothing out of the ship. How I could not have got any food, except fish and turtles and, as it was a long time before I found any of them, I would have died first. If I would have lived, it would have been like a mere savage. If I had killed a goat or a bird, I had no way to flay or open it or remove the meat from the skin and the bowels or to cut it up. I would have had to gnaw it with my teeth and pull it with my claws, like a beast.

These reflections made me very sensitive to the goodness of Providence and very thankful for my present condition, with all its hardships and misfortunes. This part I recommend to those who are apt, to contemplate in their misery, "Is any affliction like mine?" Let them consider how much worse the cases of some people are, and their life might have been, if Providence had thought fit.

I had another thought, which also gave me hope. I compared my present situation with what I had deserved and had reason to expect from the hand of Providence. I had lived a dreadful life, completely destitute of the knowledge and fear of God. I had been well instructed by father and mother. Neither had been lacking in their early attempts to infuse a religious awe of God into my mind, a sense of my duty and what the nature and end of my life required of me. But I fell early into the seafaring life, which of all lives is the poorest of the fear of God, though His terrors are always in front of them. Falling early into the seafaring life, and into seafaring company, all that little sense of religion which I had entertained was laughed out of me by my messmates, with their hardened despising of dangers and views of death, which grew habitual to me by my long absence from being able to talk with anyone like myself or to hear anything that was good.

So void was I of everything that was good that, in the greatest deliverances I enjoyed – my escape from Salé, rescue by the Portuguese captain and delivery to the Brazils and my receiving of cargo from England – I never once had the words "Thank God!" so much as on my mind and in my greatest distress I didn't have so much as a thought to pray to Him, or to say, "Lord, have mercy on me!" No, the only mention of God's name was to swear at it and blaspheme it.

I had terrible thoughts for many months because of my wicked and hardened past life. When I looked around me and considered what wisdom had come to me since I came to this place and how God had dealt generously with me – had not only punished me less than my evil had deserved, but had so plentifully provided for me – this gave me great hopes that my repentance was accepted, and that God had mercy in store for me.

With these thoughts I decided not only to resign to the will of God in my present circumstances, but to be sincerely thankful. I was still alive and should not complain, seeing I had not been completely punished for my sins. I enjoyed so many mercies which I had no reason to have expected in that place. I should never worry about my condition, but I should rejoice and give thanks daily for that daily bread, which nothing but a crowd of wonders could have brought me. I should consider I had been fed by miracle, as great as the feeding of Elijah by ravens – no, by a long series of miracles. I could hardly have named a place in the uninhabitable part of the world where I could have been castaway more to my advantage. A place where, though I had no society, I also found no ravenous beasts and no furious wolves or tigers to threaten my life, no venomous creatures or poisons and no savages to murder and devour me. As my life was a life of sorrow one way, so it was a life of mercy another and I wanted nothing to make it a life of comfort but to be able to make sense of God's goodness to me and care over me in this condition and be my daily consolation. After I understood all this, I wasn't sad anymore. I had now been here so long that many things which I had brought on shore for my help were either gone or wasted.

My ink, except a very little, had been gone some time. This I eked out with water until it was so pale, it barely left any appearance of black on the paper. As long as it lasted I used it to write down the days of the month on which any remarkable thing happened to me. By recalling times past, I remembered there was a strange concurrence of days in the various providences which happened to me, and which, if I had been superstitiously inclined to observe days as fatal or fortunate, I might have had reason to have looked on with a great deal of curiosity.

First, the same day I broke away from my father and friends and ran away to Hull to go to sea, one year after I was taken by the Salé man-of-war and made a slave. The same day of the year I escaped out of the shipwreck in Yarmouth Roads was the same day a year later I made my escape from Salé in a boat. The same day of the year I was born – the 30th of September – was the same day I had my life so miraculously saved twenty-six years later when I was castaway on this island, so that my wicked life and my solitary life both began on the same day.

The next thing to my ink being lost was the biscuit I brought out of the ship. This I had saved to the last degree, allowing myself only one cake of bread a day for over a year and I was without bread for nearly a year before I got any grain of my own. I had great reason to be thankful that I had any at all, since it was next to miraculous.

My clothes, too, began to decay. As for linen, I had none for a long time, except some shirts which I found in the chests of the other seamen and which I carefully preserved. Many times, I could bear to wear no other clothes but a shirt and it was a great help to me that I had, among all the men's clothes from the ship, almost three dozen shirts. There were also several of the seamen's thick watchcoats,[88] but they were too hot to wear and though it is true the weather was so violently hot that there was no need of clothes, I could not go quite naked. I was not inclined to, nor could I stomach the thought of it, though I was alone. I could not bear the heat of the sun when naked as well as with some clothes on. No, the heat frequently blistered my skin but with a shirt on, the air itself made some motion and whistling under the shirt, was twice as cool as without. I could never bring myself to go out in the heat of the sun without a hat. The sun, beating with such violence as it does in that place, would give me a headache as it pounded down on my head, without a hat on. If I put on my hat it would go away.

---

[88] A warm overcoat worn by sailors in cold or stormy weather.

I began to consider about putting the few rags I had, which I called clothes, into some order. I had worn out all the waistcoats[89] I had, and I now had to see if I could make jackets out of the watchcoats, along with other materials I had. I started tailoring – more like botching – since I made the most pathetic work of it. However, I made shift[90] from a couple of the waistcoats, which I hoped would serve me a long time. As for pants, I made a very sorry pair until after.

I have mentioned that I saved the skins of all the creatures that I killed – the four-footed ones – and I had them hung up, stretched out with sticks in the sun, so some of them were so dry and hard that they were good for nothing, but others were very useful. The first thing I made of these was a large cap for my head, with the hair on the outside to shoot off the rain. This I performed so well, that after I made an outfit exclusively from these skins – a waistcoat and open-kneed pants, both loose, since they were to keep me cool, not warm. I must acknowledge they were terribly made. If I was a bad carpenter, I was a worse tailor. However, if it happened to rain when I was out, the hair of my waistcoat and cap kept me very dry.

After this, I spent a great deal of time and pains making make an umbrella. I really wanted one and had a good mind to make one. I had seen them made in the Brazils, where they are very useful in the heat there and I felt the heat every bit as bad here – and sometimes worse – being closer to the equator. Besides, as I was forced to be outside often, it was very useful to me for the rain as well as the heat. I took a world of effort with it and was a long time before I could make anything hold, and after I had thought I had it, I spoiled two or three before I made one to my liking. At last I made one that worked well, though the main difficulty I found was to make it fold down. I could make it spread, but

---

[89] Vests.
[90] A long, loose-fitting undergarment.

if it did not come down and draw in, it was not portable for me except over my head, which would not do. At last, I made one to my liking and covered it with skins, hair upwards so it threw off the rain like a penthouse and kept off the sun so well that I could walk out in the hottest of the weather better than I could before in the coolest. When I had no need of it, I could close it and carry it under my arm.

I lived very comfortably, resigned to the will of God and throwing myself solely at the disposal of His providence. This made my life better than sociable. When I began to regret the absence of conversation I would ask myself, or even God Himself, was that not better than the greatest enjoyment of human society in the world?

10.

Tames Goats

I can't say that for five years after this any extraordinary thing happened to me, but I lived on as before in the same way in the same place. Besides my yearly labor planting barley and rice and curing my raisins, the main thing I worked on was a canoe, which at last I finished. By digging a canal to it six feet wide and four feet deep, I brought it the almost half mile to the creek. As for the first canoe, which was so big, I was forced to let it lie where it was as a reminder to teach me to be wiser next time. The next time, though I could not get a proper tree for it and was where I could not get the water to it without digging for half a mile, I saw it was feasible at last and I never gave up. Though I was nearly two years making both the canoe and canal, I never begrudged my labor, in hopes of having a boat to go off to sea at last.

However, though my little canoe was finished, the size was not at all close to the plan I had when I made the first – venturing over to the TERRA FIRMA over 40 miles away. The smallness of my boat put an end to that idea and now I thought no more of it. I had a boat, so my next idea was to make a cruise around the island. As I had been in one place on the other side, crossing over land, the discoveries I made in that little journey made me very eager to see other parts of the coast. Now I had a boat, so I thought of nothing except sailing around the island.

For this, I fitted a little mast to my boat and made a sail out of some of the pieces of the ship's sails which I had stored, and which I had a lot still left. Having fitted my mast and sail and tried the boat, I found she would sail very well. Then, I made little lockers at each end of my boat to put provisions, necessities, ammunition, etc., to be kept dry from either rain or the spray of the sea. I cut a little, long, hollow place inside the boat, where I could lay my gun, making a flap to hang down over it to keep it dry.

I fixed my umbrella in the step at the stern like a mast, to stand over my head and keep the sun off me like an awning. And so, every now and then I took a little voyage on the sea, but never far out and never far from the little creek. Eager to view the circumference of my little kingdom, I decided on my cruise. I supplied my ship for the voyage, putting in two dozen loaves (cakes I would call them) of barley-bread, an earthenware pot full of parched[91] rice (a food I ate a good deal of), a little bottle of rum, half a goat, gunpowder and shot for killing more, and two of the large watchcoats I had saved out of the seamen's chests, one to lie on and the other to cover me at night.

It was the 6th of November in the sixth year of my reign – or my captivity, whichever you please – that I set out on this voyage and I found it much longer than I expected. Though the island itself was not very large, when I came to the east side, I found a large ledge of rocks lie out about six miles into the sea – some above water, some under it. Beyond that a shoal of sand, lying dry about a mile farther, so I was forced to go a great way out to sea to avoid it.

When I first discovered this, I was going to give up my enterprise and come home again, not knowing how far it might force me to go out to sea and above all, doubting how I would get back again. I came to an anchor – I had made a kind of anchor with a piece of a broken grappling from the ship. Securing my boat, I took my gun and went on shore, climbing up a hill which seemed to overlook that point where I saw the full extent of it, and decided to explore.

Viewing the sea from that hill, I noted a strong and furious current, which ran to the east and came close to the point. I took more notice of

---

[91] Lightly roasted.

it because I saw there was the danger that when I came into it I might be carried out to sea by the strength of it and not be able to make the island again. Had I not got first on this hill, it would have been so, since there was the same current on the other side the island, only that it was off at a further distance and I saw there was a strong eddy[92] near the shore. Even if I could get out of the first current, I would then be in an eddy.

I stayed here two days because the wind was blowing hard, and being just contrary to the current, caused the sea to break in large waves on the point, so it was not safe for me to keep too close to the shore, or to go too far off because of the current.

The morning of the third day, the wind having died down overnight, the sea was calm and I ventured out, but I warn all rash and ignorant pilots. No sooner did I come to the point, and not even a boat's length from the shore, but I found myself in deep water and a current like a drain. It carried my boat along with such violence that all I did could not keep her on the edge of it. I found it hurried me farther and farther out from the eddy, which was on my left. There was no wind blowing to help me and all I could do with my paddles meant nothing. Now I began to give up. As the current was on both sides of the island, I knew in a few miles they must join again and then I was irrecoverably gone. I saw no possibility of avoiding it, so I had no prospect ahead except death, though not by the sea, which was calm, but from starvation. I had found a tortoise on shore, as big as I could lift and had tossed it into the boat and I had a large jar of fresh water, but what was all this when I was driven into the vast ocean, where there was no shore, no mainland or island, for a thousand miles at least?

And now I saw how easy it was for the providence of God to make even the most miserable condition of mankind worse. I looked back on

---

my desolate, solitary island as the most pleasant place in the world and all the happiness my heart could wish for was to be there again. I stretched out my hands to it with eager wishes – "Oh happy deserted island!" I said, "I will never see you again. Oh, miserable creature, where am I going?" Then I cautioned myself with my unappreciative state of mind, and that I had complained about my solitary condition. What would I give to be on shore there again! Proving we never see the true state of our condition until we see the opposite, nor know how to value what we enjoy, except when we want it. It is barely possible to imagine the dismay I was now in, being driven almost six miles from my beloved island (or so it now appeared to me to be) into the wide ocean and in the greatest despair of ever seeing it again. I worked hard until my strength was almost exhausted and kept my boat as much to the north – towards the side of the current which the eddy lay on – as I possibly could. Around noon, as the sun passed its height, I thought I felt a little breeze in my face from the south. This cheered my heart a little, especially when in about half-an-hour it blew a gentle gale. By this time, I was a frightening distance from the island and had a little cloudy or hazy weather intervened, I had been done another way, since I had no compass on board and would never have known how to steer towards the island if I had lost sight of it. But the weather continuing clear, I applied myself to get up my mast and spread my sail, staying away to the north as much as possible to get out of the current.

Just as I had set my mast and sail and the boat began to sail, I saw by the clearness of the water some alteration of the current was near. Where the current was so strong the water was foul, but noticing the water clear, I found the current subside and presently I found about half a mile to the east, a breach of the sea on some rocks. I found these rocks caused the current to part again, and as the main part of it ran away southerly, leaving the rocks to the northeast, the other turned by the rocks and made a strong eddy, which ran back again to the northwest with a very sharp stream.

They who know what it is to have a reprieve brought to them, or to be rescued from thieves just about to murder them, may guess what my present joy was and how gladly I put my boat into the stream of this eddy. With the wind also blowing, how gladly I spread my sail to it, running cheerfully in front of the wind and with a strong tide underfoot. This eddy carried me about three miles on my way back again directly towards the island, but about six miles more to the north than the current which carried me away at first, so when I came near the island, I found myself at the northern shore of the other end of the island, opposite to that which I went out from.

When I had made a couple of miles more with the help of this current or eddy, I found it was expended and served me no further. Being between two strong currents in the wake of the island, the water was calm and still having a fair breeze, I kept on steering directly for the island, though not making such good time as I did before.

About four o'clock in the evening, being within a couple of miles of the island, I found the point of the rocks which caused this disaster stretching out to the south. Throwing the current more southerly had, of course, made another eddy to the north. This I found very strong but not directly where my course lay, which was due west, but almost fully north. Having a fresh gale, I sailed across this eddy, slanting northwest and in about an hour came within a mile of the shore where, it being smooth water, I soon got to land.

When I was on shore, I fell on my knees and gave God thanks for my deliverance, deciding to lay aside all thoughts of liberation by my boat. Refreshing myself with the things I had, I brought my boat close to shore, in a little cove I had spied under some trees and laid down to sleep, being spent with the labor and fatigue of the voyage.

I was now at a great loss which way to get home with my boat! I had run through so much danger and knew too much to think of attempting it the same way I went out. I didn't know what was on the other side of the island and didn't have any mind to run any more adventures. I decided the next morning to make my way west along the shore and see if there was any creek I could lay up my frigate[93] in safety, to have her again if I wanted her. In about three miles or so coasting the shore, I came to a very good inlet about a mile over, which narrowed until it came to a very small brook. Here I found a very convenient harbor for my boat as if she had been in a little dock made on purpose for her. Here I put in, and having stowed my boat very safe, I went on shore to look around and see where I was.

I soon found I had passed a little by the place where I had been before when I travelled on foot. Taking nothing out of my boat except my gun and umbrella, as it was exceedingly hot, I began my march. The way was comfortable enough after such a voyage and I reached my old retreat in the evening and found everything standing as I left it. I got over the fence and laid down in the shade to rest my limbs, since I was very weary and fell asleep. But you who read my story, judge if you can, what a surprise I had when I was woken out of my sleep by a voice calling me by my name several times. "Robin, Robin, Robin Crusoe: poor Robin Crusoe! Where are you, Robin Crusoe? Where are you? Where have you been?"

I was so dead asleep at first, fatigued with rowing for part of the day and walking the latter part, that I did not wake thoroughly. Dozing, I thought I dreamed somebody had spoken to me, but the voice continued to repeat, "Robin Crusoe, Robin Crusoe." At last I began to wake up and was at first terribly frightened and got up extremely

---

[93] This is a joke on Defoe's part, as a frigate is a larger warship and his canoe definitely wasn't.

alarmed. No sooner were my eyes open, but I saw my parrot Polly sitting on the top of the hedge and immediately knew it was he that spoke to me in the bemoaning language I had used to talk to him and teach him. He had learned it so perfectly that he would sit on my finger and lay his bill close to my face and cry, "Poor Robin Crusoe! Where are you? Where have you been? How came you here?" and such things as I had taught him.

Even though I knew it was the parrot and could be nobody else, it was a long time before I could calm myself. First, I was amazed how the creature got here and then, how he would just stay around the place and nowhere else. When I was satisfied it could be nobody but honest Polly, I got over it and holding out my hand, I called him by his name. The sociable creature came to me and sat on my thumb, as he used to do, and continued talking to me, "Poor Robin Crusoe!" and "how did you come here?" and "where had you been?" just as if he had been overjoyed to see me again and so I carried him along home with me.

I had now had enough of rambling to sea for some time and had enough to do for many days to sit and reflect on the danger I had been in. I would have been very glad to have had my boat again on my side of the island but I didn't know how it was feasible to get it around. As to the east side of the island, which I had gone around, I knew there was no venturing that way. My heart would shrink and my blood ran cold when I thought about it. As to the other side of the island, I did not know how it might be there but supposing the current ran with the same force against the shore as it passed by on the other, I might run the same risk of being driven away from the island as I had been before. With these thoughts, I contented myself to be without a boat, though it had been the product of so many months' labor to make and of so many more to get it into the sea.

I remained in this state of mind nearly a year and lived a very sedate, retired life, as you may well suppose. I was very serene and comfortable in resigning myself to the dispositions of Providence. I thought I lived very happily in all things except that of society. I improved myself in this time in all the mechanic exercises which my necessities required and I believe I would, on occasion, have made a very good carpenter, especially considering how few tools I had.

Besides this, I arrived at an unexpected perfection in my earthenware and tried to make them with a wheel, which I found infinitely easier and better and now I made things round and shaped, which before were dirty things to look at. But I think I was never more conceited of my own performance, or more joyful of anything I found out, than my being able to make a tobacco pipe. Though it was a very ugly, clumsy thing when it was done, and only burned red, like other earthenware and would draw the smoke, I was exceedingly comforted by it since I had always used to smoke. There were pipes in the ship, but I forgot them at first, not thinking there was tobacco on the island and after when I searched the ship again, I could not find any pipes.

I also improved my wicker-ware and made an abundance of baskets, as well as my abilities allowed. Though not very handsome, they were very handy and convenient for laying things in or bringing things home. If I killed a goat, I could hang it up in a tree, flay it, dress it, cut it in pieces and bring it home in a basket. Likewise, with a turtle – I could cut it up, take out the eggs and a piece or two of the meat – which was enough for me – and bring them home in a basket, leaving the rest behind. Also, large deep baskets were the receivers of my grain, which I always rubbed out as soon as it was dry and cured, and kept it in large baskets.

I now noticed my gunpowder decreased considerably. This was a want which it was impossible for me to supply and I began seriously to consider what I must do when I would have no more powder or more particularly, how I would kill any goats. I had in my third year here, kept a young kid and bred her up tame and I was hoping to get a he-goat but I could not by any means until my kid grew to be an old goat. As I could never find it in my heart to kill her, she died of old age.

Now in the eleventh year of my residence and, as I have said, my ammunition growing low, I set myself to study to trap and snare the goats to see whether I could catch some of them alive, particularly I wanted a she-goat great with young.[94] For this I made snares to hinder them and I do believe more than once they were taken in them, but my tackle[95] was not good since I had no wire so I always found the traps broken and my bait devoured. I decided to try a pitfall[96] so I dug several large pits in the earth, in places where I had observed the goats fed, and over those pits I placed hurdles with a heavy weight on them. Several times I put ears of barley and dry rice without setting the trap and I could easily see the goats had gone in and eaten the grain as I could see the marks of their feet. I set three traps in one night and the next morning I found them, all standing with the bait eaten. This was very discouraging. I altered my traps and going one morning to see them, I found in one of them a large old he-goat. In one of the others I found three kids – a male and two females.

I didn't know what to do with the old one. He was so fierce I dared not go into the pit to him to bring him out alive, which was what I wanted. I could have killed him, but that was not my business, nor would it answer my end. I let him out and he ran away, frightened out of his wits. But I did not know then what I learned afterwards – hunger will tame a lion. If I had let him stay three or four days without food and then have carried him some water to drink and a little grain, he would have been as tame as one of the kids. Knowing no better at that time, I let him go. Then I went to the three kids and taking them one by

---

94 Pregnant
95 Equipment
96 A covered pit used as a trap.

one, I tied them together with strings and with some difficulty brought them all home.

It was a while before they would feed but throwing them some sweet grain, it tempted them and they began to be tame. If I expected to supply myself with goats' meat when I had no gunpowder or shot left, breeding some was my only way and I would have them around my house like a flock of sheep. Then it occurred to me I must keep the tame goats from the wild ones, or else they would always run wild when they grew up. The only way for this was to have an enclosed piece of ground, well fenced with a hedge to keep them in, or to keep wild ones out.

This was a huge undertaking for one pair of hands but as I saw the necessity, I had no choice. My first work was to find a proper piece of ground where there was likely to be forage for them to eat, water for them to drink and cover to keep them from the sun.

Those who understand such enclosures will think I had very little problem when I built on a place proper for all these (being a plain, open piece of savannah, as our people call it in the western colonies),[97] which had two or three little streams of fresh water in it and at one end was very woody – they will smile at my calculation when I tell them I began by enclosing this piece of ground so my hedge must have been at least two miles around. Nor was the madness of it so great as to the scope, because if it was ten miles around, I would have enough time to do it, but I did not consider my goats would be as wild in that area as if they had the whole island.

My hedge was begun and carried on about fifty yards when it occurred to me to enclose a piece about 150 by 100 yards, as it would maintain as many as I would have in any reasonable time. As my stock increased, I could add more ground to my enclosure, so I stopped.

---

[97] That would be the future United States

I was about three months hedging in the first piece. Until I had done it, I tethered the three kids in the best part of it and used to feed them to make them more familiar with it. Very often I would go and carry them some ears of barley or a handful of rice and feed them out of my hand, so after my enclosure was finished and I let them loose, they would follow me up and down, bleating after me for a handful of grain.

This answered my need and in about 18 months I had a flock of about twelve goats, kids and all. Two years later I had 43, not including several I took and killed for my food. After that, I enclosed five pieces of ground to feed them in, with little pens to drive them as I wanted and gates out of one piece of ground into another.

But this was not all. Not only did I have goat meat when I pleased, but milk too. In the beginning I did not think of milk and when I thought about it, it was really a pleasant surprise, since now I set up my dairy and sometimes had a gallon or two of milk a day. As Nature supplies food to every creature and dictates naturally how to make use of it, after many attempts and failures, I made both butter and cheese and was never in need of it afterward. I had never milked a cow – much less a goat – or seen butter or cheese made only when I was a boy, but I finally succeeded. How mercifully our Creator can treat His creatures, even in those conditions in which they seemed to be overwhelmed! How He can sweeten the bitterest providences, and give us a reason to praise Him for dungeons and prisons! What a table was here spread for me in the wilderness, where I saw nothing at first except to die from hunger!

11.

Finds Man's Footprint
on the Sand

It would have made a Stoic[98] smile to see me and my little family sit down to dinner. There was me, the majesty, prince and lord of the whole island. I had the lives of all my subjects at my absolute command. I could hang, draw,[99] give liberty and take it away, and no rebels among all my subjects. Then, to see how like a king I dined, all alone, attended by my servants! Polly, as if he had been my favorite, was the only person permitted to talk to me. My dog, who had now grown old and crazy and had found no species to multiply with, always sat at my right and two cats on either side of the table, expecting now and then a bit from my hand, as a special favor.

But these were not the two cats which I brought on shore in the beginning, as they were both dead and buried near my habitat. One of them had multiplied with some wild creature and these were two which I had preserved tame. The rest ran wild in the woods and became troublesome to me, as they would often come into my house and plunder me, until I was forced to shoot them. I had to kill a large amount and after a while, they left me. With this company and in this

---

[98] A member of the Stoic school of philosophy, who believed people should be free from passion, unmoved by joy or grief. Basically Mr. Spock on *Star Trek*.
[99] Disembowel

plentiful manner I lived. It could not be said I wanted anything but society and sometime after this, I would have too much of that.

I really wanted to use my boat, but I was very unwilling to run any more risks. Sometimes I sat planning ways to get her around the island, and other times I sat down happy enough without her. But I had a strange uneasiness in my mind and wanted to go to the hill I went up to see how the shore lay and how the current ran. This inclination increased every day and I finally decided to travel there by land, following the edge of the shore. I did, but if anyone in England met a man such as me, it would either have frightened him or raised a great deal of laughter. As I frequently stood still to look at myself, I could only smile at the notion of my travelling through Yorkshire with such equipment and clothing.

I had a large, high, shapeless cap made of a goat's skin, with a flap hanging down behind to keep the sun off me as well as the rain from running down my neck. I had a short jacket of goat's skin, the flaps coming down to about the middle of the thighs, and a pair of open-kneed pants of the same skin. The pants were made of the skin of an old he-goat, whose hair hung down so long on either side that, like pantaloons,[100] it reached to the middle of my legs. I had no socks or shoes, but had made a pair of somethings – I barely knew what to call them, like buskins,[101] to flap over my leg, and lace on either side like spatterdashes,[102] but primitively shape, as were the rest of my clothes.

I had on a wide belt of dried goat skin, which I pulled together with two thongs instead of buckles, and in a kind of a frog[103] on either side of this, hung a little saw and a hatchet instead of a sword and dagger. I had another thinner belt fastened the same way, which hung over my

---

[100] Men's close-fitting pants fastened below the calf or at the foot.
[101] A knee-high boot.
[102] A long legging worn to keep trousers clean.
[103] An attachment to a belt for holding a sword.

shoulder and at the end of it, under my left arm, hung two pouches. These were both made of goat skin and in one hung my powder, in the other my shot. On my back I carried my basket, on my shoulder my gun and over my head a large, clumsy, ugly, goatskin umbrella, which was, after all, the most necessary thing I had next to my gun. As for my face, the color was not as mulatto-like as one might expect from a man not at all careful and living within nine or ten degrees of the equator. My beard I had once let grow until it was about a quarter of a yard long but since I had scissors and razors, I had cut it pretty short, except what grew on my upper lip, which I had trimmed into a large pair of Muslim whiskers, like I had seen worn by some Turks at Salé. Of these moustaches, I will not say they were long enough to hang my hat on them, but they were long and monstrous enough so that in England they would have passed for frightful.

Dressed like this, I went on my new journey and was out five or six days. I travelled first along the seashore to where I first brought my boat on the rocks. Having no boat now to take care of, I went over the land and looking forward to the rocky point, I was surprised to see the sea smooth and quiet – no rippling, no motion, no current, at least no more than in any other place. I didn't understand this and decided to spend some time observing it, to see if nothing from the tide had caused it. I was convinced the tide was coming from the west, and joining with the current from some large river on shore, must be the cause of this current and, as the wind blew harder from the west or from the north, this current came nearer or went farther from the shore. Waiting there until evening, I went up to the rock again and I plainly saw the current as before, only that it ran farther this time – over a mile from the shore, while in my case it stayed close to the shore and hurried me and my canoe along with it.

This convinced me that I had to only observe the ebb and the flow of the tide and I might very easily bring my boat around the island again.

When I thought about putting it in practice, I had such terror in my spirits that I could not tolerate the thought of it. Instead, I decided – which was safer though more labor intensive – to build another canoe and have one for one side of the island, and one for the other.

Now I had two plantations on the island, as I called them. One was my little tent with the wall around it under the rock and the cave behind me, which by this time I had enlarged into several apartments, one inside another. As for my wall, those stakes now grew like trees and by now had grown so big and spread so much, that you could not see anyone living behind them. Near my dwelling was my farmland, properly cultivated and planted and which duly yielded me their harvest in season.

Besides this, I had my country seat, and I also now had a tolerable plantation there. First, I had my little cottage, which I kept in good repair –or specifically, I kept the hedge up to its usual height, the ladder standing always inside. I kept the trees always cut so they would spread, grow thick and wild and make better shade, which they did to my mind. In the middle of this I always had my tent standing, and under this I made a couch out of skins and other soft things and a blanket on top, with a watch-coat to cover me. And here, whenever I was absent from my chief seat, I took up in my country home.

Next to this I had my enclosures for my cattle – my goats – and I had taken an unimaginable amount of effort to fence and enclose this ground. I was so anxious to stop the goats from breaking through that I never stopped until, with infinite labor, I had stuck the outside of the hedge so full of small stakes it was more a fence than a hedge and there was barely room to put a hand between them. When those stakes grew, as they all did in the next rainy season, it made the enclosure stronger than any wall.

This will testify that I was not idle and I spared no pains to do whatever was necessary for my comfort. Keeping a breed of tame creatures would be a living storeroom of meat, milk, butter and cheese for me as long as I lived in the place, even if it were forty years. Keeping them in reach depended entirely on my perfecting my enclosures which I effectively secured. When these little stakes I had planted began to grow, they were so thick I was forced to pull some of them up again. I also had my grapes growing, which I mainly depended on for my winter store of raisins and which I never failed to preserve very carefully, since they were the best delicacy of my whole diet. They were not only enjoyable, but medicinal, wholesome, nourishing and refreshing to the last degree.

As this was also about halfway between my other habitat and the place where I had laid up my boat, I generally stayed here on my way as I frequently used to visit my boat. I kept all things belonging to her in very good order. Sometimes I went out in her to divert myself, but no more hazardous voyages – barely ever a stone's throw from the shore since I was so apprehensive of being carried away again by the currents or winds, or any other accident.

But now I come to a new part of my life. It happened around noon one day, going towards my boat I was very surprised to see the print of a man's naked foot on shore, which was plainly visible in the sand. I was flabbergasted, like I had seen a ghost. I listened, I looked round me, but could hear nothing, nor see anything. I went up on higher ground to look farther. I went up and down the shore, but it was the only one – I could see no other impression but that one. I went to it again to see if there were more and to see if it might not be my imagination but there was no room for that. There was exactly the print of a foot – toes, heel and every part of a foot. How it got there I don't know. After countless fluttering thoughts, I came home to my fortification not feeling the ground I walked on but terrified to the last degree, looking behind me every two or three steps, mistaking every bush and tree and imagining every stump at a distance to be a man. It's impossible to describe how many shapes my frightened imagination represented to me or how many wild ideas I imagined and what strange, unaccountable whimsies came into my thoughts.

When I came to my castle – or so I think I called it ever after this – I bolted into it like someone pursued. Whether I went over by ladder or went in at the hole in the rock, I can't remember. Never has a frightened hare fled or a fox into his hole with more terror than me.

I did not sleep that night. The farther I was from the reason for my fright, the greater my fears were. I was so embarrassed with my own horrible ideas, I formed nothing but dismal thoughts, even though I was now a long way off. Sometimes I thought it must be the devil and reason joined me in this. How would any other thing in human shape come to the place? Where was the vessel that brought them? Where were any other footsteps? And how was it possible a man would come there? But then, to think Satan would take human shape in such a place, where there could be no reason for it except to leave the print behind and even that for no purpose, since he could not be sure I would see it. I considered the devil would have found an abundance of other ways to terrify me than a single footprint. As I lived on the other side of the island, he would never have been so simple as to leave a mark in a place where the odds were 10,000:1 I would see it, and in the sand too, which the first surge of the sea on a high wind would have defaced entirely. All this seemed inconsistent with the thing itself and with all the notions we usually entertain of the subtlety of the devil.

Such things assisted me to argue out of all anxieties of it being the devil and I concluded then it must be some more dangerous creature – that it must be some of the savages from the mainland who had wandered out to sea in their canoes and had made the island and had been on shore, but were gone again to sea, being as unwilling to have stayed on this desolate island as I would have been to have had them stay.

While these ideas were rolling in my mind, I was very thankful that I was not there at that time or they did not see my boat, and perhaps have searched farther for me. Then terrible thoughts racked my imagination about them finding my boat and that there were people here now. If so, I would certainly have them come again in greater numbers and devour me and if they did not find me, they would find my enclosure, destroy all my grain and carry away my flock of tame goats and I would die of starvation.

My fear banished all my religious hope, all my former confidence in God which was founded on the wonderful experience of His goodness. It was as if He who fed me by miracle by His power could not preserve what He had given me by His goodness. I scolded myself for my laziness. I should have planted more grain than what would serve me until the next season, as if no accident could intervene to prevent my enjoying my crop. I was ashamed of myself and decided in future to have two or three years' grain beforehand so that, whatever might come, I would not die from a lack of bread.

How strange a chequer-work[104] of Providence is the life of man! and by what secret reasons are the actions taken as different circumstances present! Today we love what tomorrow we hate; today we seek what tomorrow we shun; today we desire what tomorrow we fear, even tremble at the fear of. I, whose only disorder was that I was banished from human society, alone, restricted by the boundless ocean, cut off from mankind, and condemned to what I call silent life. I was someone whom Heaven thought not worthy to be numbered among the living or to appear among the rest of His creatures. To have seen one of my own species would have been like resurrecting me from the dead and the greatest blessing Heaven itself, next to the supreme blessing of salvation, could give. Now I would tremble at the thought of seeing a

---

[104] A chessboard.

man and was ready to sink into the ground at the shadow or silent appearance of a man having set his foot in the island.

Such is the uneven state of human life and it afforded me many curious speculations afterwards, when I had recovered from my first surprise. I considered this was the station of life the infinitely wise and good providence of God had determined for me. As I could not foresee what the Divine wisdom might be in all this, I was not to dispute His sovereignty over me since I was His creature, and He had an undoubted right to govern and dispose of me as He thought fit. And as I was a creature who had offended Him, He had a judicial right to condemn me to what punishment He thought fit and it was my part to submit to His indignation, because I had sinned against Him. God, who was not only righteous but omnipotent, had thought fit to punish and afflict me, so He was able to deliver me. If He did not think fit to do so, it was my unquestioned duty to resign myself absolutely and entirely to His will and it was also my duty to hope in Him, pray to Him and quietly to attend to the dictates and directions of His daily providence.

These thoughts took up many hours, days, even weeks and months and one effect of my thoughts on this I cannot omit. One early morning, lying in my bed and filled with thoughts about my danger from the appearances of savages, I found it disturbed me very much. On this, these words of the Scripture came into my thoughts, "Call on Me in the day of trouble, and I will deliver you and you will worship Me." Rising cheerfully out of my bed, my heart was not only comforted but I was guided and encouraged to pray sincerely to God for deliverance. When I had done praying I took my Bible, and opening it to read, the first words I saw were, "Wait on the Lord and be of good cheer, and He will strengthen your heart." It is impossible to express the comfort this gave me. In answer, I thankfully laid down the book, and was no longer sad, at least on that occasion.

In the middle of these thoughts and anxieties, it came to me one day that all this might be a mere chimera[105] and this footprint might be my own when I came on shore from my boat. This cheered me up a little too, and I began to persuade myself it was all a delusion, that it was nothing else but my own foot and why might I not come that way from the boat, as well as go that way to the boat? I could not tell for certain where I had trod and where I hadn't and that if, at last, this was only my own footprint, I had played the part of those fools who try to make stories of specters and ghosts, and then are frightened at them more than anybody.

Now I began to gain courage and to peep around again, as I had not left my castle for three days and I began to starve. I had little or nothing indoors except some barley-cakes and water. I knew my goats wanted to be milked too, which usually was my evening diversion and the poor creatures were in great pain and inconvenience because of it. It almost spoiled some of them and almost dried up their milk. Encouraging myself with the belief this was nothing except my own footprint and that I might jump at my own shadow, I began to go outside again and went to my country house to milk my flock. To see how scared, how often I looked behind me, how I was ready every now and then to lay down my basket and run for my life – it would have made anyone think I was haunted by my conscience, or that I had been frightened recently – indeed, I had! I went my cottage a few more days and seeing nothing, I began to be a little bolder and to think it was just my imagination. But I could not persuade myself completely until I went down to the shore again to see this footprint and measure it against my own. It was evident that when I laid up my boat, I could not possibly be on shore anywhere near. Secondly, when I measured the mark with my own foot, my foot was smaller. Both these things filled my head with new

---

[105] Illusion.

imaginations, and gave me the vapors[106] again so that I shook with cold like one with a fever. I went home again, filled with the belief that some man or men had been on shore or that the island was inhabited, and I might be surprised before I was aware. I didn't know what course of action to take for my security.

Oh, what ridiculous resolutions men take when possessed with fear! It deprives them of reason. The first thing I proposed to myself was to tear down my enclosures and turn all my tame cattle wild into the woods to avoid the enemy finding them and then come back to the island in prospect of booty. Then, I would dig up my two fields so they wouldn't find the grain there and be prompted to frequent the island. Then, I would demolish my cottage and tent so they would not see any remnants of habitation and be prompted to look farther.

These were the subjects of the first night's thoughts after I was home again, while the fears which had overrun my mind were fresh and my head was full of nervousness. Fear of danger is ten thousand times more terrifying than danger itself and we find the burden of anxiety much greater than the evil which we are anxious about. I thought I looked like Saul, who complained not only the Philistines were on him, but God had forsaken him. Now I did not take measures to compose my mind – by crying to God in my distress and resting on His providence, as I had done before, for my defense and rescue. If I had done that, at least I would have been more cheerfully supported by this new surprise and perhaps carried through it with resolve.

This confusion kept me awake all night and in the morning I fell asleep, my mind tired and my spirits exhausted. I slept very soundly and awoke much more composed than I had ever been before. Now I began to think calmly and I concluded this island (which was exceptionally pleasant, fruitful, and not as far from the mainland as I

---

106 A sudden feeling of faintness.

thought) was not as entirely abandoned as I might imagine. Although there were no permanent inhabitants, there might sometimes come boats which, either by design or driven by crosswinds, might come to this place. I had lived there fifteen years now and had not met with the least shadow of any people. If at any time they would be driven here, it was probable they left again as soon as they could, seeing they had never thought fit to stay here. The most danger I could see was from an accidental landing of stragglers who were driven here against their wills and went off again with all possible speed. I had nothing to do but consider a safe retreat, in case I saw any savages land on the spot.

Now, I began to regret digging my cave so large and putting in a door which came out beyond where my fortification joined the rock. I decided to build a second fortification in a semicircle where I had planted a double row of trees about twelve years earlier. These trees were planted so thick before that they only needed a few piles driven between them to be thicker and stronger and my wall would be soon finished. I now had a double wall and my outer wall was thickened with pieces of timber, old cables and everything I could think of to make it strong. In it I had seven little holes, about as big as I might put my arm through. Through the seven holes I planted the muskets I took out of the ship. These I planted like cannon and fitted them into frames that held them like a carriage so I could fire all the seven guns in two minutes' time. This wall took many weary months to finish and I never thought myself safe until it was done.

When this was done I stuck all the ground outside my wall full of stakes from the willow-like tree which grew on the island. I believe I set nearly twenty thousand of them, leaving a pretty large space between them and my wall so I would have room to see an enemy and they would have no shelter from the young trees if they attempted to approach my outer wall.

In two years' time I had a thick grove and in six years' time I had a forest around my dwelling, growing so monstrously thick and strong that it was completely impassable. Nobody would ever imagine there was anything beyond it, much less a house. As for the way I would go in and out, it was by using two ladders now, so when the two ladders were taken down no man living could come down to me without doing himself harm and if they had come down, they were still on the outside of my outer wall.

I took all the measures forethought could suggest for my own preservation and it will be seen they were not without good reason, though I foresaw nothing at that time more than my fear suggested to me.

12.

A Cave Retreat

While doing this, I was not totally careless of my other affairs. I was very concerned about my little herd of goats. They were a ready supply for every need and began to be sufficient without the expense of gunpowder and shot and without the fatigue of hunting after wild ones. I was opposed to lose the advantage of them and to have to nurse them all over again.

I thought of only two ways to preserve them. One was to find another convenient place to dig a cave underground and drive them into it every night. The other was to enclose two or three little bits of land, remote from one another and as concealed as I could, where I could keep about a half-dozen young goats in each place so if any disaster happened to the flock in general, I might be able to raise them again with little trouble and time. Though it would require a good deal of time and labor, I thought was the most rational design.

I spent some time to find the most remote parts of the island and I found one which was as private as my heart could wish. It was a little damp piece of ground in the middle of the hollow and thick woods, where I almost lost myself once before trying to come back that way from the eastern part of the island. I found a clear piece of land, nearly three acres, so surrounded with woods that it was almost a natural enclosure. At least it did not need nearly as much labor to make it like the other piece of ground I had worked so hard at.

I immediately went to work on this piece of ground and in less than a month's time I had fenced it around so well that my flock were well secured in it. Without any further delay, I moved ten young she-goats and two he-goats to this piece and when they were there I continued to perfect the fence until I had made it as secure as the other. I did this at a more leisurely pace and it took a great deal more time. All this labor was purely at the expense of my anxieties from the man's footprint. I had never seen any human creature come near the island and I had now lived two years under this uneasiness, which made my life much less comfortable than it was before, as anyone who knows what it's like to live in the constant fear of man can imagine. My uneasiness had a great impression on the religious part of my thoughts, and this caused me great anguish. The dread and terror of falling into the hands of savages and cannibals was so heavy on my spirits that I seldom found myself in the state of mind for prayer to my Maker – at least not with the calmness and resignation of soul which I was accustomed to. Instead, I prayed to God when I was under great pain and pressure of mind, surrounded with danger and expecting every night to be murdered and devoured before morning. From my experience, a peaceful state of mind of thankfulness, love and affection is much more proper for prayer than of terror and agitation. Under the dread of impending harm, a man is no more fit to perform the duty of praying to God than he is for a repentance on a sickbed. These anxieties affect the mind as the others do the body; and the agitation of the mind is as great a disability as that of the body and much greater. Praying to God is an act of the mind, not of the body.

But I digress. After I secured one part of my little living stock, I went around the whole island searching for another private place to make another deposit. Wandering closer to the west point of the island than I had ever done and looking out to sea, I thought I saw a boat in the distance. I had found a telescope in one of the seamen's chests but not with me, and this was so remote I could not tell what to make of it though I looked at it until my eyes were not able to look any longer. Whether it was a boat or not I do not know, but as I descended from the hill I couldn't see it any longer, and I decided not to go out again without a telescope in my pocket. When I came down the hill to the end of the island where I had never been before, I was convinced that seeing the man's footprint was not such a strange thing as I imagined and it was a special gift that I was castaway on the side of the island where the savages never came. Otherwise I would have known nothing was more frequent than the canoes from the mainland, when they were a little too far out at sea, to shoot over to that side of the island for harbor. Likewise, as they often met and fought in their canoes, the victors, having taken any prisoners, would bring them over to this shore where, being all cannibals and according to their dreadful customs, they would kill and eat them.

When I came down to the shore, I was completely confounded and amazed. It is not possible to express my horror at seeing the shore spread with skulls, hands, feet and other bones of human bodies. I particularly observed a place where a fire had been made and a circle dug in the earth, like a cockpit,[107] where I supposed the savage wretches had sat down to their human feastings on the bodies of their fellow-creatures.

I was so astonished at the sight that I entertained no notions of danger for a long time. All my fears were buried in the thoughts of such an area of inhuman, hellish brutality and the evil of human nature which, though I had heard of it often, had never seen this close. I turned away from the horrid spectacle. My stomach grew sick and I was just at the point of fainting when nature discharged the disorder from my stomach. Having vomited with uncommon violence, I was a little relieved but could not bear to stay in the place a moment longer. I went

---

[107] An early 18th-century nautical term for an area in the aft lower deck of a warship where the wounded were taken.

up the hill again as quick as I could and walked on towards my own habitation.

When I was further from that part of the island I stood still awhile, amazed. Recovering and with a flood of tears in my eyes, I gave God thanks, He who had cast my lot in a part of the world where I was distinguished from such dreadful creatures as these. Though I had considered my present condition very miserable, He had given me so many comforts so I had more to give thanks for than to complain of. Above all, even in this miserable condition, I had been comforted with the knowledge of Him and the hope of His blessing, which was a joy more than equal to all the misery which I had suffered, or could suffer.

In this frame of thankfulness, I went home to my castle and became more at ease with my safety than I was ever before. I noted these wretches never came to this island in search of what they could get – perhaps not seeking, not wanting or not expecting anything here. I knew I had been here now almost eighteen years and never saw any human footsteps there before and I might be eighteen years more, concealed as I am now, if I did not expose myself to them. I had no reason to do so – my only business was to keep myself entirely concealed – unless I found a better sort of creatures than cannibals to make myself known to. I had such a disgust of the savage wretches and their wretched, inhuman custom of devouring and eating one another that I continued brooding and sad and kept inside my circle for almost two years after this. When I say my own circle, I mean my three plantations – my castle, my country seat (which I called my cottage) and my enclosure in the woods. The aversion I had to these hellish wretches was such that I was as fearful of seeing them as of seeing the devil himself. I did even go to look after my boat all this time, instead thinking about making another. I could not think of ever making any more attempts to bring the other boat around the island to me, in case

I would meet with some of these creatures at sea, because if I fell into their hands, I knew what would have been my fate.

Time, and the satisfaction I had that I was in no danger of being discovered by these people, began to wear off my uneasiness about them. I began to live in the same calm manner as before, only now I was more cautious and kept my eyes more open to danger than I did before. I was especially more cautious of firing my gun in case any of them, being on the island, would hear it. It was a stroke of luck that I had furnished myself with a tame breed of goats, and that I had no need to hunt anymore in the woods or shoot at them. If I did catch any of them after this, it was by traps and snares as I had done before. For two years after this I believe I never fired off my gun once, though I never went out without it. What was more, as I had saved three pistols out of the ship, I always carried them with me, sticking them in my goatskin belt. I also refurbished one of the large cutlasses I had from the ship and made a belt to hang it on, so that I was now a most formidable fellow to look at when I went around.

For some time, I seemed to be reduced to my former calm, sedate way of living, except for these precautions. All of this showed me more and more how far my condition was from being miserable, compared to some others – no, to many other ways of life which it might have pleased God to have made my fate. I believed how little worrying there would be among mankind if people would compare their condition with those that were worse, in order to be thankful, than to be always comparing them with those which are better.

There were not really many things which I wanted now. The frights I had about these savage wretches, and the concern I had for my own preservation, had taken off the edge of my inventiveness for my own convenience. I had dropped a good plan – which I once had thoughts about – to try to make some of my barley into malt and then try to brew myself some beer. This was really a whimsical thought, and I scolded myself often for the simplicity of it. I would require several things to make my beer that it would be impossible for me to supply. First: casks to preserve it in, which was a thing that I was never able to accomplish, though I spent not only many days, but weeks and months attempting it. Second, I had no hops to make it keep, no yeast to made it work, no copper kettle to make it boil. And yet with all these things lacking, I truly believe had not the terror of the savages intervened, I would have undertaken it and perhaps succeeded, since I seldom gave up without accomplishing something once I put my head into it. But my ingenuity now ran another way. Night and day, I could think of nothing except how I could destroy some of the monsters in their cruel, bloody entertainment and if possible save the victim they would bring here to destroy. It would take up a larger volume than this whole book to write down all the schemes I hatched for destroying these creatures, or at least frightening them to prevent them from coming here anymore. But, all this was unsuccessful. Nothing was possible, unless I was there to do it myself. And what could one man do among them, when there might be twenty or thirty of them with darts or bows and arrows, which they could shoot as accurately as I could with my gun?

Sometimes I thought of digging a hole under where they made their fire and putting five or six pounds of gunpowder in it so when they kindled their fire, it would catch fire and blow up all that was near it. But I was unwilling to waste so much powder on them, and I couldn't be sure of it going off at a certain time. At best, it would do little more than blow the fire around their ears and frighten them, but not enough to make them abandon the place. I then thought I would prepare an ambush with my three guns all double-loaded, and in the middle of their bloody ceremony attack them, when I would be sure to kill or wound a few at every shot. Then rushing in on them with my three pistols and my sword, I didn't doubt if there were twenty, I would kill them all. This notion pleased me for weeks and I was so full of it that I often dreamed of it and sometimes, I attacked them in my sleep. I went so far with it that I worked several days looking for proper places to put myself in ambuscade,[108] to watch for them and I went frequently to the place itself, which had grown more familiar to me. While my mind was filled with thoughts of revenge and a bloody killing of thirty of them, the horror I had of the place and at the barbarous wretches devouring one another reinforced my hatred. I found a place on the side of the hill where I was satisfied I could securely wait until I saw their boats coming. Then I could – even before they came on shore – move unseen into some thickets, one of which had a hollow large enough to conceal me entirely. There I could sit and observe all their bloody doings and take aim at their heads when they were so close together it would be next to impossible to miss my shot. I decided to fulfil my plan and I prepared two muskets and my shotgun. The two muskets I loaded with a pair of slugs each and four or five smaller bullets, about the size of pistol bullets. The shotgun I loaded with nearly a handful of the largest swan shot.[109] I also loaded my pistols with about four bullets each and, well provided with ammunition for a second and third charge, I prepared myself for my expedition.

After I had my plan ready and in my imagination put it in practice, I made my tour every morning to the top of the hill, to see if there were any boats on the sea coming near the island. But I began to tire of this hard duty after constantly keeping watch for a few months and coming back without any discovery. In all that time, there had not been any appearance of savages, not only on shore but on the whole ocean, as far as my eye or telescope could see.

While I kept my daily tour to the hill to look out, I also kept up the strength of my plan. I was perfectly fine with such an outrageous idea

---

[108] An ambush
[109] A large size of shot used in hunting wild birds

as the killing of thirty naked savages, for an offence which I had not thought about at all, any farther than my passions were fired by the horror of the unnatural custom of the people of that country. People who, it seems, had been hurt by Providence in His wise creation of the world, to have no other guide than their own abominable and impaired passions. They were left, and perhaps had been so for some ages, to do such horrid things and have such dreadful customs as nature, entirely abandoned by Heaven and motivated by some hellish degeneracy, allowed. But now, when I grew tired of the fruitless excursions, my opinion of the action itself began to alter. I began, with cooler and calmer thoughts, to consider what I was going to engage in. What authority did I have to pretend to be judge, jury and executioner to these men, who Heaven had thought fit for so many years to leave unpunished and to be the executioners of His judgments on one another. How had these people offended me and what right did I have to engage in the blood quarrel they shamelessly had with one another. I debated this often with myself. "How do I know what God Himself judges in this particular case? It is certain these people do not commit these acts as a crime. It is not against their own consciences and their god is not reprimanding them. They do not know it is an offence and then commit it in defiance of divine justice, as we do with almost all the sins we commit. They think it no more a crime to kill a captive taken in war than we do to kill an ox, or to eat human flesh than we do to eat mutton."

When I considered this, I realized I was certainly in the wrong. These people were not murderers, any more than those Christians were murderers who often put to death prisoners taken in battle. Or, more frequently, put whole troops of men to the sword without allowing surrender, though they threw down their arms and surrendered. Although the treatment they gave one another was so brutish and inhuman, it was really nothing to me. These people had done me no harm. If they attempted, or I saw it necessary for my preservation to attack them, something might be said for it. But, they really had no knowledge of me, and consequently no plan for me. Therefore, it would not be justified for me to attack them. This would validate the conduct of the Spaniards in all their barbarities practiced in America, where they destroyed millions of these people who, even if they were idolators[110] and barbarians and had several bloody and barbarous rites in their customs, such as sacrificing human bodies to their idols were – to the Spaniards – very innocent people. The destruction of them is spoken of with the highest disgust and detestation by even the Spaniards themselves today and by all other Christian nations of Europe as butchery, a bloody and unnatural piece of cruelty, unjustifiable either to God or man. For this the very name of a Spaniard is considered frightful and terrible to all people of humanity or of Christian compassion. It is as if the kingdom of Spain was particularly eminent in the production of a race of men who were without principles or the common bowels of pity to the miserable, which is considered the mark of generous state of mind.[111]

These considerations put me to a full stop and I began to be off my plan and to conclude I was wrong to think of attacking the savages. It was not my business to meddle with them, unless they first attacked me and it was my business to prevent. If I was discovered and attacked by them, I knew my duty. On the other hand, I argued with myself that this really was the way to not deliver myself and to entirely ruin and destroy myself. Unless I was sure to kill everyone – not only those on shore at that time, but all who came after. But, if only one of them escaped to

---

[110] Someone who worships "false gods," a definite no-no to 17th-century Christians, though this would mean any other religion but Christianity.

[111] Historical note: when Defoe wrote this, the Protestant England was at war with the Catholic Spain during the War of the Spanish Succession and since Defoe was a well-known political propagandist, consider this his little jab at the enemy.

tell their country-people what had happened, they would come by the thousands to avenge the death of their fellow man, and I would bring on certain destruction. I concluded that, neither in principle nor in policy, I should not concern myself in this affair. My business was by all possible means to conceal myself from them and not to leave any sign for them to guess there was any human on the island. Religion joined in with this sensible resolution. I was convinced now in many ways that it was not my duty when I was planning all my bloody schemes for the destruction of innocent creatures – I mean innocent to me.

As to the crimes they were guilty of towards one another, I had nothing to do with them. They were national and I should leave them to the justice of God, who is the Governor of nations and knows how to make a just retribution for national offences. This appeared so clear to me now. I was truly satisfied I was not allowed to commit no less a sin than that of willful murder. On my knees I gave humble thanks to God, who delivered me from blood-guiltiness, begging Him to grant me the protection of His care, so I would not fall into the hands of the barbarians – or I would not lay my hands on them – unless I had a clearer call from Heaven to do it, in defense of my own life.

I truly did not want to attack these wretches, so for nearly a year I never once went up the hill to look out to sea, or to know if any of them had been on shore. I did not want to be tempted to renew my plans against them or be provoked by any advantage that might present itself to attack them. The only thing I did was move my boat, which was still on the other side of the island, and carried it down to the east end of the island. I stored it in a little cove, which I found under some high rocks and where I knew – because of the currents – the savages dared not come with their boats for any reason. Along with my boat I took everything I had left with her, including a mast and sail and a thing like an anchor, which could not be called either an anchor or grapnel[112] though it was the best I could make. All these I removed, so there would not be the least shadow of discovery or appearance of any boat, or of any human habitation on the island. Besides this, I kept myself, as I said, more secluded than ever and seldom went from my cell except on my constant work – to milk my she-goats and manage my little flock which, being on the other side of the island, was out of danger. These savage people, who sometimes haunted this island, never came with any thoughts of finding anything here. Consequently, they never wandered from the coast and I do not doubt they would have been on shore several times if my fear of them had not made me cautious.

I looked back with some horror on the thoughts of what would have happened if I stumbled on them and been discovered before that. Naked and unarmed, except with one gun often only loaded with small shot, I walked everywhere, peeping and peering around the island to see what I could get. What a surprise if, instead of the footprint, I had found twenty savages, and by their swift running no possibility of escaping them! The thoughts of this sometimes sank my soul and distressed my mind so much that I could not recover right away. What would I have done? Not only would I have been unable to fight them, but I also would not have the presence of mind to do what I should. After serious thinking, I would be depressed and sometimes it would last a long time. But then I would ascend into thankfulness to Providence, which had delivered me from so many unseen dangers and had kept me from those harms which I had no way to deliver myself from.

I had often thought, when I first began to see the merciful dispositions of Heaven, of the dangers we run through in this life. How wonderfully we are delivered from harm when we know nothing about

---

[112] A small anchor with several flukes.

it. How, when we are in a dilemma, whether to go this way or that way, a secret hint will direct us this way, when we intended to go that way. When sense, our own inclination and perhaps business has called us to go the other way, a strange impression on the mind, from where and by what power we don't know, will tell us to go this way. Then we find If we hadn't listed, all would be lost. On these and many similar contemplations I made it a rule – whenever I found those secret hints, I never failed to obey the secret dictate, though I knew no other reason for it. I could give many examples of the success of this during my life, especially in the latter part of my inhabiting this unhappy island. It is never too late to be wise and I advise all men, whose lives are in store for such extraordinary incidents as mine – or even not so extraordinary – do not discount secret hints from Providence. Let them come from what invisible intelligence they will. That I will not discuss and can't explain, but certainly they are proof of the conversations of spirits and a secret communication between us and them. You will see I have some remarkable instances of such proof as can't be resisted, from the remainder of my solitary residence in this dismal place.

I believe the reader will not think it strange if I confess that these anxieties, these constant dangers I lived in and the concern that was now on me, put an end to all ingenuity and to all the plans I had for my future accommodation and convenience. I had my safety on my mind now more than my food. I would not drive a nail or chop a stick of wood now, fearing the noise would be heard. I wouldn't fire a gun for the same reason. Above all, I was painfully uneasy at making any fire in case the smoke, which is very visible in the day, would betray me. For this reason, I moved that part of my business which required fire – burning pots and pipes, etc. – into my new apartment in the woods where I found, after I had been some time, a natural cave which went in a long way and where no savage, had he been at the mouth of it, would be hardy to venture in. Certainly, neither would any other man except someone who, like me, wanted nothing a safe retreat.

The mouth of the cave was at the bottom of a large rock where, by accident – I did not see abundant reason to credit all such things to Providence – I was cutting down some thick tree branches to make charcoal. Before I go on I must tell why I was making charcoal. I was afraid of making smoke around my house and I could not live there without baking my bread or cooking my meat, so I burned some wood here, as I had seen done in England, under turf until it became charcoal. But I digress. While I was cutting down some wood here, I noticed behind a very thick branch of low brush there was a hollow. I was curious to look in, and getting with difficulty into the mouth of it, I found it was large – sufficient for me to stand upright in it and perhaps another person as well. I confess, I quickly left the cave, because when I looked farther into the darkness, I saw two broad shining eyes – I didn't know if was devil or man – which twinkled like two stars, the dim light from the cave's mouth shining directly in and making the reflection.

After a time, I recovered. I called myself a thousand fools and thought he who was afraid to see the devil was not fit to live twenty years on an island all alone and there was nothing in this cave scarier than myself. Plucking up my courage, I picked up a firebrand[113] and rushed in again with the stick flaming in my hand. I had not gone in three steps before I was almost as frightened as before. I heard a very loud sigh, like that of a man in some pain, and it was followed by a broken noise, like words half expressed and then a deep sigh again. I stepped back and was undeniably struck with such surprise that it put me into a cold sweat and if I had had a hat on my head, my hair would have lifted it off. Again, plucking up my spirits as well as I could, and

---

[113] Piece of burning wood.

encouraging myself by considering the power and presence of God was everywhere and was able to protect me, I stepped forward again and by the light of the firebrand, I saw lying on the ground a monstrous, frightful old he-goat, gasping for life and dying of old age. I kicked him a little to see if I could get him out and he attempted to get up, but was not able to raise himself. I thought he could lie there – if he had frightened me, he would certainly frighten any of the savages, if any of them would be so hardy as to come in there while he had any life in him.

I had now recovered from my surprise and began to look around me. The cave was very small – it was perhaps twelve feet deep, but in no manner of shape – neither round nor square, no hands having ever been employed in making it but those of Nature. I also observed there was a place at the farther side of it that went in further, but was so low that it required me to creep on my hands and knees to go into it. I didn't know where it went and having no candle, I stopped and decided to go again the next day with candles and a tinder-box,[114] which I had made from the lock of one of the muskets, with some wildfire in the pan.

The next day I came with six large candles– I made very good candles now from goat's tallow, but was hard pressed for candle-wick, sometimes using rags and sometimes the dried rind of a weed – and going into this low place I was forced to creep on all fours almost ten yards – which by the way, I thought was a venture bold enough, considering I didn't know how far it might go, nor what was beyond it. When I had got through, I found the roof rose nearly twenty feet. But never was such a glorious sight seen on the island, as it was to look round the sides and roof of this cave. The wall reflected a hundred thousand lights to me from my two candles. I didn't know what it was in the rock – whether diamonds or any other precious stones or gold –

---

[114] A tinderbox is a container made of wood or metal containing flint, steel, and tinder. It was the precursor of matches.

which I supposed it to be. The place I was in was a delightful grotto, though completely dark. The floor was dry and level and had small loose gravel on it, so there was no nauseous or venomous creature to be seen, neither was there any damp or wet on the sides or roof. The only difficulty in it was the entrance. However, as it was a place of security and such a retreat as I wanted, I rejoiced at the discovery and decided, without any delay, to bring some of the things I was most anxious about to this place. Particularly, I decided to bring my gunpowder and all my spare arms, including two shotguns and three muskets. I kept in my castle only five muskets, which stood mounted like cannons on my outermost fence and were ready to take out on any expedition. When I moved my ammunition, I happened to open the barrel of powder I took out of the sea and had been wet. I found the water had penetrated about three or four inches into the powder on every side, which caking and growing hard, had preserved the inside like a kernel in the shell, so I had nearly sixty pounds of very good powder in the center of the cask. This was a very pleasant discovery, so I carried it all there, never keeping more than a couple of pounds of gunpowder with me in my castle, for fear of a surprise of any kind. I also carried there all the lead I had left for bullets.

I imagined myself now like one of the ancient giants who were said to live in caves and holes in the rocks, where nobody could come at them. I persuaded myself, while I was here, that if five hundred savages were to hunt me, they would never find me – or if they did, they would not try to attack me here. The old goat whom I found expiring died in the mouth of the cave the next day and I found it much easier to dig a hole there, throw him in and cover him with earth than to drag him out, so I interred him there, to prevent offence to my nose.

13.

Wreck of a Spanish Ship

I was now in the twenty-third year of my residence on this island and was so naturalized to the place that, could I have enjoyed the certainty no savages would come and disturb me, I could have been content to spend the rest of my time there, until I laid down and died like the old goat in the cave. I also had some little diversions and amusements, which made the time pass more pleasantly than it did before. First, I had taught my Polly to speak. He talked so articulately and plain, that it was very enjoyable and he lived with me no less than 26 years. I don't know how long he lived afterwards, though I know they think in the Brazils they live a hundred years. My dog was a pleasant and loving companion to me for no less than sixteen years and then died of old age.

My cats multiplied, as I said, until I was forced to shoot several of them to keep them from devouring me and all I had. But when the two old ones I brought with me were gone and after continually shooing them and not feeding them, they all ran wild into the woods, except two or three favorites which I kept tame and whose young, when they had any, I always drowned. These were part of my family. Besides these I always kept two or three household kids around me, which I taught to feed out of my hand. And, I had two more parrots, which talked well and would all call 'Robin Crusoe,' though none like my first – but then, I didn't take pain with any of them as I had with him. I had also several tame seabirds, whose name I didn't know which I caught on shore and cut their wings.

The little stakes I had planted in front of my castle-wall had now grown to a good thick grove and these birds all lived among these low trees and bred there, which was very delightful. Because of all this, I was very satisfied with the life I led, if I could have been secured from the dread of the savages. But it was otherwise directed and it may not be wrong for all people who read my story to make this just observation: how frequently during our lives the evil we try the most to shun and is the most horrible is often the means of our rescue. I could give many examples of this during my unaccountable life, but in nothing was it more remarkable than during my last years of solitary residence in this island.

It was now December in my twenty-third year. It was the southern solstice – I can't call it winter – and the time of my harvest, which required me to be pretty much out in the fields. Going out early in the morning before sunrise, I was surprised by the light of a fire on the shore about two miles away, but not towards that part of the island where savages had been. It was on my side of the island.

I was terribly surprised at the sight and stopped in my grove, not daring to go out in case I might be surprised. Now I had no more inner peace. I feared the savages, while rambling over the island, would find my grain or any of my work, and immediately conclude there were people here and would never rest until they had found me. I went back to my castle, pulled up the ladder and made all things outside look as wild and natural as I could.

Then I prepared myself inside, putting myself on the defense. I loaded all my cannon – as I called my muskets – and all my pistols and decided to defend myself to the last gasp, not forgetting to commend myself to Divine protection and sincerely pray to God to deliver me out of the hands of the barbarians. I continued like this for about two hours and began to be impatient for intelligence abroad, as I had no spies to send out. After sitting a while longer and thinking what I would do, I was not able to bear sitting in ignorance any longer. Setting up my ladder to the side of the hill where there was a flat place, I mounted the top of the hill. Pulling out my telescope, I laid down flat on my belly and began to look for the place. I found there were no less than nine naked savages sitting around a small fire they had made, not to warm them – they had no need in the heat – but I assumed to cook some of their barbarous diet of human flesh which they had brought with them, whether alive or dead I could not tell.

They had two canoes with them, which they had hauled up on the shore and as it was low tide, they seemed to wait for the return of the tide to go away again. It is not easy to imagine the confusion I felt, especially seeing them come on my side of the island and so close to me. When I considered their coming must always be with the current, I began afterwards to be calmer, satisfied I might go out safely when the tide came in if they were not on shore already. Having made this observation, I went about my harvest work with more composure.

As I expected, as soon as the tide came back I saw them all take the boat and row away. For an hour or more before they left they were dancing and I could easily distinguish their gestures with my telescope. I could see they were stark naked, but whether they were men or women I could not tell.

As soon as I saw them leave, I took two guns on my shoulders, two pistols in my belt and my large sword by my side, and as fast as I could go to the hill where I had discovered it all. As soon as I was there – two hours later – I saw there had been three more of the savages' canoes there and looking out farther, I saw they were all together at sea, heading for the mainland. Going down to the shore I could see the marks of horror which their dismal work had left behind – the blood, the bones and part of the human flesh eaten by those wretches with merriment and sport. I was so filled with anger at the sight, I now began to premeditate the destruction of the next I saw there, whoever they were. The visits they made to this island were not very frequent, as it was more than fifteen months before any more of them came on shore again. I neither saw them nor any footsteps or signals in all that time and in the rainy seasons, they are sure not to come abroad, at least not so far.   All this time I lived uncomfortably from the constant fear of their finding me by surprise. The expectation of evil is more bitter than the suffering, especially if there is no room to shake off that expectation or those fears.

During all this time, I was in a murdering state of mind and spent most of my hours, which would have been better employed, deciding how to circumvent and attack them the next time I saw them. I didn't consider at all that if I killed one party – maybe ten or so –the next day or week or month I still had to kill another and another, AD INFINITUM,[115] until I would be no less a murderer than they were in being man-eaters, and perhaps much more so. I spent my days puzzled and anxious, expecting I would one day or other fall into the hands of these merciless creatures and if I did at any time venture abroad, it was not without looking around me with the greatest care and caution imaginable. And now I found how happy it was I had a tame flock of goats, as I dared not fire my gun on any account, especially near that side of the island where they usually came. If they had fled from me now, they would surely come again with maybe three hundred canoes in a few days, and then I knew what to expect. I wore out a year and three months before I ever saw any more of the savages. They might have been there once or twice but either they didn't stay, or I did not see them. In May, as near as I could calculate and in my 24th year, I had a very strange encounter with them.

The fear during this fifteen months' interval was very great. I slept restlessly, dreamed horrible dreams and often woke out of my sleep in

---

[115] Forever

the night. In the day, great troubles overwhelmed my mind and in the night, I often dreamed of killing the savages and of the reasons why I might justify doing it.

But let's ignore all this for a while. It was the middle of May on the sixteenth I think, as well as my poor wooden calendar would estimate. There was a strong windstorm all day, with a great deal of lightning and thunder and a very foul night after. I didn't know the cause of it, but as I was reading the Bible and had very serious thoughts about my present condition, I was surprised with what I thought was the noise of a gun fired at sea. This was a surprise of quite a different nature from any I had before and the notions this put into my head were of another kind. I quickly got up my ladder and got to the top of the hill when a flash of fire made me listen for a second gun which, in about half a minute, I heard. By the sound, I knew it was from that part of the sea where I was driven down current in my boat. I immediately considered this must be a ship in distress and that they had fired these as signals of distress to some other ship. I had the presence of mind to think, though I could not help them, they might help me. I brought together all the dry wood I could get and making a large pile, I set it on fire on the hill. The wood was dry and blazed freely and though the wind blew very hard, it burned well, so I was certain if there was any such thing as a ship, they must see it. And no doubt they did. As soon as my fire blazed up, I heard another gun and after that several others, all from the same direction. I plied my fire all night long until daybreak and when it was broad daylight and the air cleared up, I saw something at a great distance at sea, east of the island. Whether it was a sail or a hull I could not distinguish, not even with my telescope. It was too far away and the weather was still somewhat hazy out at sea.

I looked frequently all that day and soon realized it did not move. I concluded it was a ship at anchor and eager to be satisfied, I took my gun and ran towards the south side of the island to the rocks where I had been carried away by the current. Getting up there, the weather by this time being perfectly clear, I could plainly see the wreck of a ship, cast away in the night on those concealed rocks which I found when I was out in my boat. These rocks, as they slowed the violence of the stream and made a kind of counter-stream, were the reason I was saved from the most desperate, hopeless condition I had ever been in all my life. What is one man's safety, however, is another man's destruction. The rocks being completely under water, the crew did not see them and they were driven on them in the night. Had they seen the island, as I must suppose they did not, they would have tried to save themselves by taking their boat. But firing off guns for help, especially when they saw my fire, filled me with many thoughts. I imagined when they saw my fire they might have put themselves into their boat and tried to make the shore, but the sea was very high and they might have been driven away. Other times I imagined they might have lost their boat already, the sea smashing it against the ship. Other times I imagined they had some other ship saw their distress signal and had rescued them. Other times I imagined they were in their longboat, and taken by the current as I was, were carried out into the ocean, where there was nothing but misery and death and by this time might be starving and ready to eat one another.

As all these were conjectures at best so in the condition I was in, I could do no more than look at the misery of the poor men and pity them, which had still this good effect – it gave me more and more cause to give thanks to God, who had so happily provided for my comfort in this desolate place, and of two ships' crews lost at sea, not one life was spared but mine. I learned here again that it is very rare God's wisdom casts us into any misery so great unless we can see something to be thankful for and see others in worse circumstances than our own. Such certainly was the case of these men, none of whom I thought would be saved. Rationally, I had to expect they all died, unless they were rescued in the night by another ship. This was a slim possibility indeed, as I saw no sign of any such thing. I cannot explain what a strange longing I felt in my soul at this sight. "If only there was maybe one or two saved out of this ship, to have escaped to me so I might have had just one companion, one fellow-creature, to have spoken to me and to have conversed with!" I thought. In all the time of my solitary life I never felt so serious, so strong a desire for the companionship of my fellow-creatures, or so deep a regret at the want of it.

There are some impulses which, when they are unleashed by an object, carries the soul to such violent, eager embrace, that the absence of it is insupportable. Such were these solemn wishes that only one man had been saved. I believe I repeated the words, "Oh, if only one!" a thousand times and my desires were so moved by it, when I spoke the words my hands would clench together, so if I had had any soft thing in my hand I would have crushed it involuntarily. My teeth clenched so hard, for some time I could not part them again. Let the naturalists[116] explain these things and the reason for them. All I can do is to describe the fact, which was surprising even to me, though I didn't know where it came from. Doubtless, it was the effect of passionate wishes and strong ideas, realizing the comfort the conversation of one of my fellow-Christians would have been to me. But it was not to be. Either their fate or mine, or both, prevented it. Until my last year on this island, I never knew whether any were saved out of that ship and had only the agony, some days after, of seeing the corpse of a drowned boy come on shore near the shipwreck. He had no clothes on but a seaman's waistcoat, a pair of open-kneed linen drawers and a blue linen shirt, but nothing to tell me so much what nation he was from. He had nothing in his pockets

---

[116] Someone who believes only natural (as opposed to supernatural or spiritual) laws and forces operate in the world.

but two pieces of eight and a tobacco pipe, which was ten times more valuable than the coins.

It was now calm and I wanted to venture out in my boat to this wreck, not doubting I might find something on board that might be useful to me. But that did not press me so much as the possibility there might be some living creature on board, whose life I might not only save but might – by saving that life – comfort my own to the last degree. This thought clung to my heart so much I could not settle night or day and I must venture out in my boat to board this wreck. Committing the rest to God's wisdom, the impression was so strong that it could not be resisted – it must come from some invisible direction and I would be letting myself suffer further if I did not go.

Under the power of this impression, I hurried back to my castle and prepared everything for my voyage. I took some bread, a large pot of fresh water, a compass, a bottle of rum (I still had a lot of that left) and a basket of raisins. Loading myself with everything required. I went down to my boat, got the water out of her, got her afloat, loaded all my cargo in her and then went home again for more. My second cargo was a large bag of rice, the umbrella for shade, another large pot of water and about two dozen small loaves of barley cakes, with a bottle of goat's milk and some cheese, which I carried with a lot of work and sweat to my boat. Praying to God to direct my voyage, I put out. Rowing the canoe along the shore, I came at last to the extreme point of the island on the northeast side. And now I was to launch out into the ocean and either to venture or not venture. I looked on the rapid currents which ran constantly on both sides of the island and which were very terrifying to me, remembering the danger and my heart began to fail me. I expected if I was driven into either of those currents, I would be carried out to sea and perhaps out of my reach of the island again and, as my boat was small, if any little wind would rise, I would be inevitably lost.

These thoughts burdened my mind so much I began to give up on my enterprise. Having hauled my boat into a little creek on the shore, I stepped out and sat down, very thoughtful and anxious, between fear and desire, about my voyage. As I was musing, I could see the tide had turned and was coming in, so now it was unrealistic for many hours. It then occurred to me I could go up to the highest piece of ground that I could find and observe how the tide lay when it came in, so I could judge which way I would be taken. I found a little hill which overlooked the sea both ways and from where I had a clear view of the currents and which way I was to guide myself in my return. The current went out close by the south point of the island, so the current would also be close to the north shore and that I only had to keep to the north side of the island in my return, and I would do well enough.

Encouraged by this, I decided the next morning to set out with the first tide. Resting for the night in my canoe under my watch-coat, I launched out early. I headed north, a little out to sea until I began to feel the benefit of the current. The current went east and carried me quickly. It did not hurry me as the current on the south side had, which took away my ability to steer the boat. Having a strong steerage with my paddle, I went quickly for the wreck and in less than two hours I came up to it. It was a dismal sight. The ship, which by its building was Spanish, was jammed in between two rocks. Her stern was beaten to pieces by the sea. Her forecastle was stuck in the rocks and had run on with great violence. Her mainmast and foremast were broken off. But, her bowsprit[117] was sound and the head and bow appeared firm. When I came close to her, a dog appeared on her, who seeing me coming, yelped and cried. As soon as I called him, he jumped into the sea to came to me. I took him into the boat, but found him almost dead with hunger and thirst. I gave him a cake of my bread and he devoured it like

---

[117] A large mast projecting forward from the bow (or front) of a ship.

a ravenous wolf that had been starving a fortnight in the snow. I then gave the poor creature some fresh water with which, if I would have let him, he would have burst himself. After this I went on board but the first sight I had was two men drowned in the forecastle with their arms tightly around one another. I concluded that when the ship struck, the sea broke so high and so continually over her, that the men were not able to bear it and were strangled with the constant rushing in of the water, as much as if they had been under water. Besides the dog, there was nothing left in the ship that had life, or any goods, that I could see, except what were spoiled by the water. There were some casks of liquor, but I didn't know whether they were wine or brandy. They lay lower in the hold, and which, the water draining out, I could see. However, they were too big to meddle with. I saw several chests, which I believe belonged to some of the seamen and I got two of them into the boat without examining what was in them. Had the stern of the ship been stuck and the forepart broken off, I might have made another voyage. What I found in those two chests made me suppose the ship had a great deal of wealth on board. By the course she steered, she must have been bound from Buenos Aires in the south part of America towards Havana in the Gulf of Mexico and so perhaps to Spain. She had, no doubt, a great treasure in her but of no use at that time to anybody and I didn't know what became of the crew.

Besides these chests, I found about a twenty-gallon cask full of liquor, which I got into my boat with much difficulty. There were several muskets in the cabin and a large powder-horn, with about four pounds of gunpowder in it. As for the muskets, I had no need for them, so I left them but took the powder-horn. I took a fire-shovel and tongs, which I desperately wanted as well as two little brass kettles, a copper pot to make chocolate, and a gridiron.[118] With this cargo and the dog, I

---

[118] A frame of parallel metal bars used for grilling meat or fish over an open fire.

left, the tide beginning to come in again. About an hour after dark, I reached the island again, weary and fatigued. I rested that night in the boat and in the morning, I decided to store what I had in my new cave and not carry it home to my castle. After refreshing myself, I got all my cargo on shore, and began to examine my find. The cask of liquor was a kind of rum, but not like we had at the Brazils. It was not at all good. When I opened the chests, I found several things of great use to me. In one there was a fine case of extraordinary bottles, filled with fine and very good liqueurs. The bottles held about three pints each and were tipped with silver. I found two pots of very good succades or sweetmeats, [119] well fastened on the top so the salt-water had not hurt them and two more which the water had spoiled. I found some very good shirts, which were very welcome to me and about twenty white linen handkerchiefs and colored neckcloths. The handkerchiefs were also very welcome, being exceedingly refreshing to wipe my face in a hot day.

When I came to the next chest, I found there three large bags of pieces of eight, which held about eleven hundred pieces in all. In one of them, wrapped up in a paper, were six gold doubloons and some small bars of gold; I suppose they might all weigh nearly a pound.[120] In the other chest were some clothes, but of little value. By the circumstances, it must have belonged to the gunner's mate, though there was no gunpowder in it except for two pounds of fine glazed powder kept, I suppose, for charging their shotguns. Overall, I got very little this voyage that was of any use to me. As to the money, I had no use for it. It was to me like the dirt under my feet and I would have given it all for three or four pair of English shoes and stockings, things I greatly wanted but had none on my feet for many years. I did get two pair of

---

[119] Preserved or crystallized fruit.
[120] About £115,000 in total (converted into 2017 worth).

shoes, which I took off the feet of the two drowned men in the wreck and I found two more pairs in one of the chests, which were very welcome to me. They were not like our English shoes though, either for ease or service, being what we call pumps rather than shoes. I found in this seaman's chest about fifty pieces of eight, but no gold. I supposed this belonged to a poorer man than the other, which seemed to belong to some officer. I lugged this money home to my cave and stored it, as I had done before from our own ship. It was a great pity that the other part of this ship was not accessible, since I could have loaded my canoe several times over with money and if I ever escaped to England, it would lie here safe enough until I returned for it.

14.

A Dream Realized

Having brought all my things on shore now and secured them, I went back to my boat and rowed her along the shore to her old harbor, where I laid her up and made my way to my old home, finding everything safe and quiet. I began now to rest, live like I had and take care of my family affairs. For a while I lived easy enough, only I was more vigilant than I used to be, looked out more often and did not go out so much. If at any time I did move with any freedom, it was always to the east part of the island, where I was satisfied the savages never came and where I could go without so many precautions, such as the weapons I carried with me if I went the other way. I lived like this nearly two more years but my unlucky head, that always let me know it was born to make my body miserable, was all this time filled with ideas for me to get away from this island. Sometimes I thought about making another voyage to the wreck, though reason told me there was nothing left there worth the danger. I truly believe if I had the boat that I escaped from Salé in, I would have ventured to sea, bound anywhere. I have been, in all my circumstances, a memento to those who are touched with the plague of mankind where half of their miseries flow – I mean not being satisfied with the station God and Nature has placed them. Looking back on my primitive condition and the excellent advice of my father – not listening to it was my ORIGINAL SIN – my subsequent mistakes were the reasons for my current, miserable condition. Providence had very happily seated me at the Brazils as a planter, and if only it had blessed me with limited desires, I could have been happy and I might have been by this time one of richest planters in the Brazils. The improvements I had made in the little time I lived there and the increase I probably would have made if I had remained, I might have been worth a hundred thousand moidores.[121] What business had I to leave a settled fortune and a well-stocked plantation, to become a supercargo to Guinea to fetch negroes, when patience and time would have increased my wealth and I could have bought them at my own door from those whose business it was to fetch them? Though it would have cost more, the price difference was not worth the risk. This is usually the fate of young heads and consideration of the foolishness comes with age, or the dearly bought experience of time. It was this way with me now and the mistake was so deep-rooted in my mind, I could not satisfy myself staying in my place. I was continually poring over my escape from this place. Let me tell you some of my first concepts of this foolish scheme for my escape, and how, and on what foundation, I acted.

I now retired to my castle after my last voyage to the wreck, my frigate laid up and secured under water as usual, and my condition restored to what it was before. I had more wealth than I had before, but was not at all richer. I had no more use for it than the Indians of Peru had before the Spaniards came there.

It was one of the nights in the rainy season in March, the 24th year of my first setting foot on this island of solitude. I was lying in my hammock awake, healthy, no pain, no problems of the mind, no uneasiness of body, but I could by no means close my eyes to sleep. No, not a wink all night long. It is impossible to tell the countless crowd of thoughts that whirled through that great thoroughfare of the brain on this night. I ran over the whole history of my life in miniature until my coming to this island, then everything after that. In my deliberations on my case since I came on shore, I was comparing my happiness during

---

[121] Current value of this, based on what a moidore would buy in England at the time, would be £11,800,000.

my first years here with the anxiety, fear and care which I had lived in ever since I had seen the footprint in the sand. Not that I did not believe the savages had frequented the island all along and at times might have been several hundred of them on shore. But I had never known it, so I did not fear it. I had been completely satisfied – though my danger was the same – and I was as happy in not knowing my danger as if I had never been exposed to it. Then I realized, how infinitely good Providence is, which while governing mankind, has made such narrow boundaries to his sight and knowledge of things. Though he walks amid so many thousand dangers, the sight of which would distract his mind and sink his spirits, he is kept serene and calm by having the events hidden from sight and knowing nothing of the dangers which surround him.

After these thoughts had entertained me for some time, I contemplated the real danger I had been in for so many years and how I had walked around in the greatest security and tranquility, even when nothing except a hill, a large tree or the casual approach of night had been between me and falling into the hands of cannibals, who would have the same view of me as I would of a goat or turtle and have thought it no more crime to kill and devour me than I did of a pigeon or a sandpiper. I would unjustly slander myself if I said I was not sincerely thankful to my great Preserver, whose singular protection I acknowledged with great humanity, and all these unknown rescues were owed and without who I would inevitably have fallen into their merciless hands.

When these thoughts were over, I considered the nature of these wretched creatures – I mean the savages – and how in the world the wise Governor of all things would give up any of His creatures to such inhumanity – to something so much below brutality itself – to devour its own kind. But as this ended in fruitless speculations, it occurred to me to inquire what part of the world these wretches lived in? How far off the coast did they come? Why they ventured so far from home? What kind of boats they had? Why shouldn't I go over there, much as they came to me?

I never troubled myself to consider what I would do when I went there. What would become of me if I fell into the hands of these savages or how I would escape them if they attacked me? How could I reach the coast and not to be attacked by them? And if I didn't fall into their hands, what I would do for food or where I would turn my course? None of these thoughts came my way. My mind was wholly bent on going in my boat to the mainland. I looked on my present condition as the most miserable that could possibly be, that I was not able to throw myself into anything but death. If I reached the mainland I might meet with relief or I might coast along, as I did on the African shore, until I came to some inhabited country where I might find some relief. After all, I might fall in with some Christian ship that might take me in and if worst came to worst, I could die, which would put an end to all these miseries at once. All this was the fruit of a disturbed mind, an impatient state of mind, made desperate by the long continuation of my troubles and the disappointments I had met in the wreck where I had been so near obtaining what I so sincerely longed for – somebody to speak to and find out where I was and how I could escape. I was completely agitated by these thoughts. All my calm, resigned to Providence and waiting for the outlook of Heaven, seemed to be suspended. I had no power to turn my thoughts to anything but to a voyage to the mainland, which came on me with such force and recklessness, that it was not to be resisted.

This agitated my thoughts for two hours or more, with such violence that it set my blood on fire and my pulse beat as if I had a fever. Nature, as if I had been exhausted with the thought of it, threw me into a sound sleep. You would think I would have dreamed of it, but I did not, nor anything relating to it. I dreamed I went out in the morning – as usual – from my castle. I saw two canoes and eleven savages coming to land

and they brought with them another savage who they were going to eat. Suddenly, the savage they were going to kill jumped away and ran for his life. In my sleep, he came running into my little thick grove by my fortification to hide. Seeing him alone and not seeing the others hunted him that way, I showed myself to him and smiling, encouraged him. He kneeled to me, praying to me to assist him. I showed him my ladder, made him go up and took him into my cave and he became my servant. As soon as I had got this man, I said to myself, "Now I can venture to the mainland and this fellow will serve me as a pilot and will tell me what to do and where to go for provisions and where not to go for fear of being devoured and what places to venture into and what to shun." I awoke with this thought and was so overwhelmingly happy at the prospect of my escape in my dream, the disappointment I felt finding it was no more than a dream was equally overwhelming and I was extremely dejected.

I did realize this, though: my only way to attempt an escape was to try to get a savage and, if possible, it would be one of their prisoners, who they had condemned to be eaten and would bring here to kill. But there was still this difficulty: it was impossible to attempt this without attacking a whole caravan of them and killing them all. This was not only very desperate and might fail but I had also seriously debated the lawfulness of it. My heart trembled at the thought of shedding so much blood, though it was for my escape. I need not repeat the arguments against this, being the same mentioned before. I had other reasons to offer now. Those men were enemies to my life and would devour me if they could. It was self-preservation to deliver myself from this death of a life, and I was acting in my own defense as much as if they were assaulting me. Though these things argued for it, the thought of shedding human blood for my rescue was terrible and I could by no means reconcile myself with it for a long time. After many disputes with myself – these arguments, one way and another, struggled in my head a long time – the prevailing desire for liberation mastered all the rest. I decided to get one of these savages, whatever the cost. My next thing was to choose how to do it and this was very difficult. I decided to watch to see when they came on shore and leave the rest to chance, taking such measures as the opportunity would present.

I scouted as often as possible, so often that I was very tired of it. It was over a year and a half that I waited and for most of that time went out to the southwest corner of the island almost every day to look for canoes, but none appeared. This was very discouraging and began to trouble me greatly, though I cannot say it wore the edge off my desire. The longer it was delayed, the more eager I was for it. I was not careful at first to avoid the sight of these savages and avoid being seen by them, as I was now eager to attack them. Besides, I imagined myself able to manage one, or maybe two or three savages if I had them, to make them slaves, to do whatever I told them and to prevent their ever being able to harm me. I pleased myself with this affair a long time but still nothing presented itself. All my dreams and schemes came to nothing because no savages came near me for what seemed like an eternity.

About a year and a half after I entertained these notions, I was surprised one morning when I saw at least five canoes on shore on my side of the island and the people who belonged to them landed and out of my sight. The number of them broke all my measures. Knowing there was always about six in a boat, I didn't know what to think of it, or how to attack thirty men single-handed. I lay still in my castle, perplexed and discomforted. However, I put myself into the same position for attack I had previously and was ready for action, if anything had presented. Having waited for some time, listening if they made any noise, and being very impatient, I set my guns at the foot of my ladder and clambered up to the top of the hill, standing so my head did not appear above the hill so they could not see me. Looking through my telescope, I saw there were no less than thirty, they had a fire kindled and they had meat ready. I didn't know how they cooked it or what it was, but they were all dancing in their barbarous gestures around the fire.

While I was looking at them, I saw two miserable wretches dragged from the boats and were now brought out for the slaughter. I saw one of them immediately fall, knocked down with a club or wooden sword. Two or three others were at work immediately, cutting him open for cooking, while the other victim was left standing by himself until they were ready for him. Seeing himself a little at liberty and unbound, Nature inspired this poor wretch with hopes of life, and he ran away from them with incredible speed along the sand directly towards that part of the coast where my home was. I was terribly frightened when I saw him run my way, especially when I saw him pursued by the whole group. Now I expected that part of my dream was happening and he would take shelter in my grove. I could not depend on my dream and that the other savages would not pursue him there and find him. However, I kept my position and my spirits began to recover when I found there was only three men chasing him. I was more encouraged when I found he outran them. If he could hold out for half-an-hour, he would easily get away from them all.

There was between them and my castle the creek where I landed my cargoes out of the ship, which I mentioned often in the first part of my story. He would have to swim over it or the poor wretch would be captured there. When the escaping savage reached the creek, he made nothing of it and plunging in, swam through in about thirty strokes, landed, and ran with exceeding strength and speed. When the three savages came to the creek, two of them could swim but the third could not. Standing on the other side, he looked at the others, but went no farther and turned back which, as it happened, was a good choice. The two who swam were more than twice as strong swimmers as the fellow who fled from them. Now was the time to get a servant and, perhaps, a companion or assistant. I was plainly called by Providence to save this poor creature's life. I immediately ran down the ladder with all possible speed, grabbed my two guns and getting up the hill with the same speed, I crossed towards the sea. Having a very shortcut – all downhill – I placed myself between the pursuers and the pursued, hollering to the pursued who, looking back, was as much frightened of me as of them. I beckoned to him to come back and slowly advanced towards the two who followed.

Rushing on the leading savage, I knocked him down with the handle of my gun. I was unwilling to fire, because I did not want the rest to hear though at that distance it would not have been easily heard and being out of sight of the smoke, they would not have known what to make of it. Having knocked this fellow down, the other who pursued him stopped as if he had been frightened and I advanced towards him. As I came closer, I saw he had a bow and arrow and was fitting it to shoot at him. I was forced to shoot first and killed him at the first shot. The poor savage who was pursued thought he had seen both his enemies killed and was so frightened with the fire and noise of my gun that he stood still. He came neither forward nor went backward, though he still seemed inclined to flee. I shouted again to him and made signs to come forward, which he easily understood and came a little way. He stopped again, then came a little farther, then stopped again and I could see he was trembling, as if he had been taken prisoner and would be killed, as his two enemies were. I gestured to him again to come to me and gave him all the signs of encouragement I could think of. He came nearer and nearer, kneeling every ten or twelve steps, in token of acknowledgment for saving his life. I smiled at him and looked pleasant and signaled to him to come closer still. After a while, he came close to me and then kneeled again, kissed the ground and laid his head on the ground and taking my foot, he set it on his head. This, it seems, was in token of swearing to be my slave forever. I picked him up and encouraged him as best as I could.

But there was more work to do. The savage I had knocked down was not killed, but stunned with the blow and began to come to. I pointed to my new slave and showed him the other savage was not dead. He spoke some words to me and though I could not understand them, I thought they were pleasant to hear – they were, after all, the first sound of another man's voice I had heard in over twenty-five years. But there was no time for such thoughts now. The savage who was knocked down recovered and sat up on the ground. I noticed my savage began to be afraid. When I saw that, I pointed my other gun at the man, as if I would shoot him. When he saw this my savage – or so I call him now – made a motion to me to lend him my sword. He ran to his enemy and at one blow cut off his head so cleverly, no executioner in Germany could have done it sooner or better. I thought this very strange for someone who, I had reason to believe, never saw a sword in his life, except their own wooden swords. However, as I learned afterward, they make their wooden swords so sharp, so heavy and the wood is so hard, that they will cut off heads and arms with one swing. When he had done this, he came laughing to me in triumph and brought me the sword again. With an abundance of gestures I did not understand, he laid it down in front of me with the head of the savage he had killed. What astonished him most was how I killed the other Indian from so far off. Pointing to the other savage, he made signs to me to let him go to him and I told him go, as well as I could. When he came to him he stood amazed, looking at him, turning him first on one side, then on the other. He looked at the wound the bullet had made, which was in his chest. The hole it made was small and there was not a lot of blood. He picked up his bow and arrows and came back. I turned to go away and gestured to him to follow me, making signs that more savages might come after them. He made signs he would bury them so they would not be seen by the rest if they followed. I made signs to him to do that. He went to work and in an instant, he had scraped a hole in the sand with his hands big enough to bury the first in, dragged him into it and covered him. He did the same for the other. I believe he had buried them both in a quarter of an hour. Then I took him, not to my castle, but to my cave on the farther part of the island. I did not let my dream come to pass in that way. Here I gave him bread and a bunch of raisins and a cup of water, which he needed after his running. Having refreshed him, I made signs for him to go and lie down to sleep, showing him a place where I had laid some rice-straw with a blanket on it, which I used to sleep on myself sometimes. The poor creature lay down and went to sleep.

He was a comely,[122] handsome fellow, perfectly well made, with straight, strong limbs. He was not too large, but tall and well-shaped and, best as I could discern, about twenty-six years old. He had a very good expression, not fierce and surly, but seemed to have something very manly in his face and he had all the sweetness and softness of a European in his look, especially when he smiled. His hair was long and black, not curled like wool. His forehead was very high and large and a great liveliness and sparkling sharpness in his eyes. The color of his skin was not quite black, but very tawny – not an ugly, yellow, nauseous tawny, as the Brazilians, Virginians and other natives of America are, but a bright kind of a dun[123] olive-color that had in it something very pleasant, though not very easy to describe. His face was round and plump, his nose small, not flat like the negroes; a very good mouth, thin lips and his fine teeth well set and as white as ivory.

After he had slumbered, rather than slept, about half an hour he awoke again and came out of the cave to me. I was milking my goats which I had in the enclosure just by. When he saw me, he came running

---

[122] Pleasant to look at
[123] A dull greyish-brown color

to me, laying himself down again on the ground, with all the possible signs of a humble, thankful disposition, making a great many frantic gestures to show it. At last he laid his head flat on the ground, close to my foot and set my other foot on his head, as he had done before. After this he made all the signs to me of subjugation, servitude and submission imaginable to let me know he would serve me as long as he lived. I understood him in many things and let him know I was very pleased with him. In a little time, I began to speak to him and teach him to speak to me. First, I let him know his name would be Friday, which was the day I saved his life. I also taught him to say Master and then let him know that was to be my name. I also taught him to say Yes and No and to know the meaning of them. I gave him some milk in an earthenware pot and let him see me drink it and dip my bread in it, then gave him a cake of bread to do the same, which he quickly complied with and made signs that it was very good. I stayed there with him all that night but as soon as it was day, I signaled to him to come with me and let him know I would give him some clothes. He seemed very glad, as he was stark naked. As we went by the place where he had buried the two men, he pointed to the place and showed me the marks he had made to find them again, making signs to me that we would dig them up again and eat them. At this I was very angry, expressed my disgust, made as if I would vomit at the thought of it and gestured to him to come away, which he did immediately with humility. I led him to the top of the hill to see if his enemies were gone. Pulling out my telescope I looked and plainly saw the place they had been, but not them or their canoes. They were gone and had left their two comrades behind, without any search for them.

But I was not content with this discovery. Now having more courage and consequently more curiosity, I took my man Friday with me. I gave him the sword and with the bow and arrows on his back, made him carry one gun for me and I carried two for myself. Away we marched to where these creatures had been, since I wanted to gather some further intelligence. When I came to the place my blood ran cold and my heart sunk at the horror of the spectacle. It was a dreadful sight to me, though Friday made nothing of it. The place was covered with human bones, the ground dyed with their blood and large pieces of flesh left here and there, half-eaten, mangled, and scorched – all the tokens of the triumphant feast after a victory over their enemies. I saw three skulls, five hands, the bones of three or four legs and feet and an abundance of other body parts. Friday, by his signs, made me understand they brought over four prisoners to feast on – three of them were eaten and he, pointing to himself, was the fourth. He gestured there had been a great battle between them and his king and they had taken many prisoners. The victors had taken their prisoners to several places to feast on them, as was done here by these wretches.

I had Friday gather all the skulls, bones, flesh and whatever remained, and lay them together in a heap. On this he made a large roaring fire and burnt them all to ashes. I found Friday had still a hankering for some of the flesh and was still a cannibal by nature. I showed so much disgust at the thought of it and at the slightest appearance of it, that he dared not try it and I let him know I would kill him if he tried. When the remains were burned, we came back to our castle and there I went to work for my man Friday. First, I gave him a pair of linen drawers, from the poor gunner's chest I mentioned and which, with a little alteration, fit him very well. Then I made him a jerkin[124] of goatskin, as well as my skill would allow – though I was now a tolerably good tailor. I gave him a cap which I made of a rabbit skin and was fashionable enough. Now he was acceptably clothed and was very pleased to see himself almost as well clothed as his master. It is true he went awkwardly in these clothes at first. Wearing pants was very

---

[124] A sleeveless jacket.

strange to him and the sleeves of the waistcoat chafed his shoulders and the inside of his arms but I let them out a little where he complained they hurt him and getting used to them, he took to them very well.

The next day, after I came home with him, I began to consider where I would lodge him. To put myself at ease, I made a little tent for him in the vacant place between my two fences. As there was a door there into my cave, I made a formal frame and a door to it from boards, and set it up in the passage a little inside the entrance. Allowing the door to open on the inside, I barred it up in the night, taking in my ladders, so Friday could no way come at me inside my innermost wall, without making so much noise that it would wake me up. My first wall now had a complete roof over it of long poles, covering my tent and leaning up to the side of the hill, which was laid across with smaller sticks and then thatched over thickly with the rice-straw. At the hole to go in or out by the ladder I had placed a kind of trap-door which, if it had been attempted on the outside, would not have opened at all, but would have fallen and made a loud noise. As to weapons, I took them all in every night. But I needed none of this precaution. Never had a man a more faithful, loving, sincere servant than Friday, without passions, sullenness or plans, completely thankful and engaged. His affections were tied to me, like those of a child to a father and he would have sacrificed his life to save mine on any occasion. The many proofs he gave me put it out of doubt and soon convinced me I needed no precautions for my safety on his account.

This frequently made me observe with wonder how God had bestowed on his creatures the same reason, affections, sentiments of kindness and obligation, passions and resentments of wrongs, sense of gratitude, sincerity, fidelity, and all the capacities of giving and receiving good He has given to us. And when it pleases Him to offer the occasion of exerting these, sometimes they are better at applying them to the right uses than we are. This made me very sad sometimes, when the occasion presented and I thought how terrible we can be, even though we are enlightened by the great lamp of instruction, the Spirit of God and by the knowledge of His word. And why has it pleased God to hide this knowledge from so many millions of souls who, if I might judge by this poor savage, would make much better use of it than we did? But who was I to question Providence, that would hide the sight from some and reveal it to others, and expect the same result from both. I stopped my thoughts with this conclusion: we did not know by what light and law these men were condemned, but since God was infinitely holy and just, these creatures were all sentenced because sinning against that light which, as the Scripture says, was law to themselves. Such rules their consciences acknowledge to be right, though the foundation was not known to us. As we all are the clay in the hand of the potter, no pot could say to Him, "Why have you made me this way?"

But back to my new companion. I was very delighted with him and made it my business to teach him everything to make him useful, handy and helpful, but especially to make him speak and understand me when I spoke. He was the most apt scholar ever and was so happy, so constantly diligent and so pleased when he could understand me or make me understand him, that it was very pleasant for me to talk to him. Now my life began to be so easy that I began to say to myself: If I could have been safe from more savages, I didn't care if I ever left the island.

15.

Friday's Education

After a few days, to bring Friday off his horrid enjoyment of a cannibal's stomach, I should let him taste other meat. So, I took him out with me one morning to the woods. I went intending to kill a kid out of my own flock and bring it home and prepare it. But as I was going I saw a she-goat lying down in the shade with two young kids sitting by her. I stopped Friday. "Hold," I said, "stand still." I made signs to him not to move. I shot my gun and killed one of the kids. The poor creature, who at a distance had seen me kill his savage enemy, but did not know nor could imagine how it was done, was surprised, trembled and shook, and looked so amazed I thought he would have collapsed. He did not see the kid I shot at or saw I had killed it, but ripped up his waistcoat to feel if he was wounded. He thought I decided to kill him and he came and kneeled to me and embracing my knees, said a lot of things I did not understand but I could easily see the meaning was to not kill him.

I soon found a way to convince him I would do him no harm. Pulling him up by the hand, I laughed at him and pointing to the kid I had killed, and gestured to him to run and fetch it, which he did. While he was wondering and looking to see how the creature was killed, I loaded my gun again. Soon I saw a large bird, like a hawk, sitting on a tree within shot. So, to let Friday understand what I would do, I called him to me again, pointed at the bird – which I discerned was actually a parrot – then pointed to my gun and to the ground under the parrot, to let him see I would make it fall. I made him understand I would shoot and kill that bird. I fired and told him to look and immediately he saw the parrot fall. He stood frightened again, despite all I had said to him, and I found he was more amazed, because he did not see me put anything into the gun, but thought there must be some wonderful fund of death and destruction in that thing, able to kill man, beast, bird or anything near or far off. This astonishment would not wear off for a long time and I believe, if I would have let him, he would have worshipped me and my gun. As for the gun itself, he would not touch it for several days after. He would speak to it when he was by himself which, as I later learned, was to ask it not to kill him. After his astonishment had subsided, I pointed to him to run and fetch the bird I had shot, which he did, but stayed some time. The parrot wasn't dead and had fluttered away a good distance from the place where she fell. However, he found her, took her up, and brought her to me. Since I noticed his ignorance about the gun before, I took this advantage to load the gun again and not to let him see me do it, so I might be ready for any other mark that might present. But, nothing more offered at that time. I brought home the kid and the same evening I took the skin off and cut it out as well as I could. Having a pot fit for that purpose, I stewed some of the meat and made some very good broth. After I had begun to eat, I gave some to my man, who seemed very glad and liked it. One thing he found incredibly strange was to see me eat salt with it. He made a sign to me that salt was not good to eat. Putting a little into his own mouth, he made out like it nauseated him and would spit and sputter and wash his mouth with fresh water. On the other hand, I took some meat in my mouth without salt and I pretended to spit and sputter without the salt as much as he had done with. But it would not do. He would never care for salt with meat or in his broth – at least not for a long time and then only a very little.

Having fed him with boiled meat and broth, I was decided to feast him the next day by roasting a piece of the kid. This I did by hanging it over the fire on a string – as I had seen many people do in England – by setting two poles up, one on each side of the fire and one across the top and tying the string to the cross stick, letting the meat turn continually. This Friday admired very much and when he came to taste the meat, he took so many ways to tell me how much he liked it that I could not understand him. At last he told me, as well as he could, he would never eat man's flesh anymore, which I was very glad to hear.

The next day I put him to work beating some corn out and sifting it the way I used to do. He soon understood how to do it as well as I, especially after he had seen it was to make bread. After that I let him see me make my bread and bake it too and in a little time Friday could do all the work for me as well as I could do it myself.

I now began to consider, having two mouths to feed instead of one, I must provide more ground for my harvest and plant more grain than I used to do. I marked out a larger piece of land and began the fence in the same manner as before. Friday helped, and worked not only very hard, but also very cheerfully. I told him why I needed more harvest land and he appeared to understand. He also let me know he thought I had much more work on his account now than I had for just myself and he would work harder for me if I would tell him what to do.

This was the most pleasant year of all the life I led in this place. Friday began to talk well and understand the names of almost everything I asked for, and of every place I had to send him and talked a great deal to me. I now began to have some use for my tongue again which I had very little occasion for before. Besides the pleasure of talking to him, I had a singular satisfaction in the fellow himself. His simple, genuine honesty appeared to me more and more every day and I began really to love the creature and I believe he loved me more than was possible for him ever to love anything before.

I wondered if he had any desire to go back to his own country. Having taught him English so well that he could answer almost any question, I asked him whether the nation he belonged to never conquered in battle? At which he smiled, and said "Yes, yes, we always fight the better" – he meant always fight better than his opponents, and so we began the following conversation:

MASTER. You always fight the better. How were you taken prisoner then, Friday?

FRIDAY. My nation beat much for all that.

MASTER. How beat? If your nation beat them, how were you taken?

FRIDAY. They many more than my nation, in the place where me was. They take one, two, three and me. My nation over-beat them in the yonder place, where me no was. There my nation take one, two, great thousand.

MASTER. But why did your side not recover you from the hands of your enemies, then?

FRIDAY. They run one, two, three and me and make go in the canoe. My nation have no canoe that time.

MASTER. Well, Friday, what does your nation do with the men they take? Do they take them away and eat them, as these did?

FRIDAY. Yes, my nation eat mans too. Eat all up.

MASTER. Where do they take them?

FRIDAY. Go to other place, where they think.

MASTER. Do they come here?

FRIDAY. Yes, yes, they come here. Come other else place.

MASTER. Have you been here with them?

FRIDAY. Yes, I have been here (points to the northwest side of the island, which seems was their side).

So my man Friday had formerly been among the savages who used to come on shore on the farther part of the island, on the same man-eating occasions he was now brought for. After, when I had the courage to take him to that side, he knew the place and told me he was there once, when they ate twenty men, two women and one child. He could not say twenty in English, but he numbered them by laying stones in a row.

I have told this passage, because it introduces what follows. After this conversation with him, I asked him how far it was from our island to the shore and whether the canoes were often lost at sea. He told me there was no danger, no canoes were ever lost, but a little way out to sea, there was a current and wind, always one way in the morning, the other in the afternoon. This I understood to be no more than the tide, but afterwards understood it was caused by the great flow of the mighty river Orinoco, as I found afterwards our island lay in the mouth of and the land was the great island Trinidad on the north point of the mouth of the river. I asked Friday a thousand questions about the country, the inhabitants, the sea, the coast and what nations were near. He told me all he knew with the greatest openness imaginable. I asked him the names of the nations of his type of people, but could get no other name than Caribs, which I easily understood that these were the Caribbees,[125] which our maps place on the part of America reaching from the mouth of the river Orinoco to Guyana and onwards to St. Martha. He told me up a long way beyond the moon – which must be west from their country – there lived white bearded men, like me and pointed to my long whiskers. He then said they had killed many men, which I understood he meant the Spaniards, whose cruelties in America had been spread over the whole country and were remembered by all the nations from father to son.

I inquired if he could tell me how I might go from this island and get to those white men. He told me, "Yes, yes, you may go in two canoe." I did not understand what he meant by two canoe until at last, with great difficulty, I found he meant it must be in a large boat, as big as two

---

[125] Now known as the Caribbean islands of the U.S. Virgin Islands, St. Kitts and Nevis, Montserrat, Dominica, Martinique, St. Lucia, St. Vincent and Grenada.

canoes. This part of Friday's conversation I began to enjoy and from this time I entertained some hopes that I might find an opportunity to escape from this place and this poor savage might be a means to help me.

During the long time Friday had been with me, speaking to me and understanding me, I did not want to lay a foundation of religious knowledge in his mind. I asked him one time who had made him. The creature did not understand me at all, but thought I had asked who his father was. I tried a different way, and asked him who made the sea, the ground we walked on, the hills and woods. He told me, "It was one Benamuckee, that lived beyond all." He could describe nothing of this great person, but that he was very old, "much older," he said, "than the sea or land, than the moon or the stars." I asked him then, if this old person had made all things, why did not all things worship him? He looked very serious and with a perfect look of innocence said, "All things say O to him." I asked him if the people who die in his country went away anywhere? He said, "Yes, they all went to Benamuckee." Then I asked him whether those they eat went there too. He said, "Yes."

From this, I began to instruct him in the knowledge of the true God. I told him the great Maker of all things lived up there, pointing up towards heaven. He governed the world by the same power and providence by which He made it. He was omnipotent, could do everything for us, give everything to us, take everything from us and slowly, I opened his eyes. He listened with great attention and received with pleasure the notion of Jesus Christ being sent to redeem us, of how to pray to God and His being able to hear us, even in heaven. He told me one day, that if our God could hear us, up beyond the sun, he must be a greater God than their Benamuckee, who lived only a little way off and could not hear until they went up to the great mountains where he lived. I asked him if he ever went there to speak to him. He said, "No, they never went who were young men; none went there but the old men," whom he called their Oowokakee. They were, as I made him explain to me, their clergy and they went to say O (so he called saying prayers) and then came back and told them what Benamuckee said. I realized there is priestcraft even among the most blinded, ignorant pagans in the world and the policy of making a secret of religion, to preserve the veneration of the clergy, found not only in the Roman but perhaps among all religions in the world, even among the most brutish and barbarous savages.[126]

I attempted to clear up this fraud with my man Friday and told him that their old men going up to the mountains to say O to their god Benamuckee was a cheat and their bringing his word from there was even more of one. If they met with any answer or spoke with anyone there, it must be with an evil spirit. Then I gave a long sermon about the devil, his origin, his rebellion against God, his hatred of man and the reason for it, the many tricks he uses to deceive mankind to their ruin, how he tries to have us worship his darkness instead of God and how he had secret access to our passions and how he adapted his snares to our desires to make us be our own tempters and cause our destruction by our own choice.

It was not so easy to imprint right notions in his mind about the devil as it was about the existence of God. Nature assisted all my arguments of an overruling, governing Power, a secret directing Providence and of the equality and justice of paying homage to Him that made us. The was nothing like this in the notion of an evil spirit, his nature and above all, his inclination to do evil and to draw us in to do so too. The poor creature completely confused me with a natural and innocent question and I barely knew what to say to him. I had been talking a great deal about the power of God, His omnipotence, His aversion to sin, His

---

[126] This is a thinly-veiled dig at the Catholic Church, which the Protestant Defoe was not particularly fond of.

being a consuming fire to the workers of evil and how He made and could destroy us and all the world in a moment. He listened with great seriousness. After this I had been telling him how the devil was God's enemy and used all his malice and skill to defeat the good plans of Providence and to ruin the kingdom of Christ in the world.

Friday said, "You say God is so strong, so great. Is He not much strong, much might as the devil?"

"Yes, yes," I replied. "Friday, God is stronger than the devil. God is above the devil and therefore we pray to God to tread the devil down under our feet and enable us to resist his temptations and quench his fiery darts."

"But if God much stronger, much might as the wicked devil, why God no kill the devil, so make him no more do wicked?"

I was strangely surprised at this question. After all, though I was now an old man, I was only a young doctor and unqualified as a casuist[127] or a solver of difficulties. At first, I didn't know what to say, so I pretended not to hear him and asked him what he said. But he was too intent on an answer to forget his question, so he repeated it in the very same broken words. By this time, I had recovered a little and said, "God will punish him severely. He will be reserved for judgment and is to be cast into the bottomless pit, to dwell with everlasting fire."

This did not satisfy Friday. He responded to me, repeating my words. "RESERVED FOR JUDGMENT! me no understand. But why not kill the devil now, not kill great ago?"

"You may as well ask me why God does not kill you or me, when we do wicked things here that offend Him. We are preserved to repent and be pardoned."

---

[127] Someone who resolves of specific cases of conscience, duty or conduct through interpretation of religious doctrine.

He pondered some time on this. "Well, well," he said affectionately, "that well. So you, I, devil, all wicked, all preserve, repent, God pardon all."

Here again I was run down by him to the last degree. How does nature guide reasonable creatures to the knowledge of God, but nothing but divine revelation can form the knowledge of Jesus Christ and of redemption purchased for us? Nothing but a revelation from Heaven can form these in the soul. The gospel of our Lord and Savior Jesus Christ – the Word of God and the Spirit of God – promised as the guide and sanctifier of His people, are the necessary instructors of the souls of men in the saving knowledge of God and the means of salvation.

I stopped the conversation between me and my man, rising hastily, as if I was going out. Sending him for something a good way off, I seriously prayed to God that He would enable me to instruct and save this poor savage, and by His Spirit assist the heart of the poor ignorant creature to receive the light of the knowledge of God in Christ, and would guide me to speak to him from the Word of God so his conscience might be convinced, his eyes opened and his soul saved. When he came back, I spoke with him about the redemption of man by the Savior of the world and of the doctrine of the gospel preached from Heaven, specifically repentance towards God and faith in our blessed Lord Jesus.

I had, God knows, more sincerity than knowledge in all the methods I used for this poor creature's instruction. I believe all who act on the same principle will find what I did – while laying things open to him, I instructed myself in many things either I did not know or had not fully considered before, but which occurred naturally to my mind while trying to enlighten this poor savage. I had more affection now than I ever felt before, so whether this poor wild wretch was better for me or not, I had great reason to be thankful he ever came to me. My grief sat lighter on me, my home grew comfortable to me beyond measure and when I looked back on my solitary life, I had not only been moved to look up to heaven myself and to seek the Hand that had brought me here, but was now an instrument to save the life – and for all I know – the soul of a poor savage and bring him to the true knowledge of religion so he might know Christ Jesus, in whom is eternal life. When I considered all these things, a secret joy ran through every part of My soul and I frequently rejoiced I was ever brought to this place, which I had so often thought was the most dreadful thing that could possibly have occurred to me.

I continued in this thankful frame of mind for the remainder of my time and the hours of conversation between Friday and I made the three years we lived there together perfectly and completely happy, if any such thing as complete happiness can be formed in a sublunary[128] state. This savage was now a good Christian, much better than I, though I have reason to hope – and bless God for it – we were equally penitent and comforted. We had the Word of God to read and no farther off from His Spirit than if we had been in England. While reading the Scripture I always let him know, as well as I could, the meaning of what I read. And he, by his serious inquiries made me a much better scholar of Scriptural knowledge than I would ever have been with my own private reading. I also must say, from my experience on the island, was how infinite and indescribable a blessing it is that the knowledge of God and the salvation by Christ Jesus is so plainly laid down in the Word of God. A basic reading of the Scripture made me able to understand my duty was to go on to the great work of sincere repentance for my sins, having a Savior, and obedience of all God's commands – and this without any human teacher. The same plain instruction sufficiently enlightened this savage creature and make him a better Christian than most I have known in my life.

---

[128] Characteristic of this world, as opposed to a higher, spiritual one.

As to all the disputes, wrangling, strife and contention which have happened in the world about religion, whether doctrine or schemes of church government, they were all completely useless to us. For all I can see, they were to the rest of the world as well. We had the Word of God as the sure guide to heaven, and we had – blessed be God – understanding of the Spirit of God from His word, leading us into truth and making us both willing and obedient to the instruction of His word. And I cannot see what use the greatest knowledge of the disputed points of religion – which have made such confusion in the world – would have been to us, if we could have obtained it. But I must go on with the historical part of things and take every part in its order.

After Friday and I became more intimately acquainted and he could understand almost all I said to him and speak fluently in broken English to me, I acquainted him with my own history, or at least that which related to my coming to this place – how I had lived there and how long. I let him into the mystery, as it was to him, of gunpowder and bullet, and taught him how to shoot. I gave him a knife, which he was delighted with and I made him a belt to hang a hatchet from, which was not only as good a weapon, but much more useful on other occasions.

I described to him the country of Europe, particularly England, how we lived, how we worshipped God, how we behaved to one another and how we traded in ships to all parts of the world. I told him about the wreck I had survived and showed him the place where she lay, though she was all beaten to pieces and gone now. I showed him the ruins of our boat, which we lost when we escaped and which I could not move with all my strength, and it had also fallen to pieces. Seeing this boat, Friday stood deep in thought and said nothing. I asked him what it was he studied. Finally he said, "Me see such boat like come to place at my nation." I did not understand him for a long time but at last, when I had examined it further, I understood a boat like that came on shore where he lived, or as he explained it, was driven there by stress of weather. I imagined some European ship must have been cast away on their coast and the boat got loose and was driven ashore, but I was so stupid that I never once thought of men making their escape from a wreck there, so I only wanted a description of the boat.

Friday described the boat to me well enough, but I understood him better when he added with some warmth, "We save the white mans from drown." I asked if there were any white mans, as he called them, in the boat. "Yes," he said, "the boat full of white mans." I asked him how many. He told on his fingers seventeen. I asked him what became of them. He told me, "They live, they dwell at my nation."

This put new thoughts into my head. I imagined these might be the men from the ship that was cast away in sight of my island, who after the ship was struck on the rock had saved themselves and landed their boat on that wild shore among the savages. I inquired deeper what had become of them. He assured me they still lived there and had been there about four years. The savages left them alone and gave them food to live on. I asked him why they did not kill them and eat them. He said, "No, they make brother with them," which I understood to mean a truce. Then he added, "They no eat mans except when make the war fight."

It was some time after this I was on the top of the hill on the side where I had discovered the mainland of America. The weather was very serene and Friday looked very intently towards the mainland. Surprised, jumping and dancing, called out to me. I asked him what was the matter. "Oh, joy!" he said. "Oh, glad! there see my country, there my nation!" An extraordinary sense of pleasure appeared on his face, his eyes sparkled and his expression had a strange eagerness, as if he had a mind to be in his own country again. This put many thoughts into me, which at first made me not so easy about my new man Friday as I was before. I had no doubt that if Friday could get back to his own nation again, he would not only forget all his religion but all his obligation to me, would tell his countrymen about me and come back, perhaps with a hundred of them and make a feast of me, which might make him as happy as he used to be with his enemies when they were taken in war. As my suspicion increased and held for weeks, I was a little more cautious and not so familiar and kind to him as before. I was wrong. The honest, grateful creature had no such thought except what comprised a religious Christian and a grateful friend.

While my suspicion lasted, every day I was pushing him to see if he would reveal any of the new thoughts I suspected were in him. Everything he said was so honest and so innocent and I could find nothing to nourish my suspicion. Despite all my uneasiness, at last he made me entirely his own again and he did not in the least perceive I was uneasy and I could not suspect him of deceit.

On a hazy day – we could not see the continent – and walking up the same hill, I asked him "Friday, do not you wish to be in your own country, your own nation?"

"Yes," he said, "I be much O glad to be at my own nation."

"What would you do there?" I asked. "Would you turn wild again, eat men's flesh again and be a savage as you were before?"

He looked full of concern and shaking his head said, "No, no, Friday tell them to live good. Tell them to pray God. Tell them to eat bread, cattle flesh, milk. No eat man again."

"Why? They will kill you."

He looked serious, then said, "No, no, they no kill me, they willing love learn." He added that they learned a lot from the bearded men who came in the boat. Then I asked him if he would go back to them. He smiled and told me he could not swim so far. I told him I would make a canoe for him. He told me he would go if I would go with him.

"They will eat me if I go there."

"No, no," he said, "me make they no eat you. Me make they much love you." He meant he would tell them how I had killed his enemies and saved his life, so he would make them love me. Then he told me, as well as he could, how kind they were to seventeen white men – or bearded men as he called them – who came on shore in distress.

From then on, I confess I had a mind to venture over and see if I could possibly join with those bearded men, who I had no doubt were Spaniards and Portuguese. I did not doubt we would find some method to escape from there, being on the continent and a good company together, at least better than I could from an island forty miles off shore, alone and without help. After a few days, I told Friday I would give him a boat to go back to his own nation. I took him to my frigate, which was on the other side of the island and clearing it of water – I always kept it sunk in water – I brought it out, showed him and we both went in it. He was a very dexterous fellow at managing it and would make it go almost as swift as I could. When he was in, I said to him, "Well, now, Friday, shall we go to your nation?" He looked dumbfounded at me. He thought the boat was too small to go so far. I then told him I had a bigger boat. The next day I went to the place where the first boat I had made lay which I could not get into the water. He said it was big enough, but as I had not taken care of it – it had sat for 23 years – the sun had split and dried it and it was rotten. Friday told me such a boat would do very well and would carry "much enough food, drink, bread." This was his way of talking.

16.

Rescue of Prisoners from Cannibals

I was, by this time, so fixed on my plan to go over with him to the continent that I told him we would go and make a canoe as big as needed and he would go home in it. He didn't say a, but looked very serious and sad. I asked him what was the matter. He asked me again, "Why you angry mad with Friday? What me done?" I asked him what he meant. I told him I was not angry with him at all. "No angry!" he said, repeating the words several times, "Why send Friday home away to my nation?"

"Friday, did not you say you wished you were there?"

"Yes, yes," he said, "wish we both there. No wish Friday there, no master there." He would not think of going there without me.

"I go there, Friday?" I asked, "What will I do there?"

He turned very quick on me at this. "You do great deal much good," he replied. "You teach wild mans be good, sober, tame mans. You tell them know God, pray God, and live new life."

"Oh, Friday! You don't know what you're saying. I am just an ignorant man myself."

"Yes, yes, you teachee me good, you teachee them good."

"No, no, Friday. You will go without me. Leave me here to live by myself, as I did before." He looked confused again and running to one of the hatchets which he used to wear, he quickly picked it up and gave it to me. "What must I do with this?" I asked.

"You take kill Friday," he answered.

"Why must I kill you?" I asked.

He responded quickly, "What you send Friday away for? Take kill Friday, no send Friday away." This he said so sincerely that I saw tears in his eyes. I plainly saw his extreme affection for me and a firm resolution in him. I told him then and often after that I would never send him away from me if he was willing to stay with me.

I found by his speech a settled affection to me and nothing could part him from me. I also found the foundation of his desire to go to his own country was laid in his ardent affection for his people and his hopes of my doing them good. This was something I had not the least intention or desire of attempting. Still, I had a strong inclination to attempt my escape, founded on the belief there were seventeen bearded men there. Without further delay, I went with Friday to find a large tree to cut down and make a large canoe to undertake the voyage. There were enough trees on the island to build a small fleet of good, large vessels, not just canoes. The main thing I looked at was to get one close to the water so we could launch it when it was made and avoid my earlier mistake. Friday settled on a tree, since he knew much better than I what kind of wood was best. To this day I can't tell you what wood to call the tree we cut down, except that it was like the tree we call fustic[129] or between that and the Nicaragua wood, since it was the same color and smell. Friday wanted to burn the cavity of this tree out to make it a boat, but I showed him how to cut it with tools. After I had showed him how, he did very handily. After about a month's hard labor we finished it and made it very well, especially using our axes to cut and form the outside into the true shape of a boat. After this, it cost us nearly two weeks to get her along, inch by inch, on large rollers into the water. But when she was in, she would have carried twenty men easily.

---

[129] A type of mulberry tree.

When she was in the water, though she was so big, it amazed me to see with what dexterity and how swift my man Friday could manage her, turn her and paddle her along. So, I asked him if he would venture over in her. "Yes," he said, "we venture over in her very well, though great blow wind." However, I had a further plan he knew nothing of: to make a mast and a sail and to fit her with an anchor and cable. A mast was easy enough to get. I focused on a straight young cedar, which there were great plenty of on the island, and I put Friday to work cutting it down and gave him directions how to shape it. The sail was my responsibility. I knew I had old sails, or rather pieces of old sails, but as I had them 26 years and had not been very careful to preserve them, I did not doubt they were all rotten. Most of them were. Nevertheless, I found two pieces which appeared pretty good and with these I went to work. With great pains and awkward stitching – I had no needles – I made a three-cornered ugly thing like the sail I had on the boat I used to escape from Barbary.

I took nearly two months performing this task, rigging and fitting my masts and sails. I finished them completely, making a small stay and foresail, to assist if we turned into the wind. Finally, I fixed a rudder to the stern. I was a bungling shipwright, but since I knew the usefulness and necessity of a rudder, I applied myself with so much pain to do it, that at last I brought it to fruition, though considering the many stupid plans I had that failed, I think it cost me almost as much labor as making the boat.

After all this was done, I had my man Friday teach me what we needed to navigate my boat. He knew very well how to paddle a canoe, but he knew nothing about a sail and a rudder and was amazed when he saw me steer the boat with the rudder, and how the sail filled as our course changed. When he saw this, he was astonished and amazed. However, with a little use, I made all these things familiar to him and he became an expert sailor, though he did not understand the compass.

On the other hand, as there was very little cloudy weather and seldom any fog, there was little need for a compass, since the stars were always out at night and you could see the shore by day, except in the rainy seasons. Then nobody cared to move either by land or sea.

I was now in my 27th year of captivity in this place, though the three last years I had this creature with me should be left out of the account, my life being quite different than in all the rest of the time. I kept the anniversary of my landing here with the same thankfulness to God for His mercies as at first. If I had reason to acknowledge it then, I had much more so now, having additional care of Providence over me and the great hopes I had of being speedily rescued. I had an unshakable impression that my liberation was at hand and I would not be another year in this place. I went on, however, digging, planting and fencing as usual. I gathered and cured my grapes and did every necessary thing as before.

The rainy season returned, when I kept more indoors than at other times. We had stowed our new vessel as securely as we could, bringing her up into the creek. Hauling her up to the shore at highwater mark, I made my man Friday dig a little dock, just big enough to hold her and just deep enough to give her enough water to float in. When the tide was out, we made a strong dam across the end of it to keep the water out and so she lay, dry from the tide and the sea. To keep the rain off we laid a lot of tree boughs, so thick she was as well thatched as a house. We waited for November and December, when I planned to make my adventure.

When the dry season began, I was preparing daily for the voyage. And the first thing I did was to put aside a certain quantity of provisions for our voyage. I intended in a week or two to open the dock and launch out our boat. I was busy one morning on something of this kind, when I called to Friday and had him go to the seashore and see if he could find a turtle for the eggs as well as the meat. Friday had not been gone long when he came running back and flew over my outer wall, like someone who didn't feel the ground. Before I had time to speak to him he cried out to me, "O master! O master! O sorrow! O bad!"

"What's the matter, Friday?"

"O yonder there," he said, "one, two, three canoes; one, two, three!" By his way of speaking I concluded there were six, but then learned there were only three.

"Well, Friday, do not be frightened." I uplifted him up as well as I could. However, I saw the poor fellow was terribly scared. Nothing ran in his head except they had come for him and would cut him in pieces and eat him. The poor fellow trembled and I hardly knew what to do with him. I comforted him as well as I could and told him I was in as much danger as he and they would eat me as well as him. "But Friday," I said, "we must decide to fight them. Can you fight, Friday?"

"Me shoot," he responded, "but there come many great number."

"Don't worry, our guns will frighten those we do not kill."

I asked him whether, if I decided to defend him, he would defend me and stand by me and do just as I tell him. He said, "Me die when you tell me to die, master." I went and fetched a good shot of rum and gave it to him, which after all these years I still had a great deal left. After we drank, I made him take the two shotguns which we always carried and loaded them with large swan-shot, as big as small pistol-bullets. Then I took four muskets and loaded them with two slugs and five small bullets each and my two pistols I loaded with a pair of bullets each. I hung my large sword by my side and gave Friday his hatchet. When I had prepared myself, I took my telescope and went up the side of the hill, to see what I could. I quickly found there were twenty-one savages, three prisoners and three canoes and their whole business seemed to be the triumphant banquet on these three human bodies. A barbarous feast, indeed, but nothing more than was usual with them. I also noticed they had not landed where they had when Friday made his escape but closer to my creek, where the shore was low, and where a thick wood almost came down to the sea. The disgust of the inhuman errand these wretches engaged in filled me with such indignation that I came down to Friday and told him I decided to go down and kill them all and asked if he would stand by me. He had now got over his fright and his spirits were a little raised with the shot of rum I had given him. He was very cheerful and told me, as before, he would die when I told him to.

In this fit of fury, I divided the weapons between us. I gave Friday one pistol to stick in his belt and three guns on his shoulder. I took one pistol and the other three guns myself and we marched out. I took a small bottle of rum in my pocket and gave Friday a large bag with more gunpowder and bullets. I told him to keep close behind me and not to move, shoot or do anything until I told him and in the meantime not to speak a word. I headed to my right for nearly a mile, to get over the creek as well as into the woods so I could come within shot of them before I was discovered, which I had seen by my telescope was easy to do.

While I was making this march, I began to question my former decision. I do not mean I had any fear of their number, since as they were naked, unarmed wretches, it is certain I was superior to them. But it occurred to me, what reason, what occasion, much less what need did I have to go and dip my hands in blood, to attack people who had neither done or intended me any wrong? These savages to me were innocent. Their barbarous customs were their own disaster and a token of God's leaving them to such stupidity and to such inhuman courses. God did not call me to be a judge of their actions, much less an executioner of His justice. Whenever He thought fit, He would take the cause into His own hands and by national vengeance punish them as a people for national crimes, but in the meantime, it was none of my business. It was true Friday might justify it, because he was a declared enemy and at war with those very particular people and it was lawful for him to attack them, but I could not say the same for myself. These things were so warmly pressed on my thoughts as I went, I decided I would only go near them so I could observe their barbarous feast and I would act then as God would direct. Unless something offered that was more a call to me than I knew of, I would not meddle with them.

I entered the woods and, with all possible caution and silence – and Friday following close at my heels – I marched until I came to the edge of the woods next to them and only one corner of the woods lay between me and them. Here I called softly to Friday. I pointed to a large tree just at the corner of the woods and told him go to the tree, to see what they were doing. He did so and came back immediately. He told me they could be plainly viewed there and they were all around their fire, eating the flesh of one of their prisoners. Another lay tied on the sand a little from them, whom he said they would kill next. This fired my soul. He told me it was not one of their nation, but one of the bearded men. I was filled with horror at the naming of the white bearded man. Going to the tree, I plainly saw with my telescope a white man, who lay on the beach with his hands and feet tied with flags, he was a European and had clothes on.

There was a little thicket about fifty yards closer to them which, by going a little way about, I might come in undiscovered and then I would be within half a shot of them. I withheld my desire for revenge, though I was enraged to the highest degree. Going back about twenty paces, I got behind some bushes, which disguised me until I came to the thicket. Then I came to a little rise which gave me a full view of them at the distance of about eighty yards.

I now had not a moment to lose. Nineteen of the dreadful wretches sat on the ground, all huddled together, and had just sent the other two to butcher the poor Christian and bring him limb by limb to their fire. They were stooping down to untie the bands at his feet. I turned to Friday. "Now, Friday, do as I tell you." Friday said he would. "Then,

Friday, do exactly as you see me do. Fail in nothing." I set down one of the muskets and the shotgun on the ground, and Friday did the same, and with the other musket I took my aim at the savages, telling him to do the same. Then asking him if he was ready, he said "Yes."

"Then fire at them," I said, and at the same moment I also fired.

Friday's aim was so much better than mine, that when he shot he killed two of them and wounded three more. On my side, I killed one and wounded two. They were, you may be sure, alarmed. All who were not hurt jumped on their feet, but did not immediately know which way to run or which way to look, since they didn't know from where their destruction came. Friday kept his eyes on me so he would see what I did, as I instructed. As soon as the first shot was made, I threw down the piece, and took up the shotgun and Friday followed suit. He saw me cock the gun and aim. He did the same again. "Are you ready, Friday?" I asked. Again, he said yes. "Let fly then, in the name of God!"

With that I fired again among the amazed wretches and so did Friday. As our pieces were now loaded with what I call swan-shot, or small pistol-bullets, only two savages dropped but so many were wounded, they ran around yelling and screaming like mad creatures, all bloody and most of them miserably wounded. Three more fell quickly after, though not quite dead.

"Now Friday, follow me," I said, laying down the discharged pieces and taking up the musket which was loaded, which he did with a great deal of courage. I rushed out of the woods and showed myself, with Friday close behind. As soon as they saw me, I shouted as loud as I could and had Friday do so too. Running as fast as I could – which by the way was not very fast as I was loaded with arms– I headed towards the poor victim who was still lying on the beach. The two butchers who were just going to work on him had left him at the surprise of our first fire. They fled in a terrible fright to the seaside and had jumped into a canoe, which three more also did. I turned to Friday and ordered him to step forward and fire at them. He understood me immediately and running about forty yards closer, he shot at them. I thought he had killed them all, since I saw them all fall in a heap in the boat. Two of them were up again quickly. He killed two of them and wounded the third, who laid in the bottom of the boat as if he had been dead.

While my man Friday fired at them, I pulled out my knife and cut the flags that bound the poor victim. Loosening his hands and feet, I lifted him up and asked him in Portuguese what he was. He answered in Latin "Christianus," but was so weak and faint that he could barely stand or speak. I took the bottle out of my pocket and gave it him, making signs to drink and I gave him a piece of bread, which he ate. Then I asked him what country he was from and he said, "Espagniole." Recovering a bit, he let me know, by all the signs he could possibly make, how much he was in my debt for his rescue.

"Seignior," I said, with as much Spanish as I could make up, "we will talk afterwards, but we must fight now. If you have any strength left, take this pistol and sword." He took them very thankfully. As soon as he had the weapons, it was like they had put new vigor into him, and he attacked his murderers like a fury and cut two of them to pieces in an instant. Since this was all a surprise to them, the poor creatures were so frightened with the noise of our guns that they fell in amazement and fear, and had no more power to attempt their own escape than their flesh had to resist our shot. That was the case of those five who Friday shot at in the boat – as three of them fell with the injury they received, the other two fell in fear.

I kept my gun in my hand without firing – willing to keep it ready – because I had given the Spaniard my pistol and sword. I called to Friday and told him to run up to the tree from where we first fired and fetch the arms which lay there after being discharged, which he did swiftly. Giving him my musket, I sat down to load the rest again and told them to come to me when they needed. While I was loading these pieces, there was a fierce engagement between the Spaniard and one of the savages. The savage went at him with one of their large wooden swords. The Spaniard, who was weak but bold and brave as could be imagined, fought the Indian for some time and had cut two gaping wounds on his head. But the savage was a stout, strong fellow and closing in with him, had thrown him down and was wringing my sword out of his hand. The Spaniard, though prone, wisely dropped the sword and drawing the pistol, shot the savage through and killed him on the spot before I, who was running to help him, could come near him.

Friday, being now left to his liberty, pursued the fleeing wretches, with no weapon in his hand but his hatchet. With that he dispatched those three who were wounded at first and fallen, as well as any others he found. The Spaniard came to me for a gun and I gave him one of the shotguns, with which he pursued two of the savages and wounded them both. As he was not able to run, they both escaped into the woods, where Friday pursued them. He killed one of them, but the other was too nimble and though he was wounded, plunged into the sea and swam off with all his might to those two who were left in the canoe. The three in the canoe, with one wounded, were all who escaped our hands of twenty-one.

Those who were in the canoe worked hard to get out of range and though Friday made two or three shots at them, he did not hit any of them. Friday wanted to take one of their canoes and pursue them and I was very concerned about their escape back to warn the other savages. I consented to pursue them by sea. Running to one of their canoes, I jumped in and told Friday to follow me. But when I was in the canoe I was surprised to find another poor creature lying there, bound hand and foot for the slaughter as the Spaniard was, and almost dead with fear. He did not know what was happening, since he was tied so hard around the neck and heels he had not been able to look up over the side of the boat, and had been tied so long that he really had little life in him.

I immediately cut the twisted flags they had bound him with and would have helped him up, but he could not stand or speak and groaned most piteously believing he was only untied to be killed. When Friday came to him I told him speak to him and tell him of his liberation. I pulled out my bottle and made him give the poor wretch a drink which, along with the news of his being saved, revived him and he sat up in the boat. But when Friday heard him speak and looked in his face, it would have moved anyone to tears to have seen how Friday kissed him, embraced him, hugged him, cried, laughed, jumped about, danced, sang, then cried again, beat his own face and head and sang and jumped around again like a deranged creature. It was a good while before I could make him speak to me or tell me what was the matter, but when he came to himself he told me that it was his father.

It is not easy for me to express how it moved me to see what ecstasy and familial affection was in this poor savage at the sight of his father and of his being delivered from death. I can barely describe half the extravagances of his affection after this. He went in and out of the boat many times. When he went in he would sit down by him and hold his father's head close to his chest for several minutes. Then he took his arms and ankles, which were numbed and stiff from the binding and chafed and rubbed them with his hands and I gave him some rum out of my bottle to rub them with, which did them a great deal of good.

This affair put an end to our pursuit of the canoe with the other savages, who were now almost out of sight and we were lucky we did not, as it blew so hard within two hours and before they could be a quarter of their way. It continued blowing hard all night and against them from the northwest and I doubted their boat could live or that they ever reached their own coast.

But to return to Friday. He was so busy with his father I could not find in my heart to take him off for some time. After I thought he could leave him for a bit, I called him to me and he came jumping and laughing, and pleased to the extreme. Then I asked him if he had given his father any bread. He shook his head and said, "None. Ugly dog eat all up self." I gave him a cake of bread out of a little pouch I carried on purpose. I also gave him a drink for himself. He would not taste it, but carried it to his father. I had in my pocket a few bunches of raisins, so I gave him a handful for his father. Friday had no sooner given his father these raisins when I saw him come out of the boat and run away as if he had been bewitched – he was the swiftest fellow on his feet I ever saw. He ran so fast that he was out of sight in an instant. Though I called and hollered after him, away he went. In a quarter of an hour I saw Friday come back again, though not so fast as he went. As he came closer I found his pace slowed, because he had something in his hand. When he came to me I found he had been home for an earthenware jug to bring his father some fresh water and he had got two more loaves of bread. The bread he gave me, but the water he carried to his father. As I was very thirsty too, I took a little of it. The water revived his father more than all the rum or spirits I had given him, since he was fainting with thirst.

When his father had drunk, I called to him to see if there was any water left. He said yes and I told him give it to the poor Spaniard, who was in as much want of it as his father. I sent one of the loaves Friday brought to the Spaniard too, who was very weak and was resting himself on a green place under the shade of a tree. His limbs were also very stiff and very swollen with the bindings he had been tied with. When Friday came to him with the water he sat up and drank and took the bread and began to eat. I went to him and gave him a handful of raisins. He looked up in my face with all the tokens of gratitude and thankfulness that could appear in any expression. But he was so weak from exerting himself in the fight, he could not stand up on his feet. He tried to do it two or three times but was not able as his ankles were so swollen and painful. I told him to sit still, and had Friday rub his ankles and bathe them with rum, as he had done his father's.

I noticed the poor affectionate creature every two minutes turn his head around to see if his father was sitting in the same place as he left him. When Friday couldn't see him, he jumped up and, without speaking a word, ran with that swiftness that someone watching could barely see his feet touch the ground. When he came, he only found he had laid himself down to ease his limbs, so Friday came back to me. Then I asked the Spaniard to let Friday help him to the boat and then he would take him to our dwelling, where I would take care of him. But Friday was a strong fellow and took the Spaniard on his back, carrying him to the boat and set him down softly on the side of the canoe with his feet inside. Lifting him in, he set him close to his father. Stepping out again, he launched the boat off and paddled it along the shore faster than I could walk, though the wind blew hard. He brought them both safely into our creek and leaving them in the boat, ran away to fetch the other canoe. As he passed me I spoke to him and asked where he went. He told me, "Go fetch more boat." So away he went like the wind and surely, never a man nor horse ran like him. He had the other canoe in the creek almost as soon as I got to it by land. He floated me over, then went to help our new guests out of the boat, but neither of them could walk and poor Friday didn't know what to do.

To remedy this I thought, and calling to Friday to tell them to sit down on the bank while he came to me, I made a kind of hand-barrow[130] to lay them on and Friday and I carried them both up together on it between us.

But when we got them to the outside of our wall, we were at a worse loss than before, since it was impossible to get them over and I was

---

[130] A flat rectangular frame with handles at both ends that is carried by two persons, like a stretcher.

decided not to break it down. So, I went to work again and Friday and I, in about two hours' time, made a very nice tent, covered with old sails and above that with tree boughs. Here we made them two beds like I had – of good rice-straw with blankets to lie on and another to cover them on each bed.

My island was now peopled and I thought myself very rich in subjects. It was a happy thought I frequently had, of how much like a king I looked. The whole country was my own property, so I had an undoubted right of dominion. My people were completely subjugated – I was absolute lord and lawgiver. They all owed their lives to me and were ready to lay down their lives, if there had been occasion for it, for me. It was also remarkable I had only three subjects and they were of three different religions. My man Friday was a Protestant, his father was a Pagan and a cannibal and the Spaniard was a Catholic. However, I allowed liberty of conscience throughout my dominions.

As soon as I had secured my two weak, rescued prisoners, given them shelter and a place to rest, I began to think of making some provision for them. The first thing I did was to order Friday to take a yearling goat out of my flock to be killed. I cut off the hindquarter and chopping it into small pieces, I put Friday to work boiling and stewing and made them a very good dish – I assure you – of meat and broth. I cooked it outdoors, since I didn't make fire within my inner wall, and carried it all into the new tent. Having set a table there for them, I sat down and ate my own dinner with them and, as well as I could, cheered them up and encouraged them. Friday was my interpreter, especially to his father but also to the Spaniard since the Spaniard spoke the language of the savages well.

After we had dined, I ordered Friday to take one of the canoes and go and fetch our muskets and other firearms which, for lack of time, we had left on the battlefield. The next day I ordered him to go and bury the dead bodies of the savages, which lay open to the sun and would soon be offensive. I also ordered him to bury the horrid remains of their barbarous feast, which I could not think of doing myself. No, I could not bear to see them if I went that way. These tasks he performed punctually and removed any appearance of the savages being there, so when I went again, I barely knew where it was, other than the corner of the woods pointing to the place.

I then began to speak with my two new subjects. First, I had Friday ask his father what he thought of the escape of the savages in that canoe and whether we might expect their return with greater numbers. His first opinion was the savages in the boat could never live out the storm which blew that night and must have drowned or been driven south to those other shores, where they were sure to be devoured. I asked what they would do if they safely came back on my shore. He said he didn't know, but he did think they were so awfully frightened by our attack, the noise and the fire, that he believed they would tell the people they were all killed by thunder and lightning, not by the hand of man and the two who appeared – Friday and I – were two heavenly spirits, sent down to destroy them. This he knew, because he heard them all cry out in their language and say as much. It was impossible for them to believe a man could dart fire, speak thunder and kill at a distance, without lifting a hand, as they thought. This old savage was in the right. As I understood from later tellings, the savages never attempted to go over to the island again as they were so terrified with the accounts given by those four men – it seems they did escape – they believed whoever went to that enchanted island would be destroyed with fire from the gods. I didn't know this until sometime later and consequently was under continual anxiety for a long time and always kept on my guard, with all my army. As there were now four of us, I would have ventured on a hundred of them, in the open field, at any time.

17.

Visit of Mutineers

In a little time with no more canoes appearing, the fear of their coming wore off and I began to take my previous thoughts of a voyage to the mainland into consideration. I was also assured by Friday's father that – thanks to him – I could depend on good treatment from their nation. But my thoughts were put on hold when I had a serious discussion with the Spaniard. There were sixteen more of his countrymen and Portuguese, who were castaway and lived there in peace with the savages, but were in dire need of necessities and for life. I asked him about their voyage. They were a Spanish ship, bound from the Rio de la Plata to Havana. They were directed to leave their load of hides and silver there, and to bring back what European goods they could. They had five Portuguese seamen on board, who they took out of another wreck. Five of their own men drowned when the ship was first lost and these escaped through countless perils and arrived, almost starved, on the cannibal coast, where they expected to have been eaten every moment. He told me they had some weapons with them, but they were completely useless, since they had neither gunpowder nor ball.

I asked him what he thought would become of them there and if they had formed any plan of escape. He said they had many discussions about it, but having neither a vessel, the tools to build one, nor provisions of any kind, their meetings always ended in tears and despair. I asked him how he thought they would take an escape proposal from me, and if they were all here, it would be done. I told him I feared their treachery and abuse of me if I put my life in their hands. Gratitude was not an inherent virtue in man, nor did men always deal squarely when it came to favors they had received. I was not interested in rescuing them, only to be made their prisoner in New Spain after, where an Englishman was certain to be made a sacrifice, whatever reason brought him there. I would rather be delivered to the savages and eaten alive, than fall into the merciless claws of the priests and carried into the Inquisition. If they were all here I would be persuaded to build a barque[131] large enough to carry us all to either the Brazils to the south or to the islands or Spanish coast[132] to the north, unless they took me by force to their own people. Then I would be mistreated for my kindness and make my case worse than it was before.

He answered with a great deal of candor and innocence. Their condition was so miserable and they were so conscious of it, he believed they would detest the thought of using any man unkindly who would contribute to their rescue. If I pleased, he would go to them with the old man and talk with them, and return with their answer. He would make them solemnly swear that they would be absolutely under my direction as their commander and captain, and they would swear on the holy sacraments and gospel to be true to me. We would go to whatever Christian country I wanted and no other, and they would follow my orders until they landed safely in that country. I went so far as to require a contract from them for that purpose. Then he told me he would swear allegiance to me first that he would never abandon me as long as he lived until I told him to, and he would take my side to the last drop of his blood, if there was the tiniest breach of faith among his countrymen. He told me they were all very civil, honest men and they were under the greatest distress imaginable, having no weapons, clothes or any food and were at the mercy and discretion of the savages. They had no hope

---

[131] A small sailing ship.
[132] The Dominican Republic or the coast of Florida.

of ever returning to their own country and he was sure if I would undertake their relief, they would live and die by me.

On these assurances I decided to rescue them, if possible, and send the old savage and this Spaniard over to them to talk. But when we had got all things ready to go, the Spaniard himself stated an objection, which had so much prudence on one hand and so much sincerity on the other, I could only be satisfied with it. By his advice, I put off the liberation of his comrades for at least half a year. He had been with us about a month now and I had let him see how I had provided, with the assistance of Providence. He saw the stock of barley and rice I had which, though it was more than enough for myself, was not sufficient for my new family of four, much less for his 16 countrymen, if they were still alive. Most of all, it would be insufficient to supply our vessel, if we would build one, for a voyage to any of the Christian colonies of America. So, he told me it would be advisable to let him and the other two dig and cultivate some more land and plant as much seed as I could spare. We would wait another harvest so we would have grain for his countrymen, when they would come. Desire might tempt them to disagree or to think themselves not rescued, and they may think themselves out of one difficulty into another. "You know," he said, "the children of Israel, though they rejoiced at first at being delivered out of Egypt, rebelled against God Himself, when they wanted bread in the wilderness."

His caution was so reasonable and his advice so good, I could only be very pleased with his proposal, as well as satisfied with his loyalty. All four of us started digging, as well as the wooden tools we had permitted. In about a month's time, by the end of which it was seeding time, we had enough land ready to plant 22 bushels of barley and 16 jars of rice, which was all the seed we had to spare. We left ourselves barely enough food for the six months we had to wait for our crop.

Having enough people now and to put us out of fear of the savages, we went freely all over the island whenever we wanted. I marked out several trees and I sent Friday and his father to cut them down. Then I had the Spaniard – to whom I told my thoughts – to oversee and direct their work. I showed them how I had cut – with unrelenting pain – a large tree into single planks and I had them to do the same, until they made about a dozen good oak planks, nearly two feet wide, thirty-five feet long and from two to four inches thick. What extraordinary labor it took anyone can imagine.

At the same time, I attempted to increase my little flock of tame goats as much as I could. I made Friday and the Spaniard go out one day – and myself with Friday the next day – and we got about twenty young kids to breed with the rest. Whenever we shot the mother, we saved the kids and added them to our flock. But above all, the season for curing the grapes was here and I had such a remarkable quantity to be hung up in the sun, I believe had we been at Alicante – where the raisins are cured – we could have filled sixty or eighty barrels. These, with our bread, formed a large part of our food – and very good living too, I assure you, as they are exceedingly nourishing.

It was now harvest time and our crop was in good order. It was not the most plentiful increase I had seen on the island, but it was enough to answer our need. From 22 bushels of barley we brought in over 220 bushels[133] and the same proportion of the rice, which was enough if all the Spaniards had been on shore with me or to take on the voyage to any part of America. When we had secured our warehouse of grain, we went to work making more wicker-ware to keep it in. The Spaniard was very handy and dexterous at this part and often blamed me for not

---

[133] A bushel of barley would weigh 48 pounds, so 220 bushels of barley plus 220 more of rice would weigh over ten tons, a completely improbable amount.

making some things for defense of this kind of work, but I saw no need for it.

Having a full supply of food for all the guests I expected, I gave the Spaniard permission to go over to the mainland to see what he could do with those he had left behind. I gave him strict orders not to bring any man who would not first swear that he would in no way injure, fight with or attack him – that would be me – from the island, who was so kind to rescue them. They would stand by him and defend him and wherever they went would be entirely under and subjected to his command. This would be put in writing and signed by their hand. How they would do this, when I knew they had neither pen nor ink, was a question which we never asked. Under these instructions, the Spaniard and Friday's father went away in one of the canoes. I gave each of them a musket and about eight charges of gunpowder and ball, ordering them to be very good keepers of both and not to use either of them except on urgent occasions.

This was cheerful work, since it was the first time in over 27 years I was closer to rescue. I gave them bread and dried grapes that was sufficient for many days – and enough for all the Spaniards for about eight days. Wishing them a good voyage, I saw them go, agreeing on a signal they would hang out at their return, so I would know them at a distance when they came back. They went away with a fair wind on the day that the moon was full in October – as for the exact day, I don't know since I had lost count years earlier. Actually, I didn't even know the number of years though, as it proved afterwards, I found I had kept a true estimate of years.

They were gone at least eight days when a strange and unforeseen accident happened. I was fast asleep in my box one morning, when my man Friday came running in to me and called out, "Master, master, they are come, they are come!" I jumped up and regardless of danger I went, as soon as I could get my clothes on, through my thick little grove. I say regardless of danger, since I went unarmed, which was not customary. I was surprised when, turning my eyes to the sea, I saw a boat about four miles out, heading in for the shore, with a shoulder-of-mutton sail. I also observed they did not come from the mainland side of the island, but from the southernmost end of the island. I called Friday in and told him stay close, since these were not the people we looked for, and we did not know whether they were friends or enemies. I went in to fetch my telescope to see what I could make of them. Taking the ladder out, I climbed to the top of the hill. I had barely set foot on the hill when my eye plainly saw a ship lying at anchor about seven miles from me but no more than 4 miles from shore. It appeared to be an English ship and the boat appeared to be an English longboat.

I cannot express the confusion or the indescribable joy of seeing a ship – one I had reason to believe was manned by my own countrymen and consequently friends. Yet, I had some secret doubts – I could not tell where they came from – telling me to keep on my guard. It occurred to me to consider what business an English ship could have there, since it was not the way to or from any part of the world where the English had any traffic. I knew there had been no storms to drive them there in distress, and if they really were English it was most probable they were up to no good and I had better continue as I was, rather than fall into the hands of thieves and murderers.

Let no man ignore the secret hints of danger which sometimes are given to him when he may think there is no possibility of its being real. I believe such hints are given to us because they are certainly discoveries of an invisible world. If the tendency seems to be to warn us of danger, why would we not suppose they are from some friendly agent – whether supreme, or subordinate – and they are given for our good?

The present question abundantly confirmed the accuracy of this reasoning. Had I not been made cautious by this secret warning – wherever it came from – I would be done and in a far worse condition than before. I had not been long in this position before I saw the boat come near the shore, as if they looked for a creek to land at. As they did not come quite far enough, they did not see the little inlet where I used to land my rafts, instead running their boat on the beach about half a mile from me, which made me very happy. Otherwise they would have landed at my door and would soon have beaten me out of my castle, and perhaps plundered me of all I had. When they were on shore I was fully satisfied they were Englishmen – at least most of them. One or two I thought were Dutch, but it did not prove true. There were in all eleven men, three of them unarmed and tied up. When the first four of them had jumped on shore, they took those three out of the boat as prisoners. One of the three I could see was using the most passionate gestures in appeal, affliction and despair, even to extravagance. The other two, I noticed, lifted up their hands sometimes and appeared concerned, but not to such a degree as the first. I was baffled at the sight and didn't know what was going on. Friday called out to me in English, as well as he could, "O master! You see English mans eat prisoner as well as savage mans."

"Why do you think they are going to eat them, Friday? I asked.

"Yes," said Friday, "they will eat them."

"No no, Friday, "I replied. "I am afraid they will murder them, but you can be sure they will not eat them."

While this was happening, I had no thought of what the issue really was but stood trembling with the horror of the sight, expecting every moment when the three prisoners would be killed. Once, I saw one of the villains lift up his arm with a large cutlass to strike one of the poor men. I expected to see him fall every moment and all the blood in my body ran cold. I wished wholeheartedly for the Spaniard and the savage to be here, or at least that I had some way to get undiscovered and within range of those on shore so I could secure the three men. After I had observed the outrageous abuse of the three men by the insolent seamen, they ran around the island, as if they wanted to see the country. I noticed the three other men had liberty to also go where they pleased, but they all sat down on the ground, deep in thought, like men in despair. This reminded of the first time I came on shore and began to look around me; how I gave myself up for lost; how wildly I looked around me; what dreadful fears I had and how I stayed in the tree all night for fear of being devoured by wild beasts. Just as I knew nothing that night of the divine driving of the ship closer to land, so these three poor desolate men knew nothing of how close their rescue was to them, and how safe they were. We see very little in front of us in the world and how we have to depend cheerfully on the great Maker of the world. He does not leave His creatures so absolutely destitute. Even in the worst circumstances they have always something to be thankful for and sometimes are closer to relief than they imagine. Sometimes they are even brought to their rescue by that which seems to bring to their destruction.

It was at high tide when these people came on shore. While they rambled around to see what kind of a place they were in, they had carelessly stayed until the tide had left, leaving their boat aground. They had left two men in the boat who, as I found afterwards, had drunk a little too much brandy and fell asleep. One of them woke a little sooner than the other and finding the boat too far ashore for him to move it, hollered to the rest, who were straggling nearby. They all soon came to the boat, but it was past all their strength to launch her, since the boat was very heavy and the shore on that side was a soft oozy sand, almost like quicksand. In this condition, like true seamen – who are the least of all mankind given to forethought – they gave up, and away they strolled around the countryside again. I heard one of them say to another, "Leave her alone, Jack, can't you? She'll float next tide," which confirmed what country they were from. I kept hidden and quiet, not once daring to go any farther out of my castle than to my observation point on top of the hill. I was very glad how well I was fortified. I knew it was no less than ten hours before the boat could float again and by that time it would be dark. I would then be more able to see their motions and to hear their discussion, if they had any. Meanwhile, I readied myself for battle as before, though with more caution, knowing I had to deal with another kind of enemy than I had at first. I ordered Friday, who I had made an excellent marksman with his gun, to load himself with weapons. I took two shotguns and I gave him three muskets. My figure was positively fierce. I had my formidable goatskin coat on, with the large hat I have mentioned, a sword by my side, two pistols in my belt and a gun on each shoulder.

It was my plan not to make any attempt until it was dark but around two o'clock, in the heat of the day, I found they had all straggled into the woods and, as I thought, laid down to sleep. The three poor distressed men, too anxious to get any sleep had, however, sat down under the shelter of a large tree about a quarter of a mile from me, out of sight of any of the rest. I decided to reveal myself to them and learn something of their condition. Immediately I marched, my man Friday a good distance behind me, as formidably armed as I, but not quite so startling. I came as close to them as I could and then, before any of them saw me, I called out to them in Spanish, "What are ye, gentlemen?" They were startled at the noise, but were ten times more confused when they saw me, and the uncivilized figure I made. They didn't answer at all, but I thought they were going to flee so I spoke to them in English. "'Gentlemen," I said, "do not be surprised. Perhaps you have a friend nearby when you did not expect it."

"He must be sent directly from heaven," one of them said very seriously to me, pulling off his hat, "since our condition is past the help of man."

"All help is from heaven, sir," I said, "but allow a stranger to help you, as you seem to be in great distress. I saw you when you landed and when you seemed to plead to the brutes who came with you, I saw one of them lift up his sword to kill you."

The poor man, trembling and with tears running down his face, was astonished and said, "Am I talking to God or man? Is it a real man or an angel?"

"Do not fear that, sir," I answered. "If God had sent an angel to relieve you, he would have come better clothed and armed than me. Put aside your fears. I am a man, an Englishman and willing to assist you. You see I have only one servant and we have weapons and ammunition. Tell us freely, can we serve you? What is your case?"

"Our case sir is too long to tell you while our murderers are so close to us, but in short sir, I was commander of that ship. My men have mutinied against me. They have been persuaded not to murder me and have put me on shore in this desolate place with these two men – one my mate, the other a passenger – where we expected to die, believing the place to be uninhabited."

"Where are these brutes, your enemies?" I asked. "Do you know where they have gone?"

"There they are, sir," he replied, pointing to a thicket of trees. "My heart trembles for fear they have seen us and heard you speak. If they have, they will certainly murder us all."

"Do they have any firearms?"

He answered, "They had only two pieces, and one they left in the boat."

"Well then, leave the rest to me. I see they are all asleep. It is easy to kill them all, but shall we take them prisoner instead?" He told me there were two desperate villains among them who it would be unsafe to show any mercy to, but if they were held, he believed the rest would return to their duty. I asked him which they were. He told me he could not distinguish them at that distance but he would obey my plans. "Let's retreat out of their view or hearing, in case they wake up and we will discuss this further." So, they willingly went back with me until the woods protected us from them.

"Look sir,' I said, "if I proceed with your rescue, are you willing to make two conditions with me?" He anticipated my proposals by telling me that both he and the ship, if recovered, would be unconditionally commanded by me and if the ship was not recovered, he would live and die with me in what part of the world I sent him, as well as the two other men. "I only have two conditions. First, while you stay in this island with me, you will not pretend you have any authority here. If I arm you, you will give them up to me, and not be hostile to me or my people on this island, and be governed by my orders. If the ship is or may be recovered, you will carry me and my man to England free."

He gave me all the assurances the faith of man could devise that he would comply with these very reasonable demands, and would owe his life to me and acknowledge it on all occasions as long as he lived. "Well then," I said, "here are three muskets for you, with gunpowder and ball. Next tell me what you think we should do." He showed all the gratitude that he was able, but offered to be completely guided by me. I told him I thought it was very hard attempting anything, but the best method I could think of was to fire on them while they slept and if any were not killed at the first volley and offered to submit, we would save them. We therefore put it completely on God's wisdom to direct the shot. He said, very modestly, he was reluctant to kill them if he could help it, but those two were incorrigible villains and had led the mutiny on the ship. If they escaped, we would be finished, since they would go on board, bring the whole ship's crew and destroy us all. "Necessity justifies my advice, since it is the only way to save our lives." Seeing him still cautious of shedding blood, I told him they would go themselves, and manage as they found convenient.

In the middle of this discussion, we heard some of them wake up, and soon after we saw two of them on their feet. I asked him if either of them were the heads of the mutiny? He said no. "Then you may let them escape," I said. "Providence seems to have awakened them on purpose to save themselves. Now, if the rest escape you, it is your fault." This put him in action and he took the musket I had given him and put a pistol in his belt and his two comrades each put a piece in his hand. The two men who were with him made some noise, at which one of the seamen who was awake turned around. Seeing them coming, he cried out to the rest but was too late. The moment he cried out the two men fired – the captain wisely waited. They had so well aimed their shot at the men they knew, one of them was killed on the spot. The other was seriously wounded, but not being dead he rose to his feet and called for help to the others. The captain stepped up to him and told him it was too late to cry for help. He would call on God to forgive his villainy and with that word knocked him down with the stock of his musket, so he never spoke anymore. There were three more in the company and one of them was slightly wounded. By this time, I had joined them and when they saw their danger – and saw it was in vain to resist – they begged for mercy. The captain told them he would spare their lives if they would give him an assurance of their disgust of the treachery they had been guilty of, and would swear to be faithful to him in recovering the ship and taking her back to Jamaica. They gave him all the assertions of their sincerity that could be desired and he was willing to believe them and spare their lives – which I was not against, only I strongly suggested to keep their hands and feet tied while they were on the island.

While this was happening, I sent Friday with the captain's mate to the boat with orders to secure her and bring away the oars and sails. Eventually three straggling men, who were (happily for them) apart from the rest, came back when they heard the guns fired. Seeing the captain, who was their prisoner and now their conqueror, they agreed to be tied up as well, and so our victory was complete.

The captain and I inquired into one another's circumstances. I began first and told him my whole history, which he heard with an attention bordering on amazement, particularly the wonderful way I found provisions and ammunition. As my story is a whole collection of wonders, it affected him deeply. But when he reflected from there on himself and how I seemed to have been preserved there with the sole purpose of saving his life, tears ran down his face and he could not speak another word. After this discussion, I took him and his two men into my apartment, leading them in at the top of the house, where I refreshed them with my food and showed them all the inventions I had made during my long, long time in that place.

All I showed them and all I said to them was completely amazing. Above all, the captain admired my fortification and how perfectly I had concealed my retreat with a grove of trees, which being planted nearly twenty years earlier and growing much faster than in England, was quite the little forest, so thick that it was impassable in any part except the one side where I had made my little winding passage. I told him this was my castle and my residence, but that I also had a home in the country, as most princes have, where I could retreat on occasion and I would show him another time. Right now though our business was to consider how to recover the ship. He agreed with me, but told me he was at a loss what to do. There were still 26 men on board who, having entered into a cursed conspiracy which meant certain death if they were captured, would be hardened by desperation. They would carry it on, knowing if they were subdued they would be hanged as soon as they returned to England and so there would be no attacking them with so small a number as we were.

I pondered for some time what he had said and found it was a very rational conclusion. Therefore, something had to be decided on quickly to draw the men on board into a trap as well as prevent their coming and destroying, us. It occurred to me the ship's crew will soon start to wonder what had happened to their comrades and the boat, and would certainly come armed looking for them. The captain said this was rational. I told him the first thing we had to do was to pierce the boat on the beach so she wasn't seaworthy and take everything out of her. We went on board, took the weapons which were left and whatever else we found there – a bottle of brandy, one of rum, a few biscuit-cakes, a horn of gunpowder and a large lump of sugar, all of which was very welcome to me, especially the brandy and sugar, which I hadn't any for years.

When we had carried all these things on shore, we knocked a hole large enough in her bottom so even if they were strong enough to overcome us, they could not take the boat. I didn't really think we would be able to recover the ship but my view was, if they went away without the boat, I knew we could make her seaworthy again, at least enough to carry us to the Leeward Islands and call on our friends the Spaniards, as they were still in my thoughts.

18.

The Ship Recovered

While we were planning and had heaved the boat on the beach so the tide would not float her off, we heard the ship fire a gun and wave her ensign[134] as a signal for the boat to return. But no boat moved, and they fired several more times, making other signals for the boat. At last, when all their signals and firing proved fruitless, we saw them through my telescope hoist another boat out and row towards the shore. As they approached, we saw there were no less than ten men in her and they had firearms with them.

As the ship was almost six miles from shore, we had a full view of them as they came – even their faces. The tide put them a little to the east of the other boat and they rowed up on shore to the same place where the other had landed. Because of this we had a full view of them, and the captain knew each one and the characteristics of all the men in the boat. There were three very honest fellows who, he was sure, were led into this conspiracy by the rest. As for the boatswain and the rest, they were despicable and were no doubt made desperate by the mutiny. The captain was terribly worried they would be too powerful for us. I smiled at him and told him men in our circumstances were past fear and seeing what I had seen, whatever the consequence – life or death – would be a relief. I asked him what he thought of the circumstances of my life, and whether a rescue was not worth attempting? "And where, sir," I said, "is your belief of my being preserved here on purpose to save

---

[134] Flag

your life, which elevated you a little while ago? For my part, there seems to be only one thing wrong in all of it."

"What is that?' he asked.

"As you say there are three or four honest fellows among them who should be spared. Had they been all of the wicked part of the crew I would have thought God's wisdom had singled them out to deliver them to you, but believe me, every man who comes ashore is our own, and shall die or live as they behave to us." As I spoke with a raised voice and cheerful expression, I found it greatly encouraged him, so we vigorously went to work.

We had, on the first appearance of the boat, considered separating our prisoners and we had certainly secured them efficiently. Two of them, of whom the captain was less confident, I sent with Friday and the first mate to my cave, where they were remote enough and out of danger of being discovered. Here they left them bound but given food and candles and promised – if they stayed quietly – to give them their freedom in a day or two, but if they attempted to escape they would be put to death without mercy. They faithfully promised to patiently stay and were very thankful to have food and light.

The other prisoners were not as lucky. Two of them were kept restrained because the captain could not trust them. The other two were taken into my service on the captain's recommendation, and on their solemn oath to live and die with us. With them and the three honest men there were seven well-armed men and I had no doubt we would be able to deal with the ten who were coming, considering the captain had said there were three or four honest men among them. As soon as they got to where their other boat lay, they ran their boat on to the beach and all came on shore. I was glad to see this as I was afraid they might have left the boat anchored offshore, with some men in her to guard her and then we would not be able to seize the boat. Once on shore, the first thing they did was all run to their other boat. It was easy to see they were very surprised to find her stripped of everything and a large hole in her bottom. After they had considered this, they hollered with all their might, to try to make their companions hear but there was no point. Then they came together in a ring and fired a volley of their small arms, which we heard and the echoes made the woods ring. But it was all for nothing. Those in the cave, we were sure, could not hear and those in our keeping, though they heard it well enough, dared not answer them. They were so astonished at this – as they told us afterwards – they decided to go to their ship again and let them know the men had been murdered and the longboat damaged. They immediately launched their boat again and got on board.

The captain was amazed and confounded at this, believing they would board the ship again and set sail, giving up their comrades as lost and so he would still lose the ship he had hoped to recover.

They had not been long from shore when we noticed them all coming on shore again. They decided to leave three men in the boat and the rest go on shore, to go up into the country to look for their fellows. This was a great disappointment to us, as now we were at a loss what to do – seizing those seven men on shore would be no advantage to us if we let the boat escape. We had no choice but to wait and see what might present. The seven men came on shore and the three who remained in the boat put her off a good distance, anchoring the boat to wait for them so it was impossible for us to come at them in the boat. Those who came on shore kept close together, marching towards the top of the little hill which overlooked my home and we could see them plainly, though they could not see us. We would have been very glad if they would have come closer to us, so we could have fired at them or they would have gone farther off, so we could come out. But when they were on the brow of the hill where they could see into the valleys and woods which lay towards the northeast and where the island lay lowest. They shouted and hollered until they were weary. Not caring, it seems, to venture far from the shore or from one another, they sat down together under a tree to consider it. Had they gone to sleep there, as the other part of them had done, our job would be done, but they were too full of worry to go to sleep, though they could not tell what danger they had to fear.

The captain proposed to me that if they were to fire a volley again, we would rush them just when their pieces were discharged and they would certainly surrender and we would have them without bloodshed. I liked this proposal, provided it was done while we were near enough to come up to them before they could load their pieces again. But this did not happen and we lay still a long time, indecisive of what course to take. After a while, I told them there would be nothing done, in my opinion, until night. Then, if they did not return to the boat, perhaps we might find a way to get between them and the shore and might be able to trick those in the boat to get on shore. We impatiently waited a long time for them to move and were very uneasy when, after long consultation, we saw them all get up and march down towards the sea. It seems they had such awful fears of the danger of the place that they decided to board the ship again, give their companions up for lost and go on with their intended voyage.

As soon as I saw them go towards the shore, I imagined they had given up their search and were going back again. The captain, as soon as I told him my thoughts, was ready to sink at the thought. I proposed a strategy to get them back again and which answered my end to a tittle. I ordered Friday and the captain's mate to go over the little creek westward, towards the place where the savages came on shore when Friday was rescued. As soon as they came to a little rise about half a mile away, I told them to holler as loud as they could and wait until the seamen heard them. As soon as the seamen answer them, they would holler again and then, keeping out of sight, turn around, always answering when the others hollered, to draw them as far into the island

and among the woods as possible and then turn around again as I directed them.

They were just going into the boat when Friday and the mate hollered. They heard them and answering, ran along the shore westward towards the voice they heard. They were stopped by the creek, where the water was high and they could not get over, so called for the boat to come up and get them over, as I expected. When they had got themselves over, the boat had gone a good way into the creek and they took one of the three men out of her to go along with them, leaving only two in the boat. This was what I wished for. Immediately leaving Friday and the captain's mate to their business, I took the rest with me. Crossing the creek out of their sight, we surprised the two men before they were aware – one of them lying on the shore and the other in the boat. The fellow on shore was dozing. The captain, who was leading, ran in and knocked him down, then called out to the man in the boat to surrender or die. They needed very few arguments to persuade a single man to yield, when he saw five men on him and his comrade knocked down. Besides, this was one of the three who were not so enthusiastic in the mutiny as the rest of the crew and was easily persuaded not only to surrender but to join with us. In the meantime, Friday and the captain's mate so well managed their business with the rest that they drew them, by hollering and answering, from one hill to another and from one wood to another, until they were not only tired, but left them where they were sure they could not get back to the boat before it was dark. They were also very tired by the time they came back to us.

We had nothing to do now except watch for them in the dark and attack. It was several hours after Friday came back before they reached their boat and we could hear the leader long before, calling to those behind to hurry up. We could also hear them answer and complain how sore and tired they were and not able to come any faster, which was very welcome news to us. Finally, they came up to the boat. It is impossible to express their confusion when they found the boat aground in the creek after the tide went out and their two men gone. We could hear them call one another in a pitiful way, saying they were on an enchanted island and either there were inhabitants in it and they would all be murdered, or there were devils and spirits and they would all be carried away and devoured. They hollered again and called their two comrades by name many times, but no answer. After a while we could see them, by the little light there was, running around desperately and sometimes they would go and sit down in the boat to rest themselves, then come ashore again and do the same thing over again. My men would have loved for me to give them permission once it was dark to kill them. I was only willing to spare them and kill as few of them as I could and I was especially unwilling to risk killing any of our men, knowing the others were still well armed. I decided to wait and see if they separated and to make sure, I drew my ambush closer and ordered Friday and the captain to creep on their hands and knees, as close to the ground as they could so they wouldn't be discovered and get as close to them as they could before they fired.

They had not been long when the boatswain, who was the ringleader of the mutiny and had now shown himself the most dejected and dispirited of all, came walking towards them with two more of the crew. The captain was so eager at having this principal rogue close by, he hardly had the patience to let him come close enough to be sure. When they came closer, the captain and Friday rose to their feet and attacked. The boatswain was killed on the spot. The next man was shot in the body and fell next to him, though he did not die until an hour or two after. The third ran. At the noise of the fire I immediately advanced with my whole army, which was now eight men – myself, the generalissimo; Friday, my lieutenant-general; the captain and his two men and the three prisoners of war whom we had trusted with arms. We came on them in the dark so they could not see how many there was of us and I made the man they had left in the boat, who was now one of us, call them by name, to try to bring them to a meeting and reduce them to terms of surrender. This happened just as we desired, as their condition made them very willing to capitulate. He calls out as loud as he could to one of them, "Tom Smith! Tom Smith!"

Tom Smith answered immediately, "Is that Robinson?"

The other answered, "Aye, aye. For God's sake Tom Smith, throw down your arms and surrender or you are all dead men."

"Who must we yield to? Where are they?" asked Smith.

"Here they are," he said. "Here's our captain and fifty men with him, who have been hunting you for the last two hours. The boatswain was killed, Will Fry is wounded and I am a prisoner, and if you do not surrender, you are all done."

'Will they give us quarter[135] and then we will yield."

"I'll go and ask, if you promise to surrender," said Robinson.

He asked the captain, and the captain himself then called out, "You, Smith, you know my voice. If you lay down your arms immediately and submit, you will have your lives, all except Will Atkins."

On this Will Atkins cried out, "For God's sake captain, give me mercy. What have I done? They have all been as bad as I" – which, by the way, was not true. It seems this Will Atkins was the first man to grab the captain when they first mutinied and treated him barbarously while tying his hands and spoke in injurious language.[136] However, the captain told him he must lay down his arms and trust to the governor's mercy – which meant me, as they all called me governor. They all laid down their weapons and begged for their lives. I sent the man who had talked with them and two more, who bound them all. Then my great

---

[135] Mercy.
[136] He swore at him.

army of fifty men, which with those three was only eight, came up and seized them and their boat, though I kept myself and one more out of sight for reasons of state.

Our next work was to repair the boat and think of seizing the ship. As for the captain, now that he had leisure to discuss with them, he disagreed on the villainy of their treatment of him, the wickedness of their plan and how certainly it would bring them to misery, distress and perhaps the gallows in the end. They all appeared very penitent and begged for their lives. As for that, he told them they were not his prisoners, but the commander of the island's. They thought they had put him on shore on a barren, uninhabited island, but it had pleased God to direct them to one that was not, and the governor of the island was an Englishman. He might hang them all if he pleased, but as he had given them all mercy, he supposed he would send them to England, to be dealt with there as justice required – except Atkins, who the captain was commanded by the governor to prepare for death and he would be hanged in the morning.

Though this was all fiction, it had its desired effect. Atkins fell to his knees to beg the captain to plead with the governor for his life and all the rest begged him, for God's sake, not to be sent to England.

It now occurred to me the time of our rescue had come and it would be an easy thing to have these fellows take the ship. I retired in the dark from them, so they wouldn't see what kind of a governor they had and called the captain to me. When I called – at a good distance – one of the men was ordered to say to the captain, "Captain, the commander calls for you."

The captain replied, "Tell his excellency I am coming." This completely amazed them and they all believed the commander was nearby with his fifty men. When the captain came to me, I told him my plan for seizing the ship, which he felt was brilliant and decided to execute it the next morning. But, to accomplish it with more art and to be sure of success, I told him we must divide the prisoners. He would take Atkins and two more of the worst of them, and send them restrained to the cave where the others lay. This was committed to Friday and the two men who came on shore with the captain. They imprisoned them in the cave and it was a dismal place, especially to men in their condition. The others I ordered to my cottage. As it was fenced in and they were bound, the place was secure enough, considering they were on their best behavior.

To those men I sent the captain in the morning to meet with them, to tell me whether he thought they could be trusted to go on board and surprise the ship. He talked to them of the injury done to him, of the condition they were now in, and though the governor had mercifully spared their lives, if they were sent to England they would all be hanged in chains. If they would join us and attempt to recover the ship, he would have the governor's permission for their pardon.

Anyone may guess how readily such a proposal would be accepted by men in their condition. They fell on their knees to the captain and promised they would be faithful to him to the last drop, they would owe their lives to him and would go with him all over the world as long as they lived. "Well," said the captain, "I must go and tell the governor what you say, and see what I can do to get him to consent to it." He told me the state of mind he found them in and that he truly believed they would be faithful. However, so we might be very secure, I told him he would go back again and choose five to be his assistants and the governor would keep the other two with the three who were sent as prisoners to the castle – my cave – as hostages for the loyalty of those five. If they proved unfaithful, the five hostages would be hanged in chains on the shore. This looked severe and convinced them the governor was serious and they had no choice but to accept it. It was now the business of the prisoners, as much as of the captain, to persuade the other five to do their duty.

Our strength was now organized this way for the expedition. First, the captain, his mate, and passenger. Second, the two prisoners of the first gang, on the word of the captain, I had given their liberty and trusted them with weapons. Third, the other two who I had kept tied in my cottage until now, but on the captain's motion had now released. Fourth, these five just released, making twelve in all, except for the five we kept prisoners in the cave as hostages.

I asked the captain if he was willing to venture with these men on board the ship, but leave myself and my man Friday to watch the prisoners. I did not think it was wise of us to leave, having seven men left behind. It was hard enough for us to keep them apart and supply them with food. As to the five in the cave, I decided to leave them, though Friday went in twice a day to supply them with necessities. I made the other two carry provisions to a certain distance, from where Friday took them.

When I showed myself to the two hostages, it was with the captain, who told them I was the person the governor had ordered to look after them and it was the governor's order that they would not move unless told by me. If they did, they would be taken into the castle and held in irons. We never revealed to them I was governor. I now appeared as another person and spoke of the governor, the garrison, the castle and so on, on all occasions.

The captain now had no difficulty before him, except readying his two boats – including plugging the hole in one – and manning them. He made his passenger the captain of one with four of the men, and he, his mate and five more went in the other. They came up to the ship around midnight. As soon as they came within call of the ship, he made Robinson hail them and tell them they had brought off the men and the boat, but that it was a long time before they had found them, chatting until they came to the ship's side. The captain and the mate entering first with their weapons, immediately knocking down the second mate and carpenter with the butt-end of their muskets, followed closely behind by their men. They secured the rest of the men who were on the main and quarter decks and began to fasten the hatches, to keep down those who were below. The men on the other boat entered at the forechains,[137] secured the forecastle of the ship and the scuttle[138] which went down into the galley, making three the men they found there prisoners. When this was done and all safe on deck, the captain ordered the mate and three men to break into the roundhouse, where the new rebel captain was. He had heard the commotion and with two men and a boy had grabbed firearms. When the mate split open the door with a crowbar, the rebel captain and his men fired at them and wounded the mate with a musket ball, breaking his arm, and wounded two more of the men, but killed nobody. The mate, calling for help, rushed into the round-house, wounded as he was and with his pistol, shot the rebel captain through the head, the bullet entering at his mouth and coming out again behind one of his ears, so that he never spoke another word. At this the rest surrendered, and the ship was taken successfully without any other lives lost.

As soon as the ship was secured, the captain ordered seven guns to be fired, which was the signal agreed on to give me notice of his success. You may be sure I was very glad to hear this, having sat watching on the shore waiting until nearly two o'clock in the morning. Hearing the signal plainly, I laid down. Being a very fatiguing day, I slept very sound until I was surprised with the noise of a gun. Startled, I heard a man call me "Governor! Governor!" I knew the captain's voice. Climbing to the top of the hill, there he stood and pointing to the ship, he embraced me in his arms, "My dear friend and deliverer," he said. "There's your ship. She is all yours and so are we, and all that belong to her."

---

[137] The forward chains of a ship.
[138] A small hatchway in the deck of a ship

I looked at the ship and there she was, less than half a mile from shore. At first, I was ready to sink down with the surprise. I saw my escape visibly put into my hands, all things easy and a large ship ready to take me away where I pleased. For some time, I was not able to answer him, but as he had taken me in his arms I held close to him, or I would have fallen to the ground. He understood the surprise, and immediately pulled a bottle out of his pocket and gave me a swig of liqueur, which he had brought on purpose for me. After I had drunk it, I sat down on the ground. Though it brought me to myself, it was a good while before I could speak a word to him. All this time the poor man was as ecstatic as me. He said a thousand kind things to me, so I could compose myself. But the flood of joy in my chest put all my spirits into confusion. At last I broke into tears and a little while after I recovered my speech. Then I embraced him as my deliverer and we celebrated together. I told him he was sent by Heaven to deliver me and the whole transaction seemed to be a chain of wonders. Such things were the testimonies we had of a secret hand of Providence governing the world and evidence the eye of an infinite Power could search into the remotest corner of the world and send help to the miserable whenever He pleased. I did not forget to lift my heart in thankfulness to Heaven, because what heart would not bless Him, who had not only provided for me in such a wilderness, but from whom every relief must always be acknowledged.

When we had talked a while, the captain told me he had brought me a little refreshment – such as the ship had – and such as the wretches who had been so long his masters had not plundered. He called out to the boat and told his men to bring ashore the things that were for the governor. It was as if I was not going to be leaving with them, but as if I was staying on the island. First, he brought me a case of bottles full of excellent liqueurs, six very large bottles of Madeira wine, two pounds of excellent tobacco, twelve good pieces of the ship's beef and six pieces of pork, a bag of peas, and about a hundred pounds of biscuit. He also brought me a box of sugar, a box of flour, a bag full of lemons, two bottles of lime juice and an abundance of other things. Besides these – and a thousand times more useful to me – he brought me six clean new shirts, six very good neckcloths, two pair of gloves, one pair of shoes, a hat and one pair of stockings, as well as a very good suit of his own, which he had barely worn. In other words, he clothed me from head to foot. It was a very kind and delightful present – as anyone may imagine to one in my circumstances – but is unbelievable how such a kind present could be so unpleasant, awkward and uneasy as it was to me to wear such clothes at first.

After these ceremonies were past and after all his good things were brought into my little apartment, we began to consult what was to be done with the prisoners. It was worth considering if we should take them with us or not, especially two of them, who he knew were hopelessly rebellious to the last degree. The captain said he knew they were such rogues that there was no changing them and if he did take them it must be in irons, as criminals, to be delivered over to justice at the first English colony he came to. I found the captain was very anxious about it. I told him if he desired, I would ask the two men if they wanted to be left on the island. "I would be very glad if you would do that," said the captain.

"I will send for them and talk with them for you." I had Friday and the two former hostages – as their comrades kept their promise – go to the cave and bring up the five men, restrained as they were, to the cottage and keep them there until I came. After some time, I came there dressed in my new clothes and now I was called governor again. With the captain by my side, I had the men brought before me and I told them I had a full account of their villainous behavior to the captain, how they had run away with the ship and were preparing to commit further robberies, but Providence had trapped them and they had fallen into the pit which they had dug for others. I let them know by my orders the ship had been seized and they would soon see their new "captain" had received the reward for his villainy and they would see him hanging from the yardarm. As to them, I wanted to know why I should not execute them as pirates, as by my rank they could not doubt I had authority to do.

One of them answered for the rest and they had nothing to say except: when they were taken, the captain promised them their lives and they humbly begged for mercy. I told them I didn't know what mercy I could show them, as I had decided to leave the island with all my men and was going with the captain to England. As for the captain, he could not take them to England except as prisoners in irons to be tried for mutiny, the consequence of which, they must know, would be the gallows. I could not say what was best for them, unless they wanted to take their chances on the island. If they wanted that, as I was leaving the island, I was inclined to spare their lives, if they thought they could live on shore. They seemed very thankful for it and said they would much rather stay there than be taken to England to be hanged.

However, the captain seemed to have some difficulty and did not want to leave them there. I was a little angry with the captain and told him they were my prisoners, not his. I would be good to my word and if he did not consent to it, I would set them free as I found them, and if he did not like it he could catch them again – if he could. On this they appeared very thankful and I set them free. I told them to go into the woods, to the place where they came and I would leave them some firearms, some ammunition and some directions how they could live well if they thought fit. After this, I prepared to go on board the ship but told the captain I would stay that last night to prepare my things. I told him to go on board in the meantime, to keep all right in the ship, and send the boat on shore the next day for me. Also, I ordered him, at all cost, to take the dead rebel captain and hang him from the yardarm, so these men would see him.

When the captain was gone I called the men to my apartment and had a serious discussion with them on their circumstances. I told them they had made a right choice. If the captain had taken them away, it is certain they would be hanged. I showed them the rebel captain hanging from the yardarm of the ship and told them they could expect the same.

When they had all declared their willingness to stay, I told them I would let them into the story of my living there, to make it easy for them. I gave them the whole history of the place and of my coming to it. I showed them my fortifications, the way I made my bread, planted my grain, cured my grapes and all that was necessary to make their lives easy. I also told them the story of the seventeen Spaniards who were to be expected, for whom I left a letter and made them promise to treat them the same as each other. Here it may be noted the captain, who had ink on board, was greatly surprised I never hit on a way of making ink from charcoal and water, as I had done things much more difficultly.

I left them my firearms – five muskets, three shotguns and three swords. I still had more than a barrel of gunpowder left – after the first year I used only a little and wasted none. I gave them a description of the way I managed the goats, directions to milk and fatten them and to make both butter and cheese. I gave them every part of my own story and told them I would ask the captain to leave them two more barrels of gunpowder and some garden seeds, which I told them I wished I had. Also, I gave them the bag of peas the captain had brought me to eat and told them to be sure and plant them.

19.

Return to England

Having done all this I left them the next day and went on board the ship. We immediately prepared to sail, but did not leave that night. Early the next morning, two of the five we were leaving on the island swam to the ship's side, complaining bitterly about the other three. For God's sake, they begged to be taken on board, fearing they would be murdered. The captain pretended to have no power without me. After some difficulty, and their solemn promises to change, they were taken on board. They were thoroughly whipped, after which they proved very honest and quiet fellows.

Sometime after this, the longboat was ordered on shore with the things promised to the men. To this the captain – at my request – had their chests and clothes added, which they took and were very thankful for. I also encouraged them, telling them if I could send a vessel to rescue them, I would not forget them.

When I left this island, I carried on board as mementos the goatskin cap I had made, my umbrella and one of my parrots. Also, I didn't forget to take the money I mentioned earlier, which had uselessly been with me so long, it had now grown tarnished and could hardly pass for silver until it had been rubbed and handled. And so, I left the island on the 19th of December – as I found by the ship's account – 1686, after I had been on the island 28 years, two months and nineteen days, rescued from this second captivity the same day of the month I escaped in the longboat from the Moors of Salé. After a long voyage, I arrived in England June 11, 1687, having been absent for 35 years.

When I came to England it was as if I had never been known there. My benefactor and faithful steward, whom I had trusted my money with, was alive but had fallen on bad luck. She had become a widow a second time and was very low in the world. I made sure she didn't worry about what she owed me, assuring her I would give her no trouble. On the contrary, in gratitude for her former care and faithfulness to me, I helped her as my little stock could afford – which at that time would allow me to do only a little for her. I assured her I would never forget her kindness to me, and I didn't forget her when I had sufficient funds to help her. After, I went down to Yorkshire, but my father and mother were dead and family was extinct, except I found two sisters and two children from one of my brothers. As I had been given up for dead long ago, there had been no provision made for me, so I found nothing to relieve or assist me, and the little money I had would not do much for me to settle in the world.

I did meet with one piece of gratitude which I did not expect. The master of the ship – who I had so happily rescued, as well as his ship and cargo – gave an excellent account to the ship's owners of how I had saved the lives of the men and the ship. They invited me to meet them and some other merchants. Together, they complimented me on my performance and presented me with almost £200.[139]

But looking back on the circumstances of my life and how little this would go towards settling me in the world, I decided to go to Lisbon and see if I could get some information on the state of my plantation in the Brazils, and what became of my partner who – I had reason to suppose – had also given me up for dead. I went to Lisbon, where I arrived in April 1688, my man Friday reliably accompanying me in all these ramblings and proving a most faithful servant on all occasions. When I came to Lisbon, to my satisfaction I found my old friend, the

---

[139] Relative to the average wages of a worker, this would be worth £388,800 in 2017.

captain of the ship who first rescued me off the shore of Africa. He had now grown old and no longer sailed, having put his son – who was not a young man – into his ship, and who still used the Brazil trade. The old man did not know me and indeed I hardly knew him. But soon he remembered me when I told him who I was.

After some powerful expressions of the old acquaintance between us, I inquired about my plantation and my partner. The old man told me he had not been in the Brazils for about nine years, but he could assure me when he left, my partner was still alive. The trustees I had left were both dead, though he believed I would have a very good account of the improvement of the plantation. On the belief I had drowned, my trustees had given my plantation over to the procurator-fiscal,[140] who had seized it, giving one-third to the king and two-thirds to the monastery of St. Augustine, to be expended for the benefit of the poor and for the conversion of the Indians to the Catholic faith. If I or anyone appeared to claim the inheritance it would be restored, though the annual production, being distributed to charitable uses, could not be restored. He assured me the agent of the king's land revenue and the steward of the monastery had taken great care all along that every year my partner gave a faithful account of the produce, of which they had received my part. I asked him if he knew how well the plantation was doing and whether he thought it would be worth looking after or if I went there, would I have a problem getting my fair half of the produce. He didn't know to what degree the plantation was improved, but he did know my partner was now exceedingly rich from his part of it and, to the best of his memory, he had heard the king's third – which was granted to some other monastery – amounted to more than two hundred moidores[141] a year. As to me possessing it again, there was no

---

[140] Coroner or public prosecutor.
[141] About £23,600 today.

question. My partner was still alive to witness my title and my name was enrolled in the register of the Brazils. He told me the survivors of my two trustees were very fair, honest people and very wealthy, and he believed I would not only have their assistance, but would find a very considerable sum of my money in their trust, being the farm's production while their fathers held the trust before it was given up which, as he remembered, was for about twelve years.

I was a little concerned and uneasy at this explanation and asked the old captain why the trustees would dispose of my effects like this, when he knew I had made my will and had made him my heir.

He told me that was true, but as there was no proof I was dead, he could not act as executor until they were certain of my death. Besides, he was not willing to meddle with something so remote. He had registered my will and put in his claim. He could have given any account of my being dead and taken possession of the ingenio – as they call the sugar-house – and given his son, who was now at the Brazils, orders to execute it. "But," the old man said, "I have one piece of news to tell you, which you may not like. Believing you were lost, your partner and trustees did offer to me the first six or eight years' profits, which I received. At that time there was large disbursements for increasing the facilities – building an ingenio and buying slaves – and it did not amount to nearly as much as it produced after that. However, I will give you a true account of what I have received and how I have disposed of it."

After a few more days talking with this ancient friend, he brought me an account of the first six years' income from my plantation, signed by my partner and trustees, and always delivered in goods, such as bales of tobacco, chests of sugar, rum, molasses and other by-products of a sugar plantation. Every year the income increased considerably but, as the expenditures were large, at first the sum was small. The old man let me see he was in debt to me for 470 moidores of gold, as well as sixty chests of sugar and fifteen double rolls of tobacco, which were lost in his ship when he was shipwrecked coming home to Lisbon about 25 years ago. The good man then began to complain of his misfortunes and how he had been forced to use my money to recover his losses and buy a share in a new ship. "My old friend," he said, "I will not leave you penniless. As soon as my son returns from the Brazils you will be fully satisfied." He pulled out an old pouch and gave me 160 Portugal moidores in gold and title to the ship – he owned one-quarter – and put both in my hands as security for the rest.

I was too moved with the honesty and kindness of the poor man to be able to bear this. Remembering what he had done for me, how he had rescued me at sea, how generously he had treated me on all occasions and particularly how sincere a friend he was now to me, I could hardly stop weeping. I asked him if his circumstances allowed him to spare so much money right now and if it would hinder him? He told me it might be a little difficult for him, but it was my money and I would want it more than he.

Everything the good man said was full of warmth and I could barely hold back my tears while he spoke. I ended up taking 100 moidores and asked for a pen and ink to give him a receipt for them. I gave him back the rest, and told him if I ever had possession of the plantation I would return the other to him as well – which I unquestionably did afterwards. As to the bill of sale from his son's ship, I would not take it by any means. If I wanted the money, he was honest enough to pay me.

When this was done, the old man asked me how I would claim my plantation. I told him I would go over there myself. He said I could do so if I pleased, but if I did not want to, there were ways to secure my rights and immediately have the profits. As there were ships in Lisbon ready to go to Brazil, he made me enter my name in a public register, with his affidavit swearing I was alive and I was the same person who bought the land for the plantation. This was proven by a notary and he directed me to send it – with a letter in his writing – to a merchant he knew there, then suggested I stay with him until an account returned.

Never was anything more honorable than these proceedings. In less than seven months I received a large packet from my trustees' survivors and the merchants who I went to sea for originally, in which was the following:

An account of the production of my plantation, from the six years when their fathers had balanced with my old Portugal captain. The balance appeared to be 1,174 moidores in my favor. Secondly, there was the account of four more years, before the government stepped in. The balance of this, as the value of the plantation increased, was 19,446 crusadoes, or about 3,240 moidores. Thirdly, there was the Prior of St. Augustine's account, who had received the profits for over fourteen years. The prior[142] was not able to account for what was disposed of by the hospital and very honestly declared he had 872 moidores not distributed, which he acknowledged was mine. The government refunded nothing.

There was a letter from my partner, congratulating me very warmly on my being alive, giving me an account of how the estate was improved and what it produced a year. He included particulars on how many acres, what was planted and how many slaves there were on it. Making twenty-two crosses for blessings, he told me he had said many AVE MARIAS to thank the Blessed Virgin that I was alive. He very eagerly invited me to come over and take possession of my share and in the meantime to give him orders where he could deliver my possessions if I did not come myself. He concluded the letter with a sincere declaration of his friendship and that of his family, and sent as a present seven fine leopards' skins, which he had received from Africa – by some other ship which, it seems, had made a better voyage than me. He also

---

[142] Head of a Prior, like an abbot to an abbey.

sent me five chests of excellent candies and a hundred pieces of gold, not quite as large as moidores. By the same fleet my two trustees shipped me 1,100 chests of sugar, eight hundred rolls of tobacco and the rest of the whole account in gold.

I can say now the latter end of Job was better than the beginning. It is impossible to express the feelings in my heart when I found all my wealth around me – as the Brazil ships come in fleets, the same ships which brought my letters brought my goods, which were safe in Lisbon before the letters were in my hand. I turned pale and grew sick, and if the old man hadn't run and fetched me a liqueur, I believe the sudden surprise of joy would have killed me on the spot. After that I was actually very ill for some time until a physician was sent for. When the real cause of my illness was known, he ordered me to be let blood, after which I had relief and grew well. I truly believe though, if I had not been eased by a vent given in that manner to the spirits, I would have died.

I was now master of over £5,000[143] sterling and had an estate in the Brazils, making over £1,000 a year, which was as good as in England. I was now in a condition which I barely knew how to understand or how to compose myself for the enjoyment of it. The first thing I did was to pay back my good old captain, who had been charitable to me in my distress, kind to me in my beginning, and honest to me at the end. I showed him all that was sent to me and told him that, next to the wisdom of Heaven, it was all due to him. Now it was my duty to reward him, which I would do a hundred times over. First, I returned the hundred moidores. Then I sent for a notary, and had him draw up a general release from the 470 moidores he owed me, in the fullest and firmest manner possible. After that I had a document drawn up, empowering him to be the receiver of the annual profits of my plantation, and made a grant of one hundred moidores a year to him

---

[143] About £825,000 today.

during his life and fifty moidores a year to his son after him for life. I was now even with the old man.

I now had to consider which way to steer my course and what to do with the estate Providence had put into my hands. I had more to deal with now than I had in my time on the island where I wanted nothing except what I had, and had nothing except what I wanted. Now I had a great responsibility and my business was how to secure it. I didn't have a cave now to hide my money in or a place where it might lie without lock or key, until it grew moldy and tarnished before anybody would meddle with it. On the contrary, I didn't know where to put it or who to trust with it. My old patron – the captain – was honest and that was the only refuge I had. My interest in the Brazils seemed to summon me there, but I could not think of going there until I had settled my affairs and left my effects in some safe hands behind me. At first, I thought of my old friend the widow, who I knew was honest and would be fair to me, but she was much older, poor and for all I knew might be in debt, so I had no alternative but to go back to England myself and take my effects with me.

It was some months before I decided this and as I had rewarded the old captain fully to his satisfaction, I began to think of the poor widow, whose husband had been my first benefactor and she, while it was in her power, my faithful steward and instructor. The first thing I did was get a merchant in Lisbon to write to his correspondent in London, not only to pay a bill, but to go find her and take her £100 from me and to talk with her, and comfort her in her poverty by telling her she would, if I lived, have a further supply. At the same time, I sent my two sisters in the country £100 each. They were not poor, but were not in very good circumstances – one was a widow and the other had a husband who was not as kind to her as he should be. But among all my relations or acquaintances I could not decide who I should give the majority of my wealth so I could go to the Brazils and leave things safely behind. This puzzled me greatly.

I once had a mind to go to the Brazils and settle there, as I was naturalized to the place, but I had some doubt in my mind about religion, which pulled me back. However, it was not religion that kept me from going there right now. As I had made no qualm of being openly Catholic while I was among them, when I began to think of living and dying among them, I began to regret having professed myself a Papist[144] and thought it might not be the best religion to die with.

But as I have said, this was not the main thing that kept me from going to the Brazils. I decided at last to go to England where, if I arrived, I would make some acquaintance or find some relations who would be faithful to me. So, I prepared to go to England with all my wealth.

To prepare for going home, I first decided to answer the letters giving a fair and faithful account of things I had from the Brazils. To the Prior of St. Augustine, I wrote a letter full of thanks for his unbiased dealings and the offer of the 872 moidores which he had not disbursed. I wanted five hundred given to the monastery and the rest to the poor, desiring the good padre's prayers for me. I next wrote a letter of thanks to my two trustees, with all the acknowledgment so much justice and honesty called for. As for sending them any present, they were far above having any need for it. Lastly, I wrote to my partner, recognizing his industriousness in improving the plantation and his integrity in increasing the worth of the sugar-works. I gave him instructions for his future management of my portion and to send whatever became due to the old captain, until he heard from me more specifically, assuring him it was my intention to settle there for the remainder of my life. To this I added a very attractive present of some Italian silks for his wife and

---

[144] Derogatory term for Catholic.

two daughters, with two pieces of fine English broadcloth[145] – the best I could get in Lisbon – five pieces of black felt and some Flanders lace of a good value.

Having settled my affairs, sold my cargo and turned all my belongings into bills of exchange,[146] my next difficulty was which way to go to England. I was accustomed to the sea and yet, I had a strange aversion to go to England by sea at that time, though I could give no reason for it. The anxiety grew on me, and though I had shipped my baggage, I changed my mind – not once but three times.

It is true I had been very unfortunate traveling by sea and this might be one of the reasons, but let no man brush off the strong impulses of his own thoughts in these instances. Two of the ships I would have traveled on, and on which my baggage traveled came to misfortune. One was taken by the Algerines[147] and the other was lost on the Start, near Torbay and everyone drowned except three.

Stressed in my thoughts, my old captain, compelled me not to go by sea, but either by land to the Groyne,[148] and cross over the Bay of Biscay to La Rochelle in France, where it was an easy and safe journey by land to Paris, then to Calais and Dover, or to go up to Madrid, and all the way by land through France. I was so biased against going by sea at all, except from Calais to Dover, that I decided to travel all the way by land. As I was not in a hurry and did not mind the cost, this was by far the more pleasant way. To make it more so, my old captain brought an English gentleman, the son of a merchant in Lisbon, who was willing to travel with me. After, we picked up two more English merchants and two young Portuguese gentlemen, the last only going to Paris. In all there were six of us and five servants – the two merchants and the two

---

145 Fine twilled cotton.
146 Promissory note or IOU.
147 Algerians.
148 Present-day A Coruña, a city in Galicia, Spain.

Portuguese, contenting themselves with two servants in total, to save money. As for me, I got an English sailor to travel with me as a servant, besides my man Friday, who was too much a stranger to be a servant on the road.

In this style, I set out from Lisbon. Our company being very well mounted and armed, we made a little troop and they did me the honor of calling me captain, because I was the oldest man, as well as I had two servants and was the origin of the whole journey. As I have not bothered you with any of my sea journals, I will also not bother you now with my land journals, but some adventures that happened to us in this tedious and difficult journey I must not forget.

Being strangers to Spain, when we came to Madrid we wanted to see the court of Spain and what was worth observing. But since it was the latter part of the summer, we rushed away and set out from Madrid around the middle of October. When we came to the edge of Navarre, we were alarmed at several towns on the way when we heard so much snow was falling on the French side of the mountains, that several travelers were forced to come back to Pamplona after having attempted the hazardous crossing.

When we came to Pamplona itself, we found it was true, and to me – who was used to a hot climate where I could barely put any clothes on – the cold was insufferable. It was more painful than surprising to be ten days out of Old Castile, where the weather was not only warm but very hot, and immediately feel a wind from the Pyrenees so severely cold that is was intolerable and we were in danger of losing our fingers and toes to frostbite.

Poor Friday was really frightened when he saw the mountains covered with snow and felt cold weather, which he had never seen or felt before in his life. To make matters worse, when we came to Pamplona it continued snowing with so much violence and so long, the people said winter had come before its time. The roads, which were difficult before, were now quite impassable. The snow lay in some places too thick for us to travel, and being not hard frozen, as is the case in the northern countries, we couldn't go without being in danger of being buried alive. We stayed at least twenty days at Pamplona with no likelihood of getting better – it was the most severe winter all over Europe in memory – so I proposed we go to Fontarabia and from there take a ship to Bordeaux, which was a very small voyage. But, while I was considering this, four French gentlemen came in. While stopped on the French side of the pass, they had found out a guide who had brought them over the mountains so they were not very inconvenienced by the snow, crossing the country near Languedoc. Where they met snow in any quantity, they said it was frozen hard enough to hold them and their horses. We sent for this guide, who told us he would take us the same way with no threat from the snow, provided we were sufficiently armed to protect ourselves from wild beasts. He said in these heavy snows it was frequent for some wolves to show themselves at the foot of the mountains, starving from a lack of food. We told him we were well prepared for such creatures if he would keep us from the two-legged wolves, which we were told we were in most danger from, especially on the French side of the mountains. He satisfied us there was no danger of that kind the way we were going, so we willingly agreed to follow him, as did the twelve other gentlemen and their servants who had been forced to come back again.

We set out from Pamplona with our guide on the 15th of November. I was surprised when, instead of going forward, he took us back twenty miles on the same road we came from Madrid on. We passed two rivers and came into the plains and found ourselves in a warm climate again, where the country was pleasant and no snow to be seen. He made a sudden turn to his left and approached the mountains another way. Though it is true the hills and precipices looked dreadful, he made so many detours, meandered and led us by such a winding way, that we obliviously passed the height of the mountains without being burdened with the snow and unexpectedly he showed us the pleasant and fruitful provinces of Languedoc and Gascony – green and flourishing, though at a great distance – and we had some rough way to still pass.

We were a little uneasy, however, when we found it snowed one whole day and night so fast that we could not travel, but he told us to stay calm and we would soon be past it all. Indeed, we began to descend every day and to come more north than before and so, relying on our guide, we went on.

It was about two hours before night and our guide was ahead of us and just out of sight when three monstrous wolves rushed out – and after them a bear – from a hollow way adjoining to a thick forest. Two of the wolves headed for the guide and had he been farther ahead, he would have been devoured before we could have helped him. One of them fastened on his horse and the other attacked the man with such violence that he didn't have the time or presence of mind to draw his pistol, but hollered and cried out to us at the top of his voice. My man Friday was next to me and I told him to ride up and see what was the matter. As soon as Friday saw the man, he hollered out as loud as the other, "O master! O master!" but like a bold fellow, rode directly up to the poor man and with his pistol shot the wolf in the head that attacked him.

It was lucky for the poor man that it was my man Friday. Being used to such creatures in his country, he had no fear of them, instead going up close to him and shot it, while any other of us would have fired at a farther distance and perhaps either missed the wolf or shot the man.

It was enough to have terrified a bolder man than I. Undeniably, it alarmed all our company when, with the noise of Friday's pistol, we heard on both sides the most dismal howling of wolves. The noise, doubled by the echo of the mountains, appeared as if there was an extraordinary number of them and perhaps there was only a few and we had no cause for concern. However, as Friday had killed this wolf, the other that had fastened on the horse fled, without doing any damage, having happily fastened on his head where the studs of the bridle had stuck in its teeth. But the man was badly hurt, as the raging creature had bit him twice, once in the arm and the other time a little above his knee. Though he had made some defense, he was trying to stay on his horse when Friday came up and shot the wolf.

The noise of Friday's pistol made us quicken our pace and we rode up as fast as the way, which was very difficult, would allow us. As soon as we were clear of the trees, we clearly saw what had happened and how Friday had helped the poor guide, though we did not immediately determine what kind of creature he had killed.

20.

Fight Between Friday and a Bear

Never was a fight managed so bravely and in such a surprising manner as that which followed between Friday and the bear, which gave us all – though at first we were surprised and afraid for him – the greatest diversion imaginable.

As the bear is a heavy, clumsy creature and does not gallop as the wolf does, he has two particular qualities, which generally rule his actions. First, men are not his proper prey – he usually does not attempt them unless they attack first him or he is excessively hungry. If you do not meddle with him, he will not meddle with you. But you must take care to be very civil to him and give him the road, since he is a very nice gentleman. He will not go a step out of his way for a prince. If you are really afraid, your best to look another way and keep on going. Sometimes if you stop, stand still and look constantly at him, he takes it as an insult. If you throw or toss anything at him, even a bit of stick as big as your finger, he thinks himself abused and sets all other business aside to pursue his revenge and will have satisfaction on this point of honor. That is his first quality. His second major one is if he is offended once, he will never leave you – night and day – until he has his revenge and will follow you at a good round rate until he overtakes you.

My man Friday had rescued our guide and when we came up to him he was helping the hurt and frightened man off his horse. Suddenly, we spied the bear come out of the woods and a monstrous one it was, the biggest by far I had ever seen. We were all surprised when we saw him, but when Friday saw him, it was easy to see joy and courage in the fellow's expression. "O! O! O!" Friday said, pointing to him. "O master, you let me go, me shakee the hand with him. Me makee you good laugh."

I was surprised to see the fellow so pleased. "You fool," I said, "he will eat you up."

"Eatee me up! eatee me up!" said Friday, "me eatee him up. Me makee you good laugh. You all stay here, me show you good laugh." So down he steps and takes off his boots and a moment later puts on a pair of pumps – as we call the flat shoes they wear and which he had in his pocket. He gave my other servant his horse and with his gun he ran, swift like the wind.

The bear was walking softly away and didn't interfere with us, until Friday coming close called out to him, as if the bear could understand him. "Hark ye,[149] hark ye," Friday said. "Me speakee with you." We followed at a distance, since we were on the Gascony side of the mountains and entered a vast forest, where the country was plain and pretty open, though it had many trees scattered here and there. Friday came up to the bear quickly. He picked up a large stone and threw it at him, hitting him on the head. He did him no more harm than if he had thrown it against a wall. It answered Friday's goal though. The rogue was so devoid of fear that he did it purely to make the bear follow him and show us some laugh, as he called it. As soon as the bear felt the blow and saw him, he turned around and came after him, taking very long strides and shuffling on at a strange rate which would have put a horse to an ordinary gallop. Away ran Friday and he headed towards us as if he was running for help. We all decided to fire at the same time on the bear and rescue my man, though I was angry at him for bringing the

---

[149] Listen you!

bear back towards us when he was going about his own business another way. I was especially angry when he turned the bear toward us, then ran away. I called out, "You dog! Is this you making us laugh? Come here and take your horse, so we can shoot the creature."

He heard me and cried out, "No shoot, no shoot. Stand still and you get much laugh."' As the nimble creature ran two feet to the bear's one, he turned suddenly on one side of us, and seeing a large oak fit for his purpose, he signaled us to follow. Doubling his pace, he nimbly got up the tree, laying his gun down on the ground about five or six yards from the bottom of the tree. The bear soon came to the tree and we followed at a distance. The first thing he did was stop at the gun and smell it, but he left it and scrambled into the tree, climbing like a cat, though a monstrously heavy one. I was amazed at the foolishness of my man and could not for the life of me see anything to laugh at, until seeing the bear get up the tree, we all rode near to him.

When we arrived at the tree, there was Friday on the small end of a large branch and the bear about halfway to him. As soon as the bear got out to that part where the limb was weaker, he said "Ha! Now you see me teachee the bear dance." He began jumping and shaking the bough and the bear began to totter, but stood still and began to look behind him, to see how he would get back. We laughed heartily. But Friday was not done with him. Seeing him stand still, he called out to him again, as if he had supposed the bear could speak English, "What, you come no farther? You come farther." He stopped jumping and shaking the tree and the bear, as if he understood what he said, did come a little farther. Then he began jumping again and the bear stopped again. We thought now was a good time to knock him in the head, and called to Friday to stand still and we would shoot the bear. But he cried out seriously, "Please! Please! No shoot, me shoot soon enough." To make a long story short, Friday danced so much and the bear stood so awkward, we continued laughing, but still could not imagine what the fellow would do. At first, we thought he hoped to shake the bear off, but we found the bear was too cunning for that. He would not go out far enough to be thrown down, but instead held on with his broad claws and feet, so we could not imagine what would be the end of it and what the joke would be at last. But Friday put us out of doubt quickly. Seeing the bear clinging to the bough and he would not be persuaded to come any farther, "Well, well," Friday said, "you no come farther, me go. You no come to me, me come to you." and he went out to the smaller end, where it would bend with his weight and gently let himself down, sliding down the bough until he came close enough to jump down on his feet. He ran to his gun, picked it up and stood still.

"Well Friday," I said to him, "what will you do now? Why don't you shoot him?"

"No shoot,' he replied, "no yet. Me shoot now, me no kill. Me stay, give you one more laugh." And so, he did. When the bear saw his enemy had left, he came back from the bough where he stood, but did it very cautiously, looking behind him every step and coming backward until he got into the body of the tree. Then, with his hind end first, he came down the tree, grasping it with his claws and moving one foot at a time, very leisurely. Just before he could set his hind foot on the ground, Friday stepped up close to him, clapped the muzzle of his piece into his ear and shot him dead. Then the rogue turned around to see if we did not laugh and when he saw we were pleased, he began to laugh very loud. "How we kill bear in my country," says Friday.

"That's how you kill them?" I asked. "You have no guns."

"No," he said, "no gun, but shoot great much long arrow."

This was a good diversion for us, but we were still in a wild place and our guide was still badly hurt and we barely knew what to do next. The howling of wolves ran through my head and except the noise I once heard on the shore of Africa, I never heard anything that filled me with so much horror.

These things, and the approach of night, called us off or else Friday would have had us take the skin of this monstrous creature off – which was worth saving – but we had almost ten miles to go and our guide hurried us along, so we left him and went forward on our journey.

The ground was still covered with snow, though not so deep and dangerous as on the mountains. We heard afterwards the ravenous creatures were coming down into the forest and plain country, pressed by hunger to look for food and had caused a lot of trouble in the villages, where they surprised the country people, killed many sheep and horses and some people too. We had one dangerous place to pass and our guide told us if there were more wolves we would find them there. This was a small plain, surrounded by woods on every side and a long, narrow lane, which we were to pass to get through, then we would come to the village where we were to lodge. It was half-an-hour until sunset when we entered the woods and a little after sunset when we came into the plain. We met with nothing in the first woods, except in a little meadow where we saw five large wolves cross the road full speed, one after another, as if they were chasing some prey. They took no notice of us and were gone out of sight in a few moments. Our guide, who was a fainthearted fellow, told us to keep alert, since he believed there were more wolves coming. We kept our weapons ready and our eyes watching, but we saw no more wolves until we came through that wood and entered the plain. As soon as we came into the plain, we were able to look around us. The first thing we saw was a dead horse – or more exact, a poor horse which the wolves had killed and at least a dozen of them were still at work picking his bones clean. We did not think it was a good idea to disturb them at their feast and they didn't take much notice of us. Friday would have attacked them, but I would not tolerate this, as I thought we were more likely to have other business on our hands.

We were barely halfway over the plain when we began to hear the wolves howl in the woods on our left in a horrifying manner. Soon after we saw about a hundred coming directly towards us, most of them in a line, as regularly as an army drawn up by experienced officers. I barely knew how to deal them, but found the only way was to draw ourselves close together. So there wouldn't be too much interval, I ordered every other man to fire and the others would stand ready to give them a second volley immediately if they continued to advance on us. Those who had fired first would not load their fusee again, but stand ready with a pistol, as we were all armed with a fusee and a pair of pistols each. This way we were able to fire six volleys at a time. However, we had no necessity. After firing the first volley, the enemy made a full stop, terrified with the noise as well as with the fire. Four of them were shot in the head and dropped. Several others were wounded and went bleeding off, as we could see by the snow. They stopped, but did not immediately retreat. Remembering I had been told the fiercest creatures were terrified at the voice of a man, I had everyone holler as loud as they could. The notion was not altogether wrong, because they began to retreat and turn around. I then ordered a second volley to be fired in their rear, which made them gallop and away they went to the woods. This gave us leisure to reload our pieces again and so we didn't lose any time, we kept going. We had just loaded our fusees and made ourselves ready when we heard a terrible noise in the same woods on our left, only it was farther onward and the same way we were going.

Night was coming and the light began to be dusky, which made it worse on our side. The noise increasing, we could easily distinguish it was the howling and yelling of those hellish creatures. Suddenly, we saw three troops of wolves, one on our left, one behind us and one in our front, and we seemed to be surrounded by them. However, as they did not attack us, we kept moving forward as fast as we could make our horses go which, the way being very rough, was only a good hard trot.

We were in view of the entrance of the woods through which we were to pass at the farther side of the plain. But we were greatly surprised, when coming nearer the lane, we saw a confused number of wolves standing just at the entrance. Unexpectedly, at another opening of the woods, we heard the noise of a gun and looking that way, out rushed a horse with a saddle and bridle on him, flying like the wind, and about sixteen wolves full speed after him. The horse had the advantage, but as we supposed he could not hold it at that rate, we didn't doubt they would catch up with him.

Here we had a horrible sight. Riding up to the entrance where the horse came out, we found the carcasses of another horse and two men, devoured by the ravenous creatures. One of the men was no doubt the same we heard fire the gun, since there was a gun just by him recently fired. As to the man, his head and the upper part of his body was eaten. This filled us with horror and we didn't know what course to take. The creatures made our decision for us, as they gathered around us quickly, in hopes of prey. I truly believe there were three hundred of them. At the entrance into the woods there lay some large timber, which had been cut down the summer before. I drew my little troop in among those trees, and placing ourselves in a line behind one long tree, I advised them all to dismount and keeping that tree in front of us as a breastwork,[150] stand in a triangle, enclosing our horses in the center. We did so and it was well we did. Never was there a more furious charge than what the creatures made on us in this place. They came on with a growling kind of noise and mounted the piece of timber, as if they were only rushing on their prey. This fury of theirs was mainly caused by their seeing our horses behind us. I ordered our men to fire as before, every other man. They took their aim so sure that they killed several of the wolves at the first volley, but there was a necessity to keep a

---

[150] A low temporary defense

continual firing, since they came on like devils, those behind pushing on those in front.

When we had fired a second volley of our fusees, we thought they stopped a little and I hoped they would have gone off. Our respite was brief and others came forward again, so we fired two volleys from our pistols. I believe in these four firings we had killed about eighteen of them and injured twice as many, and yet, they came on again. I was reluctant to spend our shot too hastily, so I called my servant – not my man Friday, as he was better employed quickly reloading my fusee and his own while we were engaged. I called my other man, and giving him a horn of gunpowder, I had him lay a wide line along the piece of timber. He did so, and barely had time to get away when the wolves came up to it. I snapped the flint from an unloaded pistol close to the powder and set it on fire. Those that were on the timber were scorched and seven of them jumped in among us with the force and fright of the fire. We dispatched these in an instant and the rest were so frightened with the light, which the night made more terrible, they drew back. At this, I ordered our last pistols to be fired off in one volley and after that we gave a shout. The wolves turned tail and we immediately charged on nearly twenty wounded ones we found struggling on the ground and cut them with our swords. The crying and howling they made was better understood by their fellows, so they all fled.

We had killed about sixty of them and had it been daylight we would have killed many more. The field of battle now cleared, we moved forward again as we had still nearly three miles to go. We heard the ravenous creatures howl and yell in the woods as we went and sometimes we imagined we saw some of them but with the snow dazzling our eyes, we were not certain. In another hour we came to the town where we were staying, which we found terribly scared and in arms. The night before, the wolves and some bears had broken into the village and put them in such terror they were forced to keep guard night and day to preserve their cattle and, of course, their people.

The next morning our guide was so ill and his limbs so swollen with the festering of his two wounds, he could go no farther. We were forced to take a new guide and go to Toulouse, where we found a warm climate, a fruitful, pleasant country, no snow, no wolves, nor anything like them. When we told our story at Toulouse, they told us it was nothing out of the ordinary in the great forest at the foot of the mountains, especially when snow lay on the ground. They asked what kind of guide we had who would attempt to bring us that way in such a severe season and told us it was surprising we were not all devoured. When we told them how we placed ourselves and the horses in the middle, they chastised us and told us it was fifty to one we had not all been destroyed, since it was the sight of the horses which made the wolves so furious, but at other times they are really afraid of a gun. Raging because they were so hungry, their eagerness to come at the horses had made them senseless of danger and if we had not continually fired and used the gunpowder against them, the odds would have been that we would have been torn to pieces. If we were content to sit on horseback and fired as horsemen, they would not have tried to take the horses when men were on their backs. If we had stood together and left our horses, they would have been so eager to devour them, and we would have come away safe, especially having our firearms and being so many of us. For my part, I was never so sensitive to danger in my life. Seeing over three hundred devils come roaring and open-mouthed to devour us and having nothing to shelter us or retreat to, I gave myself up as lost. As it was, I believe I will never cross those mountains again. I think I would much rather go five thousand miles by sea, even if I was sure to meet with a storm once a week.

I have nothing uncommon to take notice of in my passage through France – nothing except what other travelers have said. I travelled from

Toulouse to Paris and without waiting long landed safe at Dover the 14th of January, after having had a severe cold season to travel in.

I had now come to the center of my travels and had in a little time all my newly-discovered estate safely around me, the promissory notes I brought with me paid in full.

My principal guide and privy-counsellor was my good ancient widow who, in gratitude for the money I had sent her, took great pains and spared no expense for me. I trusted her entirely and was completely at ease with the security of my belongings. Truly, I was very happy from the beginning, and now to the end, in the unspotted integrity of this good gentlewoman.

And now, having decided to dispose of my plantation in the Brazils, I wrote to my old friend at Lisbon. He offered it to my trustees' survivors, who still lived in the Brazils. They accepted the offer, and sent 33,000 pieces of eight[151] to a correspondent of theirs at Lisbon to pay for it.

In return, I signed the bill of sale they sent from Lisbon and sent it to my old man, who sent me notes for 32,800 pieces of eight, reserving the payment of 100 moidores a year to the old man the fifty to his son, as promised. And so, I have given the first part of a life of fortune and adventure – a life of Providence's gameplaying and of a variety which the world has seldom seen, beginning foolishly but closing much more happily than any part of it ever gave me to hope for.

Anyone would think in this state of complicated good fortune I was past running any more hazards – indeed I had been, if other circumstances had agreed. But I was accustomed to a wandering life, had no family or many relations. I was rich, and though I had sold my estate in the Brazils, I could not keep that country out of my head and had a good mind to go back. I especially could not resist the strong

---

[151] About £3.3 million today.

inclination I had to see my island and to know if the poor Spaniards were there. My true friend, the widow, discouraged me and prevailed for almost seven years, preventing my running abroad, during which time I took my two nephews into my care. The eldest I bred up as a gentleman and gave him a payment in addition to his estate after my death. The other I placed with the captain of a ship and after five years, finding him a sensible, bold, enterprising young fellow, I put him into a good ship and sent him to sea. This young fellow drew me in afterwards, as old as I was, to further adventures myself.

In the meantime, I settled myself here. I married – not to my disadvantage or my dissatisfaction – and had three children: two sons and a daughter. My wife died and my nephew came home successfully from a voyage to Spain. His insistence, and my inclination to go abroad prevailed and engaged me to go in his ship as a private trader to the East Indies in 1694.

In this voyage, I visited my new colony on the island, saw my successors the Spaniards, had the old story of their lives and of the villains I left there. How at first, they insulted the poor Spaniards, how they afterwards agreed, disagreed, united, separated and how at last the Spaniards were forced to use violence against them. How they were subjects to the Spaniards, how honestly the Spaniards used them – a history as full of variety and wonderful accidents as my own, particularly their battles with the Caribbeans, who landed several times on the island, and the improvement they made on the island itself and how five of them made an attempt on the mainland and brought away eleven men and five women prisoners, by whom I found about twenty young children on the island.

Here I stayed about twenty days, left them supplies, particularly weapons, gunpowder, shot, clothes, tools and two workmen I had brought from England – a carpenter and a blacksmith.

Besides this, I divided the lands into parts for them, reserved the whole property to myself, but gave them such parts as they agreed on. Settling all things with them and making them promise not to leave the place, I left them there.

From there I went to the Brazils. From there, I sent a boat with more people to the island. Besides other supplies, I sent seven women, proper as servants or wives to any who would take them. As to the Englishmen, I promised to send them some women from England, with a cargo of necessities, if they would apply themselves to planting, which I could not perform any longer. The fellows proved very honest and diligent after they were mastered and had their properties set apart for them. From the Brazils, I also sent them five cows, three of them being pregnant, some sheep and some hogs, which when I came again had increased considerably.

All these things, with an account of how three hundred Caribbees invaded and ruined their plantations, how they fought with that many twice, were at first defeated, one of them killed, and at last, a storm destroyed their enemies' canoes, they starved or killed almost all the rest and renewed and recovered the possession of their plantation and still lived on the island, with some very surprising incidents and some new adventures of my own, I shall give a farther account of in the Second Part of my Story.

www.ingramcontent.com/pod-product-compliance
Lightning Source LLC
Chambersburg PA
CBHW061024120726
47910CB00006B/2088